NEW VISION
PUBLICATION
PRESENTS

Cooper

Tit 4 Tat

A NOVEL BY

ALONZO L. STRANGE

This novel is a work of fiction. Any references to real people, events, establishments, or locales are intended only to give the fiction a sense of reality and authenticity. Other names, characters, and incidents occurring in the work are either the product of the author's imagination or are used fictitiously, as those fictionalized events and incidents that involve real persons. Any character that happens to share the name of a person who is an acquaintance of the author, past or present, is purely coincidental and is in no way intended to be an actual account involving that person.

ISBN: (10) 0982677200
ISBN: (13) 978-0-9826772-0-9
Cover design: www.mariondesigns.com
Inside layout: www.mariondesigns.com
Editors: Linda Williams and Dolly Lopez

Tat 4 Tat a novel/Alfonzo L. Strange

NEW VISION
PUBLICATION

P.O. Box 2815
Stockbridge, GA 30281
www.newvisionpublication.com

First Printing May 2010
Printed in Canada

10   9   8   7   6   5   4   3   2   1

Dedication

This book is dedicated to my son Devin M. Bice and my daughter Myah A. Bice. You two are my world and I can't express that enough. Ya'll were the true inspiration for this book. I love both of ya'll very much!

Acknowledgement

First and foremost, I would like to give all praises to God for keeping me focused. Without him none of this would have happened. I have to give special thanks to my mother for believing in me, when everyone else didn't and for staying by my side through it all. Thanks Mom!

To: My two beautiful children, Devin B. and Myah B. Even though I wasn't in your lives physically doesn't mean I wasn't thinking of you mentally!

To: All of those at Fairton FCI, Leavenworth and Loretto that helped and believed in this book. People like: Quadir "Gotti", Ivan Keith, Karriem "KB" Barrow, who had a very important part in this book. You are not forgotten homie, I got you! My people at Leavenworth U.S.P that helped me bring this book to completion: Jay "J. Dub" Wakins, Kendall "Bear", my writing partner, T. Frasier who gave me the confidence to finish this project. Thanks lil' homie, I didn't forget you "Frasier Boy." We have a lot to do!

To: All my homies in Loretto FCI, those that I came to call friends: Rob "OC" from Canada, Troy Green,

"Frankie" Perez, "E-Money" from Bad News VA, "Chico" Thomas from Queen City NC, my lil' homie Latif, and of course my good friend Muza. Without your connection, I would have never be in this situation, thanks. If I didn't mention you then you know why!

To: Those that have been by my side through this journey. I have to definitely acknowledge Tania P. from Charlotte NC. Girl, you held me down like a trooper and for that, I'll be forever grateful. To my homie Helen W. in Atlanta, you have always been there for me even before all of this. That's why I call you my true friend. Thanks.

To: My girl Sherida H. from Alabama, I know I've put you through a lot and all of the times you wanted to give up on me, but didn't, I just want to say thank you for believing in me. Remember what I said to you. "It gets greater later!" Believe me you are someone that is so special in my life and I will never forget you. Without your love and understanding, I probably wouldn't have gotten through all these years.

All of ya'll hold a special place in my heart, I just want ya'll to know that!

To: The readers of this book, I hope you love this book as much as I loved writing it.

To: Everyone that I let read it before it was even done, thanks for you honest opinions. Ya'll helped me write a good book.

To: All of the women that let me get away. "My Exes" thanks for letting me go. I probably would have made a mistake by marrying the wrong girl. Ya'll didn't deserve me anyway.

To: Keith for giving me the opportunity to share my talent with the rest of the world and to be a part of the New Vision Publication family. To you I am forever grateful.

Now: I have to give a special shout-out to my Editor,

my POA, my good friend Linda Williams. Thanks for believing in me. Thanks for making my dreams come true, and thanks for letting my name be known. You are truly an Angel in my eyes!

They say, "What doesn't kill us only makes us stronger," so I have to thank the agent that helped to put me in prison. Agent Tateo, instead of punishing me, you only helped me to realize my true potential. Thank You.

Peace,

A.L. Strange

Prologue

Henry was sitting in his black Pathfinder across from the Castle Hill housing projects sipping on a bottle of Old English Malt Liquor and puffing on a blunt of Buddah laced with Black Magic (angel dust). He was contemplating whether or not he should call the girl he met while he was at the club "Bentley" Saturday night. He took her to IHOP for breakfast, and then they drove around until they ended up at the same spot that he was sitting at right now. He gave her a ride home, since her friends weren't ready to leave when she was. She appreciated it. So in return, she gave him her number and a peck on the lips with the promise of hooking up later. That was a week ago.

He only called her once and was unable to reach her. He was in the area, so he decided to try and catch her at home since he knew where she lived. Before he did anything, he reached into his glove compartment and pulled out an opened pack of Newports that contained a piece of folded up aluminum foil. Inside it was a gram of Fishscale (cocaine). He took his pinky finger, dipped his fingernail into it, and scooped a nice sized amount out of it. He placed the nail up to his nose and sniffed it up into his right nostril. Then he repeated the same process for the left one. "Ahhh, that's it!" Henry said out loud to himself as he tilted back his head to allow the coke to take its full effect. Now that his mind was right, he pulled out his Motorola cell phone from his jacket and proceeded to dial her number.

It rang five times and, just as he was about to push the off button, her voice came over the receiver.

"Hello!" She sounded a little excited as if she was doing something and the phone startled her. Henry looked at his Gucci watch and saw that it read 3:36 p.m. He cleared his throat and quickly said, "Yeah ah, what's up?" His mind was racing to find the right words to say, but he couldn't. She thought that she recognized the voice, but wasn't sure. So all she could say was,

"Who's this?" At that moment, the young man that had his head between her thighs stopped what he was doing and looked up, causing her to look at him with an attitude as if saying, "Why you stop?! Keep going." So he placed his head back in between her legs and continued what he was doing.

"It's Henry, what's up? You too busy to talk right now?" Henry asked as he watched some guys scoping his kitted out jeep. He leaned forward a little reaching under his seat to retrieve his Glock .40 with the rubber grip handle.

"One minute," she says with the phone pressed up against her right ear and shoulder. Her head was tilted back as the young man gently nibbled on her clit. Her mind was definitely in another world. She realized that someone was on the phone when she heard a car's horn blaring in the receiver.

"Hello! Hello!"

"Yeah, I'm here," Henry said with an attitude. "I'm sorry, can you hold on for a minute?" She asked with a sense of urgency. "Yeah al-ight," Henry replied as his patience was running short.

In a quick motion, she dropped the receiver so that she could press the mute button, but instead, she pressed the speed redial. While she thought the phone was on mute, Henry was hearing everything that was going on with her and her lover.

Henry was furious as he listened to someone fucking the bitch that he was trying to get with, but the more he listened, the more excited he became. He sat in his truck, unzipped his Levi's, pulled out his dick, and proceeded to slowly stroke himself knowing that no one could see through his dark tinted windows. He couldn't believe she had the audacity to put him on hold while she was getting her freak on!

Her screams made him stroke himself faster as he envisioned himself being the one that was causing the pleasure that she was feeling. "Turn around! Turn around!" Henry heard the male voice say. "Whose pussy is this?! POW! The young man demanded as he slapped her on her ass while banging her head into the headboard. "It's your pussy!" Her voice quivers as she was about to cum.

"Ohhh Shit!!! Ahh! Oooohh! Oh Shit…"

Henry's hand moved faster up and down his shaft as he heard her reaching her peak. He too was at the point of no return and grunted as he released his seed causing it to splatter on his grey leather steering wheel. "Shit! Fuck!" he yelled realizing what he had done.

He reached into the glove compartment to grab some tissue to clean himself and wipe off the steering wheel. He listened some more and waited for her to come back to the phone. He heard her telling the guy that she just got finished fucking that she had to check on something, and then she remembered that she left someone on hold. "Oh my God!" she says, not realizing how long she had him waiting. "I hope he hung up!" she said out loud.

She went to the phone and noticed that the mute light wasn't on. She picked up the receiver and said,

"Hello, are you still there?" Henry replies in a tone that makes her feel bad for having him on hold for so long.

"Are you finished yet?" She's embarrassed because she knows he heard her love making session with her man.

"You fucking bitch!" Henry blurts out in a sarcastic tone of voice that made her skin crawl.

"Excuse me!" She screams back at him.

"Fuck You Bitch!" Henry replies once again.

"Oh no you did-" she begins to say as Henry clicks the off button on his cell phone.

Henry was furious at how she thought she could play him like that. "What! She thinks I'm a fuckin' joke or somethin', huh?" Henry said in a rage to himself. As he drove off, he vowed that he would get even and knew just how to do it.

ONE

Sonya woke up with the sun shining through her bedroom window and the sound of horns blaring from the traffic below. As she looked around, she noticed her blankets were all tangled up from the constant tossing and turning she must have done during the night. She glanced at her clock on the end table and realized that it was only six forty in the morning. Her alarm wasn't to go off for another twenty minutes. "What the hell am I doing up this early?" she said in an irritated tone of voice.

As she proceeded to get herself up out of the bed, placing her feet into her slippers, and grabbing for her robe that she kept close by, she listened a minute to see if Myah was awake yet. *"She must still be in bed,"* she thought to herself as she made her way to the bathroom. "Ahhh," she said, feeling a sense of relief as she urinated. She found herself holding it in ever since she had awakened.

Her body felt tired, which was strange, since she went to bed early last night. Nevertheless, she had to get herself together if she was going to make it to that job interview that she had at nine. Sonya wasn't a morning person and it showed as she dragged herself out of the bathroom, after brushing her teeth and washing her face. She walked back into her bedroom and glanced at the clock once more to make sure she was still on schedule. "Good! I made it before the alarm went off." With five minutes to spare, Sonya looked around in her closet to find something suitable to wear for her interview. "BEEP! BEEP! BEEP!" The sound of the alarm made her jump and drop the skirt that she had picked out to wear. "Oh shit," she mumbled under her breath as she rushed out of her closet towards the irritating noise. Sonya hit the off button and walked to the door to see if Myah had gotten up yet. She didn't hear or see any movement. So she went back to her closet and picked up the skirt that she dropped and searched around for something to match with it. "Ahh, here we go," she said after finding a cream color silk blouse that she knew would go well with the beige knee-high length skirt she had on her arm. "I know just the shoes to complete this ensemble," Sonya blurted out excitedly as she placed the outfit on the bed and got down on her hands and knees to look under her bed for those high-heeled shoes she wore just three days ago.

Just as she was about to get up, she felt as if someone was watching her. She turned her head around and saw Myah standing behind her sucking her thumb looking straight at her. "Myah, how many times have I told you not to do that?"

"Do what?" Myah asked as she rocked back and forth still sucking her thumb.

"Not to sneak up behind me like that!"

"Mommy, I don't feel good." Sonya stood up and turned towards her to feel her forehead to see if it felt warm.

"Ohhh baby, you have a fever," Sonya said as she quickly ran to the bathroom to get the thermometer. Myah stood in the doorway of her mother's bedroom and watched as her mother ran around trying to find whatever she was looking for.

Once Sonya found what she wanted, she walked back into the room and told Myah to sit down on her bed, as she placed the thermometer into her mouth. After a few minutes, she read the numbers and was startled to see that Myah's temperature was 101!

She put Myah back in the bed and went to the bathroom to get her washcloth. "Well, there goes my day," Sonya said out loud to no one in particular. By the time she finished getting her a cool towel and staying with Myah until she was asleep, it was 9:23 a.m. The interview that she was supposed to go on would have to be cancelled and, school was definitely out of the question.

Since Sonya was a single parent, she knew that she would have to make sacrifices for her daughter. She was the sole provider and caretaker. So she didn't get out much. Diallo, Myah's father, was killed in a drug deal gone bad right after she was born. He provided for them through the drug game, which Sonya was never fond of. Every chance she got, she would let it be known. Diallo's mind was set on making sure that his family was financially secure, even if it meant staying in the streets all night to make it happen.

Now that he was gone, Sonya makes sure that Myah never forgets who her father was. The few pictures that she did have of him were placed throughout their apartment as constant reminders for the both of them.

Sonya had never really gotten over the death of Diallo, but she knew that she would have to be strong for their daughter. Her surroundings weren't the best place to raise a child, especially by herself, but it was all that she could afford at the present time.

Sonya was taking advantage of the welfare system

while at the same time pursuing her goal of being a registered nurse. While Myah was at day care, she was taking classes at the local community college. Her friends all knew how serious she was about improving her situation, for herself and her daughter.

Even though she was a single mother, she was human and needed to unwind once in a while. So, she dedicated the weekends for just that. Friday and Saturday were her hangout days. These days she would spend with her girlfriends, but mostly with Tony, a guy that she met at school a couple of months ago.

Just as she was about to go and check on Myah, the phone rang startling her. She walked into her bedroom, reached down on her bed, and picked it up. "Hello," she said.

"Hey boo, what's up?" a male voice said. Sonya recognized the voice immediately, which perked her up a little. It was Tony. She always liked the way that he carried himself. She was fascinated by how mature he was to be only twenty-two years of age. The sound of his voice always did something to her, but she tried her best to down play it, trying not to sound too excited.

"Hey, what's up, Tony?" she says, nonchalantly.

"I know it's kinda early, but I was wondering if you wanted to get something to eat before class?" he said in a sexy voice. Sonya had totally forgotten about class, but she knew that she wasn't going to make it anyways.

"Ohhhh, I can't," Sonya replied knowing she would love to. "Myah has a fever."

"Is she aight?" Tony asked in a concerned voice. "I don't know. She's sleeping now, so I have to wait to see if her temperature went down when she wakes up."

"I'll be over there in fifteen minutes!"

"That's o—." Before she could finish, he had hung up and all she heard was the dial tone.

Since Tony was determined to come over, Sonya went back to her bedroom to get dressed. She stepped into the bathroom, flipped the light on, and was greeted by her reflection in the mirror. *"Damn!* I look good," she said as she admired herself. At twenty-four years old, Sonya was a very attractive woman. She kept herself up pretty well and after having Myah at nineteen, she worked out at least three times a week paying special attention to her stomach and thighs. In the long run, the hard work paid off.

After finishing up in the bathroom, Sonya went into her bedroom, found a pair of biker shorts and a long T-shirt to slip into since she wasn't going anywhere. She decided to look in on Myah to see if she was up yet. *"Good, she's still sleeping,"* she thought to herself as she kissed her on her forehead and turned to head back to her room. Before she could make it, the doorbell rang causing her to turn around abruptly.

"Who is it," she asked as she approached the door.

"It's me," a voice replied.

Even though she knew it was Tony, out of instinct, she looked through the peephole anyways. "Hold on a minute," she said as she fumbled with the chain lock on the door. Once the door was open, she moved aside to, invite him in. Without hesitation, Tony walked in, gave her a hug and kiss, and waited until she closed the door to say something.

"How's she doing boo?"

Sonya turned towards him and replied, "She's sleeping, but I think she'll be okay." As she stood in front of him, he noticed what she was wearing. Looking her up and down, he liked what he saw, and the bulge in his jeans proved it.

Tony always felt that Sonya was a classy woman and being that she was two years older than him, she didn't dress or act like most of the chicken heads that he was use to dealing with around the hood. In fact, Sonya wasn't like any of the girls he knew at all. He put her on a pedestal and in his eyes, she could do no wrong. Sonya normally dressed conservatively, but every once in a while, she would dress provocatively just for Tony.

By the look that Tony was giving her, Sonya sensed what he was thinking. She looked down at herself following where his eyes were looking and said, "Since I wasn't going anywhere, I just threw on something comfortable." Tony smiled as she emphasized the word comfortable. He knew what that meant. They walked over to the living room couch where he took off his coat and sat down.

"You want something to drink," she asked as she made her way towards the kitchen.

"Yeah, just get me a glass of Kool-Aid." As Sonya turned around to go into the kitchen, Tony kept his eyes glued to her ass. Her T-shirt was above the waistline exposing her thick round hips and voluptuous behind in her biker's shorts. His dick started to get hard again the more he stared at her. "Damn!" was all he could say when she disappeared around the wall.

"What was that," she yelled back thinking that he was saying something to her.

"Nah, I didn't say nothin'."

Sonya did hear what he said and knew that he was looking at her ass as she walked away. She saw the bulge in his jeans when he looked at her at the door. They hadn't had sex in a couple of days. So, she knew where his mind was. She was going to give him what he wanted since the same thoughts were running through her mind.

Tony never had a problem getting girls. In fact, he was a ladies' man when it came to putting his game down. However, anytime he was around Sonya, he acted like a young teenager dating for the first time. Even after weeks of dating her, he was uncomfortable making the first move when it came to initiating sex between them. Today was going to be different. After seeing what she was wearing, his mind was made up. He was going to get some pussy before he left her apartment. But little did he know, Sonya was thinking the same thing as well.

When Sonya returned from the kitchen, she handed him the glass of cherry Kool-Aid, sat down on his lap, and purposely grinded her ass into his crotch.

"Whoa!" was all Tony could say before Sonya wrapped her arms around his neck and planted soft kisses all over his face and lips. To his surprise, Sonya was just as horny as he was.

Sonya loved the feel of his body, especially when she got him excited. She couldn't help but notice that he was about to split the front of his jeans by the way his dick was pressing into her ass. She knew that he was uncomfortable sitting in the position that he was in. So, she slowly got up off his lap, grabbed him by the hand, and led him into her bedroom.

Once they were inside and the door was closed, Tony grabbed Sonya around the waist and pulled her close to his body pressing his lips against hers causing her to lean into him. His tongue played inside her mouth as her moans gave him the confidence to go further. He laid her across the satin comforter that covered her king sized bed and continued to kiss her lips and ears while at the same time, using his right hand to explore under her T-shirt causing her nipples to become hard from his gentle touch. Sonya couldn't take it anymore. So she reached for the buttons on his jeans trying to get them loose.

Tony knew what she was trying to do. So, he stopped, lifted his body off of hers, and undid his pants without saying a word. Tony's eyes lit up as he pulled off Sonya's t-shirt exposing her firm breasts since she wasn't wearing a bra. Sonya was so comfortable with herself that she never even thought about what her body looked like when she was around Tony. The first time they had sex, Tony was amazed at how confident she was with her body. In the past, the girl's he's been with usually tried to cover themselves up, fearing that he would disapprove of them, but Sonya was different. In fact, she paraded around as if she was by herself. Even now, she still acts the same way.

When she came out of her t-shirt and stood in front of him, his eyes roamed up and down taking in the splendid scenery that she was offering. Her cocoa complexion was like the color of coffee with a touch of cream. Her skin was flawless from head to toe, not a blemish was on any part of her body. Her long, dark curly hair flowed down to the middle of her back. The biker shorts that she was wearing were like a second skin on her. They showed every contour of her hips and thighs. The print of her pussy was a perfect v-shape. Sonya's stomach was as flat as a board unlike some girls he knew that had kids at a young age and developed a pouch just below their stomach.

The one thing that caught Tony's attention the most about Sonya was her eyes. They were hazel-green and almond-shaped, which gave her that exotic appearance he loved so much. Overall, Sonya was the total package. She was a 12 on a scale of 1 to 10.

As Tony stood there admiring her beauty, Sonya was wondering if he was alright because he looked like he was in a trance. "Tony, Tony," she whispered causing him to blink his eyes a few times before responding.

"Yeah, what's up?" "What's wrong with you," she asked concerned.

"I was just thinking how lucky I am to be with such a beautiful woman." That response made Sonya blush. He pulled her close, bent down, placed his lips on her neck, and worked his way down until he reached her breasts. Cupping the right one into his hand, he planted soft kisses on it as she lay across the bed with him gently on top of her. Tony caressed her breasts with his hands and played with her nipples while she moaned from the sheer pleasure of his gentle touch. The feeling was too much for her to handle. So he moved up trying to get him to stop, but Tony knew that she was enjoying it. He took his right hand and pulled down her shorts placing his middle finger inside the wet lips of her pussy while at the same time massaging her clit with his hands.

This was driving Sonya crazy. She had to control herself since she knew that Myah was right down the hall. She knew that if she was to truly let go, it would cause Myah to wake up. So she grabbed a pillow that she had on the bed and bit into it to muffle her screams. "Ahhh, Ohhh, Ahhh" was all she could say as Tony continued to play in her pussy. Sonya was on the verge of cumming when Tony suddenly stopped and moved his head in between her thighs to taste her sweet nectar. When he placed his tongue on her clit, that was all it took for her to go over the edge. The combination of his tongue and hot breath was what caused her to orgasm so hard that she started shaking as if she was having a seizure. "Ohhh my God," was what she screamed as Tony's tongue continued to suck on her clit.

Once her orgasm subsided, she sat up and pushed him back on the bed so that she could return the favor. Tony was shocked by how aggressive she became as she tried her best to get his pants off so that she could suck his dick the way that he had sucked her clit.

She wasn't a pro at oral sex, but Sonya knew enough to please him. After the first couple of times, she had gotten good at it and now to him, she was the best he had so far.

"She acts as if she has something to prove," Tony thought to himself as she pulled his dick out of his boxers and attacked it like she needed it in order to live.

The warmth of her mouth caused Tony to groan softly as he closed his eyes and felt her lips and tongue working up and down his dick. She flicked her tongue against the head of it making Tony shiver a little from the pure pleasure of it. He held on to her head as she moved up and down trying to get him to release his seed into her mouth.

The more she continued to move, the more Tony wanted to explode. Finally, the feeling was too much for him. He couldn't hold out any longer. He came so hard that it caused Sonya to gag from the amount that he released in spurts. She tried her best to swallow it all, but some of it still managed to spill out of the corners of her mouth dripping onto his nuts and legs.

She continued to suck until his orgasm was done before she let him loose. Sonya gathered herself, got up off the bed, and went into the bathroom. She then rinsed out her mouth and wet a washcloth to bring back to Tony so that she could clean up the mess they had made. They rested for a few minutes, and then proceeded to fuck until exhaustion.

As they were about to go a second round, the phone rang causing Sonya to reach for it. Tony looked up as she tried to grab the phone and said, "Don't answer it! Let it ring." "It might be important," Sonya replied as she let it ring two more times. Tony was positioned between her with her legs over his shoulders. He was in the process of blowing on her clit when he heard the phone, and she tried to move. After the fourth ring, Sonya told him to just keep going and she'll get rid of whoever it was. With that, Tony placed his face back down and continued to lick her clit while she answered the phone.

"Hello!"

TWO

The 911 call came in at 5:17 p.m. Officer Williamson was the first on the scene to witness the horrific sight of a young woman's life destroyed. Neighbors were in the hallway gathering outside of the apartment that he was in.

As Williamson called for the Homicide Detectives, he thought he heard something in one of the rooms towards the back of the apartment. With his gun drawn, he shouted to whoever it was,

"This is the police! Come out with your hands in the air now!" From what he saw in the bedroom, he wasn't taking any chances. So he cautiously walked with his back against the wall towards the origin of the noise or at least where he thought it came from and opened the door. To his surprise, it was a kid's room. So now he had to wonder where the child was during all of this.

While he surveyed the room, he heard rustling coming from behind the closed closet door. With his gun still in his right hand, he opened the door with his left and was startled when he saw a little girl staring up at him with tears in her eyes.

Sirens were heard for blocks and Williamson knew

that the place was about to be crawling with activity. He helped the child out of the closet after convincing her that he was the good guy.

Senior Det. Moody, from the Homicide Division, was on the scene within fifteen minutes of the call. His partner Det. Stevens, a ten year veteran with the NYPD, wasn't too far behind. After parking behind a blue and white, they made their way up to the third floor carefully eyeing the crowd of onlookers for anyone that might look suspicious. Years of experience has taught them that a lot of killers like to stick around to see if there were any witnesses or what the police theories might be. "Cases like this are always the most difficult to solve unless someone comes right out to confess," Det. Stevens said to his partner as they surveyed the interior of the apartment. They made their way over to the officer that was the first on the scene to find out all the details before they inspected for themselves.

Officer Williamson was standing next to a young girl that couldn't have been no older than four or five years of age. Det. Moody thought as he and Stevens walked towards them. With all the activity that was going on, no one noticed the young man in the doorway watching as the police and forensic team went about their job of dusting for fingerprints, looking through the victim's personal effects, and questioning the immediate neighbors, the ones that might have possibly heard if someone other than the victim was in the apartment.

Irk was one of the tenants that lived three floors up. He was twenty-two years old and hung around with a tough crowd. His reputation was already legendary in the streets for carrying a gun that he didn't hesitate to use. He was one of Diallo's soldiers before he died. Since he was good to him, Irk vowed that he would look out for his peeps as long as they stayed in the building. This was a promise that he made to himself since Diallo looked out for him when he was coming up. Even though Sonya never knew where the five hundred dollars came from every month, he knew that it helped her and Myah. As long as they stayed in the projects, the envelopes continued to come.

Irk played it smart and never let it be known that he was the one doing it simply out of respect for Diallo, but it was no secret that he liked Sonya and the way that she carried herself. In fact, everyone in the building liked her, but no one dared cross that line. Not only because she was Diallo's girl, but because she was protected.

"How protected could she have been if something like this could happen to her," Irk thought to himself as he just watched the activity going on in Sonya's apartment.

"Excuse me young man. Can you please step behind the yellow line so that you won't contaminate the crime scene," a woman said as she walked past him into the apartment, shutting the door behind her. The last thing that Irk saw was the look on Myah's face, a look that he would never forget.

Medical Examiner Diane Smith walked into the apartment just as Det. Moody was beginning to inspect the corpse lying on the bed. "Don't you dare touch a thing Detective," Diane playfully yelled out once she was inside the bedroom door. Moody knew who the voice belonged to before he even turned around to respond.

Everyone else that was present quickly jumped as if they were doing something wrong. It was like they got caught with their hands in the cookie jar. She strolled over with her black leather medical bag and stood next to Det. Moody who was now taking notes on a pad that he pulled out of his suit jacket and acted as if he didn't even hear he

Without turning around he said, "Ah, if it isr' late arriving Dr. Smith. I'm sure you were stu' or better yet, at another crime scene right?"

"Actually, I was just about to have dinner with my family when I received the call, but I'm sure you wouldn't know anything about that Detective since homicide is all you know." Moody eyed her with disdain and went about his examination of the body. Smith knew that she had hit a sore spot with that comment especially since she knew that he was recently divorced from his second wife.

It was common knowledge that police officers had one of the highest divorce rates in the country. Moody and Smith worked almost all of the cases that came to his precinct. It was if they were a team, and both of them were bullheaded when it came to who had authority when conducting a crime scene investigation.

Usually the police would wait for the Medical Examiner to arrive and do their job before touching and collecting any evidence, but a few times, Smith came to a crime scene where the body was moved before she had a chance to do her job. Most of the time, well all of the time, she would blame Moody since he was the Senior Detective in charge.

While they were in the bedroom, someone called for the Detectives to come into the living room area.

"Hey Det. Moody, Stevens, can ya'll come in here for a minute," a young officer yelled through the open bedroom door. The two Detectives walked towards the door, leaving Dr. Smith with the body. As they made their way into the living room, Officer Williamson was sitting on the couch with the little girl next to him trying to get her to say what she said a minute ago to him.

"Myah, tell these nice gentlemen what you just told me, okay?"

"Yeah. My mommy was screaming and she was telling him to stop, but he wouldn't stop," Myah said as she kept her head down trying not to look at the Detectives. Det. Moody was the first to say something.

"What was the bad man doing to your mommy that she wanted him to stop," he asked trying to talk like he was a kid, so that she could relate to him.

"He was hitting my mommy. So, I ran into my room cause I was scared," Myah replied as the Detectives looked in shock.

"Do you know who was hitting you mommy...what's her name," Det. Moody asked Officer Williamson.

"It's Myah, sir."

"Do you know who was hitting your mommy, Myah," he asked again as he tried to think of more questions to ask without scaring her. He was used to adults telling him details, but not a five year old that just lost her mother.

"No, I don't know who that bad man was," Myah managed to say without looking at him.

"Did he look like him," Moody asked pointing to Stevens who was an African-American, brown-skinned man with short black curly hair and a medium build. He was trying to get her to describe her mother's killer, if she did, in fact, see what he looked like.

"No, he was bigger than him. He had a cut on his face right here," Myah pointed to Steven's right cheek to indicate where the cut was.

"About how long was this cut, Myah?"

"Like this," she said as she slid her finger across her face showing that the cut was about three to four inches long.

"Was he taller than him, Myah?"

She shook her head to say yes which lead Moody to believe that the killer had to be at least six-two, or better since Steven was six-one.

Now Moody had a vague description, the best he could have hoped for considering the age of the witness.

Everything that Myah said, Det. Stevens wrote down.

"Good job Officer Williamson. If you get anything else, please let us know. You might want to take this little girl to the Dept. of Social Services since we don't know who to call yet. Let's try to keep her name out of the news. We don't want whoever did this to know we have an eyewitness," Moody said as he and Stevens started to walk back towards the bedroom to finish their examination of the body before they left for the precinct. Officer Williamson agreed and took the task of taking Myah himself.

Back in the bedroom, Dr. Smith was the first to notice that the victim had sex before or while the attack was occurring. Semen stains were spotted on the left thigh of the victim's leg.

"Do we even know the name of this poor girl gentlemen," Dr. Smith asked as she collected samples of the semen on a swab, placed it into a glass tube, and snapped it shut.

"Yeah. Her name is Sonya Johnson. She was twenty-four years old, and as it appears, a single mother. From what the neighbors say, she was one of the good ones. She wasn't into drugs, didn't hang around with a lot of people, and she was attending community college right here in the Bronx. She worked as a nurse's aide at the hospital. But damn! I never saw her there before. I would have remembered a face like that," Det. Stevens said to no one in particular.

"So, she just took care of her kid and went to school, huh," Det. Moody asked to his partner.

"It appears that way," he replied.

"What about the kid's father," Dr. Smith asked as she gathered her things to leave.

"That's what we're trying to find out now. No one seems to know anything about him," Stevens answered.

"Well someone must have really hated her to do something like this. I'll do a thorough autopsy once I get the body. I'll be able to tell you more about the cause of death," Det. Smith added. Moody stepped aside to let her pass, but before she could leave the room, he stopped her and said, "You know, we really have to stop meeting like this." With that, she smiled and walked out the door.

After Dr. Smith finished her examination of the body, she gave permission for the body to be moved to the morgue.

Meanwhile, Det. Stevens was walking around the bedroom trying to find anything that might give him an idea of who the killer might have been.

"They always leave a clue. It's just up to us to find it," he said to himself as he searched the carpet around the bed.

Pictures were taken of the crime scene and of the body before it was placed in the body bag and transported to the coroner's van. The blanket and sheets were gathered for further inspection along with anything that may have been considered vital to the case.

"Hey Jimmy, I think I found something," Det. Stevens said excitedly causing Det. Moody to walk over to where he was bending down.

"Do you see what I see," Stevens asked as he looked into Det. Moody's eyes with a hint of excitement. A small black beeper was lying near the base of the nightstand.

"Joey, take a picture of this," Moody commanded the photographer. After Joe DeGrassio, from the forensic team, took a couple of pictures of the beeper, Stevens picked it up with a latex gloved hand and placed it into a clear plastic sealable bag labeled "Evidence."

"I think he left his calling card, huh?"

"I think you might be right, Stevens. Now all we have to do is trace it back to the owner," Det. Moody stated as he turned towards the door and yelled to the officers and forensic personnel that were milling around.

"Alright fellas, let's clean this place up. I want everything noted and sealed off. Call me if you find anything else." With that said, he and Stevens walked towards the apartment door and left, leaving them inside.

In the car, they made notes of their findings and drove off to get something to eat. They wanted this murder solved within the next forty-eight hours. With the beeper in their possession, they were hours ahead of the game.

THREE

Myah was taken to the Dept. of Social Services only after her mother's body was taken by the coroner. Officer Williamson started to get attached to her. It wasn't hard to after spending a few hours with her. She started to trust him, even held little conversations with him-about her school and how she was sick that day.

It broke his heart when he had to finally bring her to the Social Services' emergency house. As he put her into his squad car, the only thing she wanted was her mother.

"Where's my mommy? Is she coming too? I want my mommmmmy!" she screamed as Officer Williamson closed the door on the passenger side of his cruiser and walked around to the driver's side. Once he was in, she looked at him with tears in her eyes and said,

"Is that bad man coming to get me?"

"No, no honey. That bad man isn't coming to get you." His eyes started to water as he thought about how innocent and vulnerable Myah really was.

The drive took about twenty minutes since traffic was heavy. When they finally arrived at the house and got out, he walked her up the few steps to the front and rang the doorbell. After a few seconds, a woman who looked to be in her mid-forties, came to the door and greeted them with a smile. She was expecting them since Officer Williamson called ahead to make sure they were prepared.

"Hey there young lady, how old are you," Mrs. Forrester asked bending down trying to get to the same level as Myah.

"Five," she said as she turned towards Officer Williamson trying to hide her face with his leg. Officer Williamson smiled and scooped her up in his arms and held her close to his chest hoping that it would comfort her.

Mrs. Forrester walked back inside as Officer Williamson followed behind. As they stood in the foyer, Williamson asked her, "Would it be a problem if I stopped by now and then to check on her, so she'll have a familiar face to see."

"No, that's fine officer. That's very considerate of you," Mrs. Forrester said watching how Myah's eyes lit up whenever he looked at her.

"Thanks, this little girl has been through a lot, and I just want to make sure that she'll be okay wherever she goes."

"She looks like she's a strong young lady. I'm sure she has some family somewhere. I'm going to start my search first thing in the morning," Mrs. Forrester said as she smiled and lead him to the door.

I'll be here tomorrow around six o'clock when my shift ends. Is that too late," Williamson asked holding the door open.

"Heavens no! The kids will be up and running around until about seventy-thirty." As soon as she said that, another lady, younger than Mrs. Forrester came into the room and took Myah in the back. Williamson looked at the way that Myah tried to fight the lady and knew that he was going to miss her. They both turned around just as

Myah called for him to get her, but before he could take a step to help her, Mrs. Forrester stopped him by holding his arm and shook her head no. "It's best if you just let her go. She'll be fine, believe me." With that, Williamson turned back around and left the house. As he headed for his cruiser, he fought with himself not to turn around, because if he did, he knew he would not be able to leave her.

At the precinct, the two detectives compared notes and decided to call Dr. Smith concerning the results of the autopsy. "You better talk to her Stevens. You know she doesn't like me," Det. Moody said as he sat at his desk rewriting the notes he took at the crime scene.

"You know what Jimmy? You and Diane have a love/hate relationship. You love her and she hates you!" They both laughed at Stevens' poor attempt of a joke while he picked up the phone and proceeded to dial the City Morgue.

After a couple of rings, a young lady with a pleasant voice answered, "Hello, Dr. Smith's office. How may I help you?"

"Yeah, this is Det. Stevens from the 43rd precinct Homicide Division, I need to speak with Dr. Smith please."

"One moment Detective." As he waited for the good doctor to pick up the phone, he looked over towards a picture on his desk of his wife and kids and thought about how young and beautiful the victim was. "*Damn*," was all he could manage to say before Dr. Smith's voice came on the phone,

"Hello."

"Yeah Doc, this is Detective Stevens. I was just calling to find out the results of the autopsy. Di..." Before he could finish his sentence, Dr. Smith cut him off and asked,

"Is Det. Moody there with you?"

"Yes ma'am, he's right here." Det. Stevens answered as he looked in Moody's direction who was looking at him trying to eavesdrop on the conversation.

"Well tell that chicken shit that he could have called himself, no offense to you Detective."

"None taken Doc. I'll tell him exactly what you said."

"To answer your question Detective Stevens, I haven't gotten a chance to do anything as of yet, but if ya'll want to come down and watch, you're more than welcome to," Dr. Smith added knowing that they would probably decline the offer. No one likes to come to the morgue since it represented death. But what Det. Stevens said next really surprised her.

"I think we'll do just that Doc. We'll be there in about twenty minutes."

Det. Stevens hung up the phone and turned towards Moody with a smile on his face. Det. Moody already knew that Diane had said something sarcastic, and he couldn't wait to hear it from his partner.

"Well Jimmy, she wants us to come down and watch. Oh, before I forget, she also said to tell you that you could have called yourself 'You chicken shit!' Those were her exact words."

"Man, I hate that bitch," Det. Moody said as he stood up to put his jacket on. He grabbed his badge and pager from his desk and then made sure that his police issued nine millimeter hand gun was secured in the holster under his arm.

"Why does she hate you so much partner?"

"We used to date back in the day, and she never got over the fact that I decided to marry someone else."

"Oh, you never told me that. Now I understand, she's bitter about the breakup, huh?"

"Nah, she's bitter because I opted to marry someone

else, but somehow I forgot to tell her that I was still engaged to Susie while we were together. So, every chance she gets, she lets me have it."

"Well, you know what they say about a woman scorned," Det. Stevens added as a joke.

"Yeah, I know. Let's go before it gets too late." With that said, they both walked out of the office to make their way downtown.

The city morgue, which was located in the heart of the Bronx, was one building that you didn't have to worry about anyone hanging around or having trouble finding a parking spot because it was too crowded. The smell of death floated in the air like a halo, but the fact remained, it was one of the cleanest buildings in the Bronx.

They went to the front and entered through the two glass doors that read City Morgue. In the middle of the lobby was a vestibule that housed the security station. The two detectives walked up to the desk where a middle-aged black man standing at about six-three, weighing every bit of two fifty was waiting for them to check in.

"Hey Rob, how's it going," Det. Moody asked as he handed the pen over to his partner to sign the sheet.

"Hey Detectives. It's still as boring now as it was the last time I saw you," the bulky security guard replied as he leaned against the console.

"It's been like what, three days since the last time I saw you," Moody asked trying to make the guard laugh a little.

"Ha ha ha, aren't you the funny one. The Doc is waiting for ya'll in room eight. Ya know the way, I'm sure," Rob said smiling as they started to walk towards the stairs.

"Rob, you really must tone it down some. You're too bubbly for this job," Stevens added looking back at the guard as they were about to turn the corner.

Once they were in the basement, they made their way down the long corridor leading to the back of the building. They passed rooms that housed the city's murder victims, accident victims, and those that their time had just expired. It got cooler the further they walked until they finally reached room BM008. Det. Stevens knocked on the big steel door and waited for someone to come up.

"Come in," a voice shouted from the other side causing Stevens to jump a little.

"I know you're not spooked about being in here partner," Det. Moody asked with a sly smirk on his face.

"I don't care how long I've being doing this job, this place still gives me the creeps whenever I come here."

"Well, get over it and let's go." They opened the door and were instantly hit with a burst of cool air as it came from the cooling system's vents along the top of the ceiling.

The room was like an ice box and it brought chills to both men. They looked towards the gurney that Dr. Smith was at and walked over to her.

"Now gentlemen, you know that you have to put on the scrubs and face masks before coming over here. All the things you'll need are right behind you on that counter. Please wash your hands and cover yourself up so you don't contaminate my area," she said in her usual sarcastic tone that Moody was so used to.

"Wow! Do you feel the daggers being thrown our way partner," Stevens commented in a hush tone as they turned and walked over towards the counter to retrieve the items that Dr. Smith had left for them. Moody took off his jacket and said,

"It doesn't bother me one bit, not one bit."

Both men placed their jackets on the coat rack and adorned the scrubs, the rubber gloves, and face masks before they entered Dr. Smith's domain again. They all gathered around the gurney that the body was on and proceeded to start the autopsy.

Each step was documented and recorded, but during the weighing of the organs, Det. Stevens had to excuse himself. It wasn't a mystery that he was starting to feel a little sick. It gave Det. Moody time alone with Dr. Smith that he really didn't want.

As she cut the recorder off without him knowing, Dr. Smith placed her tools down and turned towards him with a look that he hasn't seen in awhile.

"Jimmy, I don't want to go through this shit that we're going through. It's obvious that we're gonna have to work together unless one of us decides to transfer someplace else." Det. Moody's facial expression told her that he was confused by what she was saying. So she just laid it all out on the table while they were still alone in the room together.

"We have to decide if we are going to work together and co-exist in harmony, or we can keep at it until one of us decides enough is enough and is forced to move on. The choice is yours." Det. Moody didn't want this to continue the way it was going simply because he too was tired of it. The past was the past, but he refused to back down and let her think that she had gotten a victory over him. Now this! Of course he wanted to work together, and as she put it, "co-exist in harmony." So, he weighed his options and agreed with what she said.

"You're right Diane. I'm tired of fighting with you. The past is the past. What's done is done, right?" As he waited for her to respond, he noticed that she seemed vulnerable, and that made him want to hold her close, but before he could react, she looked at him and said,

"Let's try to be civil to each other, at least while we're working together." Moody knew that she still had feelings for him, but now that she was married, it was impossible to gain what they used to have. At that moment, Det. Stevens walked back into the room looking refreshed and ready to continue.

After the autopsy was completed, they found out that the victim had sex with two different individuals the day of the murder. She was severely beaten to death with a series of punches to the head and face area. There was no evidence of drug or alcohol use in her system, but the question still remained, "Why was she murdered?" Det. Moody reminded Stevens that they needed to find who the beeper, they found in the apartment, belongs to. At least, part of that question would be answered. Moody knew that it might be the key to breaking this case wide open.

Back at the precinct, the two detectives went about their investigation. They also tried to get some of their other duties done as well. Moody couldn't shake the fact that they were missing something that they either overlooked or just didn't see yet. The only clues that they had to go on besides the beeper, which he thought belonged to the killer, was the semen samples and the vague description that the little girl gave them. "He was tall and had a cut right here...", was all Moody kept thinking over and over again. Without a suspect to question, he knew that it was going to be difficult to put this case to rest and bring justice for that little girl who lost her mother.

Every case tells a story. Finding it out was what Det. Moody was good at. "Hey Jimmy, I have a name and address of the person that the beeper belongs to," Det. Stevens yelled from across his desk while he was in the process of ripping a page out of his notepad. He had just finished getting off the phone, and from the look on his face, he was excited by what he learned from the beeper company's sales clerk.

"Anthony J. Moore lives at 711 Walton Ave. Apt. 5-V. The clerk also said that he was in there three days ago to pay his bill," Det. Stevens was excited because he felt that he may be their killer. "Well, we should go pay a visit to this Mr. Anthony J. Moore. What you think?" Det. Moody replied.

"Let's find out why was his beeper on the victim's floor, the day that she was murdered," he added as he got up from his desk to put on his jacket.

"Maybe we should have a squad car go over there just in case our suspect tries to run," Stevens stated.

"Nah, I have a feeling that he'll behave himself. Now let's go before you try to persuade me to call in the National Guard too," Moody added as they walked side by side out of the precinct to their unmarked Crown Victoria to find their only suspect in the case.

The drive over to Walton Avenue took only fifteen minutes, but to Det. Moody, it seemed like it took forever. In his mind, he kept thinking about the scene in the victim's bedroom, and the brutal way she was murdered. *"No one should have to die like that"* was what he kept thinking to himself. He knew that he shouldn't be showing any emotions, especially after all the years of doing this job. It should have been easy for him to dismiss it and go about his business, but the fact was, every case bothered him, especially when it involved women and children.

As Det. Stevens pulled into the parking lot across the street from the building that Mr. Moore allegedly resided at, he did a quick survey of the area and noticed that everyone was out in full force. People were milling around talking, walking, and obviously selling and buying drugs. He wasn't here to figure out the landscape or who was who in these projects. Their main goal was to find Anthony Moore and bring him in for questioning.

FOUR

Anthony was standing in his bedroom looking in the mirror that was hanging above his dresser trying to get himself ready before his mother came home from work. He had just finished taking a shower and was now putting on a pair of black Levi's denim jeans and a tan leather braided belt. As he sat on his bed to put on his peanut butter colored Tims, he looked in his closet to find a shirt that would go with the jeans he was wearing. Leaving his Tims unlaced, he walked over to the mirror and admired his chiseled chest and abs from the daily work-outs he did at the gym. He slipped his twenty-eight inch Gucci link gold chain with the gold and diamond encrusted Jesus medallion over his head and watched how it hung against his chest in the mirror.

He heard his sister in the kitchen and thought to himself, "Playing in the refrigerator, no doubt."

"Hey An-gieeee," he screamed trying to get her attention.

"Whaaat," she yelled back in her sarcastic tone of voice.

"Won't you make me a sandwich real quick."

"Oh, now you're crippled, huh? The last I remember,

your hands were working just fine."

"Come onnnnn. I'm still getting dressed," he said as he chose a black hooded sweatshirt to complete his outfit.

"No! What part don't you understand? The N, or the 0," she replied, rolling her eyes in her head.

"Ah-ight, I'll remember that. You'll need me to do something sooner or later."

They lived on Walton Ave Apt. 5-V. He was twenty-two and his sister was twelve. Their mother, who was at work, didn't come home until five o'clock. Their father left them when Angela was born and has never been back since.

Tony, as his family and friends called him, was the man of the house. Tony was waiting for his mother to come home, so he could go on the block and kick it with his homies a little. Between school and work, his days were pretty much full. Now that he and Sonya were becoming serious, he didn't have the time to hang out with his homies like he use to. Tonight was going to be different. Since Sonya was going to spend time with her daughter, he was going to chill with his boys.

They always ragged on him about being "pussy whipped". So when he called his boy Big Dee and told him that he wanted to do something tonight, Big Dee couldn't believe it. They made plans, after calling up a couple more of his peeps, to head to the club. The only problem was that he had to be back early because of a test he had to get up for the next morning.

Before he put on his shirt, he splashed on some Cool Water cologne and made sure that his hair was straight. He heard someone knock on the front door. He automatically knew that it wasn't for him. "That's probably for Angie, one of her crazy ass girlfriends wanting her to come out, or wanting to spread some gossip," he said out loud to himself. He went over to his boom box near his window and pressed the play button on the tape recorder in order to listen to Rakim's new joint *Check Out My Melody.* "My names the R.A.K.I.M. Yo, I'm not on the list, but what I'm saying, I got rhymes like a scientist..." Tony was lip syncing the words as he went back over to his mirror to put on his hoodie. Before he could pick it up, he heard Angie scream his name,

"An-tho-nyy!"

As soon as the two detectives stepped out of their unmarked car, the first thing they noticed was how quickly those same people that were just milling around minutes before when they drove up, were now trying their best to disappear.

Once they were inside of Mr. Moore's building, they took the stairs to the fifth floor and headed down the dimly lit hallway towards apartment 5-V. The hallway was deserted which made it easier to get their job done. Det. Moody knocked three times and waited for someone to answer. Det. Stevens had one hand on his service gun while the other hand was clutching his notepad.

"Who is it," a young girl's voice yelled from behind the door.

"It's Det. Moody from the Homicide Division. Is there an Anthony Moore living here?" Just as he was finishing his sentence, the door opened up revealing a young girl between the ages of 10-13 years old.

"Can I help you," was all she said as they stood in the hallway trying to look inside of the apartment.

"Who you said you wanted," she asked one more time as if she didn't hear them the first time.

"I'm looking for Anthony Moore. Does he live here," Moody replied, this time with his eyes looking around her and into the apartment to see if he saw anyone else. She turned her head around without moving away from the door and yelled,

"An-tho-nyyy! The police are here!" Angie motioned for the two detectives to come in. Once they were inside, she closed the door and walked towards the kitchen to finish whatever she was doing before she was disturbed. A young light-skinned man emerged from down the apartment's hallway wearing a pair of black jeans, and on his feet were a pair of construction boots. He wasn't wearing a shirt, but dangling from his neck was a gold chain with a religious medallion on it. The first thing that both detectives noticed was that Anthony didn't have a cut or any marks on his face at all.

"Is there a problem Officers," Tony quickly asked walking towards them with his hands held up as they stood staring at him trying to make sense of it all. Once they realized that everything was safe, Det. Stevens let his hand drop from his gun and waited for Det. Moody to speak.

"Are you Anthony J. Moore?"

"Yes, I am. What seems to be the problem?" Tony asked again.

"Do you know a Sonya Johnson, Mr. Moore?"

"Yes, I do. Why? Is there something wrong?" Tony asked with a worried look on his face. Both detectives could sense that this suspect was obviously unaware of what happened within the last thirty-six hours.

"Mr. Moore, do you mind coming with us down to the precinct for further questioning," Det. Moody asked while his partner was looking around the immediate area at the pictures on the table.

"Well, I'm here with my sister. Wait! What is this about?" Tony screamed.

Det. Moody stopped him in mid-sentence and told him that he was not at liberty to discuss any details at this time, but if he could come with them, he would find out soon enough. As much as Det. Moody wanted Anthony to be the killer, it seemed unlikely.

Anthony called his next door neighbor, Mrs. Smith, to ask if it was alright for his sister to stay at her place for a couple of hours until his mother got off of work.

"Sure Anthony, bring her over," Mrs. Smith said while standing in her kitchen frying chicken. Anthony hung up the phone and told his sister to get what she needed because she was going to stay at Mrs. Smith's until he came back.

"I'll come back to get you if I get back before mommy comes home alright?"

"Whatever," his sister said with a serious attitude since she couldn't do what she wanted to if she was going to stay over Mrs. Smith's.

Detective Moody studied Anthony's body language from afar. From what he observed, Anthony seemed genuinely concerned about the well-being of Sonya. Det. Moody and his partner walked on both sides of Anthony as he walked his sister to the neighbor's apartment. It was a short walk down the hall. Once his sister went inside and closed the door, the two detectives gave each other their infamous wink. This was the code to go into the Good Cop/Bad Cop routine. "*Damn*, we might have this case closed before dinner time," Det. Moody whispered to his partner.

Tony could not imagine anything being wrong with Sonya since he had just made love to her the day before. "Lord, please let Sonya be alright," he said out loud to himself, wondering if the detectives heard him.

The detectives stopped about three feet from the elevator and slammed Anthony up against the wall.

"Assume the position asshole," Det. Stevens said while slapping the metal cuffs on his wrists.

"Owww, the damn cuffs are too tight," Anthony shrieked as he tried to maneuver his arms so that he could stop the cold metal from digging into the bones in his wrists. Det. Moody loosened the cuffs slightly hoping that Anthony would take that as a sign that he was on his side. As the detectives led Anthony out of his building, news reporters and television cameras met them.

"Oh, shit," Anthony said while lowering his head so that he could hide from the cameras. Det. Moody felt sorry for the young man, so he placed Anthony's coat over his head. It seemed as if they were walking in slow motion. The walk to the unmarked car seemed like it took forever. The rowdy crowd thickened as the detectives tried to hurry their number one suspect to their car.

"Let him go muthafuckers! He ain't do nuthin' wrong," a drunken man screamed as the detectives secured Anthony in the back seat of their Crown Victoria.

"Pull off Moody before I bust a cap in one of these lowlifes," Det. Moody smiled as he pulled off thinking that his partner was crazy enough to actually try to go to war with the projects.

Anthony remained silent the entire ride to the precinct. He kept his eyes closed hoping that when he opened them, this whole ordeal would be just a bad dream. Suddenly, he felt the car screech to a startling halt. He opened his eyes immediately, only to see civilians and news reporters rushing in their direction. "Damn it, we have to use the emergency entrance," Det. Stevens screamed to his partner as he made a sharp left turn into the police officer's garage.

"Who the hell leaked that we had a suspect," Stevens wondered out loud.

Anthony gave a sigh of relief as he was escorted into the police barracks to be questioned. He was actually scared, so scared that he felt that his bowels would give out on him at any second. *"There's nothing to be afraid of. You didn't do anything,"* Anthony secretly told himself trying to psyche himself up.

"Have a seat Mr. Moore and make yourself comfortable," Det. Stevens said to Tony motioning him to sit down. "Mr. Moore, I'd like to ask you a few questions and please think about them before answering, okay?"

"Okay," Anthony responded eagerly.

"First things first. Are you willing to fully cooperate with us honestly?"

"Yes, I'll do whatever it takes to help you."

"Good. We need you to sign this waiver stating that you have been advised of your rights, and you are willing to waive those rights, so that you can assist us in finding the perp, or perpetrators."

"Perpetrators! What perpetrators," Anthony asked nervously as his forehead started to sweat.

"Look asshole, we don't have the time, or the patience to play the hundred fuckin' question game. So either sign the form, or we'll haul your ass off to Riker's Island and put you in a cell with the real predators, who'll love ripping your virgin asshole to shreds," Det. Stevens bellowed like a crazed lunatic.

Anthony was uncuffed so that he could sign the waiver form. The detectives weren't taking any chances, so Stevens handcuffed his left arm onto the arm of the plush office chair that he was sitting in. Stevens turned the tape recorder on, so that they could get Anthony's full confession on tape.

"Please, state your full name for the record."

"Anthony J. Moore."

"Are you giving this statement voluntarily?"

Anthony paused for a few seconds without answering

Det. Stevens gave him the evil eye.

Anthony then snapped out of his zone and replied, "Yes!" A young African-American woman then entered the room to join the two detectives in the interrogation of Mr. Moore.

"How do you know Sonya Johnson?"

Anthony closed his eyes, so that he could concentrate on the questions that he was being asked.

"She is my girlfriend. Is she alright?" Anthony asked even though in his heart, he knew something was terribly wrong.

"No, she's not alright," Det. Stevens said with an attitude. "When was the last time you saw her?"

"Yesterday afternoon. I left her apartment at about four forty-five."

"So tell me, you like beating the shit out of poor innocent single mothers trying to support their kid?"

"Excuse me," Anthony said in a puzzled tone. "I love that girl, and I treat her daughter as if she is my own."

"Is that right," Det. Stevens asked sarcastically.

"Yes sir! As a matter of fact, I can tell you everything we did yesterday," he added, looking directly into his eyes. As Anthony began to speak, the woman that came into the room earlier began taking notes on her notepad. When he looked closer at the attractive woman, he noticed that her name tag, which was clipped on the front pocket of her blouse, read Rosalyn Hines (Clinical Psychologist). Anthony turned his attention back to Det. Stevens and began to explain the last day that he spent with is girlfriend. "I came over because she told me that her daughter had a fever. I thought that she might need help since she was there by herself. Once I got there, Myah was already asleep. We talked for a minute then she went to check on Myah to see if she had awakened, which she didn't. We started to fool around on the couch until she led me to her bedroom. One thing led to another, and we ended up having sex. She wanted me to stay, but I had to get home since my sister was home alone. I swear to God that I never put my hands on her. You can ask her, she'll tell you," Anthony confidently pleaded. For some strange reason, everyone in the room believed his story except Det. Stevens. He decided to press further.

"So tell me Mr. Moore, did you have unprotected sex with Ms. Johnson?"

"Yes I did sir. We always had unprotected sex since we agreed on having a monogamous relationship." At that point, Det. Stevens conscience told him that they might not have the right guy, but he wanted to ruffle his feathers a little more before he let him off the hook.

"Mr. Moore, would you be willing to let us fingerprint you and take a DNA sample?" He was hoping that Anthony would give him a sign that he was guilty.

"Sure, I'll do whatever you want to help you find whoever beat up my girlfriend," he replied naively.

"Uncuff him, Stevens. It seems that we have made a terrible mistake," Moody said reluctantly. As the cuffs were taken off of Anthony, a rookie officer brought him a KFC dinner.

"We figured you might be hungry, so we ordered you the chicken dinner special along with a Pepsi. Anthony was so hungry that he thanked them as he devoured his meal.

"Now tell us Mr. Moore, did you see anything out of the ordinary when you were leaving Ms. Johnson's apartment?" Again, Anthony closed his eyes and tried his best to visualize the last night he spent with Sonya. "Just think about what happened when you were in the apartment and what happened when you left," the Clinical Psychologist said trying to help Anthony remember any pertinent information that might help the detectives locate their potential suspect.

Anthony thought about the events the day before. He suddenly recalled Sonya getting a phone call. "Oh shit," Anthony suddenly exclaimed as he remembered all the weird shit that happened. "While Sonya and I were fu... excuse me, making love, she got a phone call," Anthony said with an embarrassed look on his face.

"Who called her and what time did this person call," the detectives asked excitedly.

"I don't know who called. All I know is that Sonya started acting strangely."

"What do you mean, she started acting strangely? Strangely how," Ms. Hines asked with her facial expression showing no emotion.

"Well, she started whispering while she was talking, and she never hung up the phone. So I figured it was one of her girlfriends because she put them on hold."

"How do you know she never hung up the phone," Det. Moody asked looking at Anthony suspiciously.

"I know that because I saw her press the mute button while I was sexing her from behind, and I saw when she dropped the phone on the floor." Anthony's sexual confession caused Ms. Hines's face to become flustered. "When I was leaving, I saw a black Pathfinder across the street from her projects. I wouldn't have paid it any mind ordinarily, but it was the only jeep on the block."

"Tell me more about this jeep," the two detectives said in unison.

"The Jeep had a booming system, and the guy was gritting on me when I passed it crossing the street," Anthony replied feeling comfortable assisting the authorities.

"So what happened next?"

"I gritted back on his ass to let him know I wasn't no

punk either!"

"Did you get a good look at him," Stevens asked Anthony as if his life depended on his answer.

"Well, all I know is that this dude must have been to Riker's or something because he had a long scar on his cheek, like someone cut him in the face," he said as he wondered why everyone looked so excited. "Oh, I remember some of his license plate number. He had a blue light going around the outside of it. The first three letters were H-E-N." The detectives jumped up and ran up to Anthony and shook him.

"Are you sure," they asked praying that they heard him right.

"I'm positive."

Det. Moody ran out of the room to put an APB on a black Pathfinder with the license plate that had H-E-N on it.

"I want you to take my card and call us if you remember anything else, okay?"

"So you mean I'm not under arrest" Anthony asked unsure if they were trying to trick him.

"No, you're not under arrest. As a matter of fact, you may be the only adult witness we have."

"Can you tell me what hospital my girlfriend is, so I can go see her?"

The detectives both held their heads down as they delivered the bad news.

"I'm sorry to inform you that Ms. Johnson was found murdered in her apartment about an hour after you left her. Someone raped and beat her to death in front of her daughter," Det. Stevens said with compassion in his voice.

Anthony stood up and screamed, "Noooo, she isn't dead. I was just with her yesterday! You're fuckin' lying!" Det. Stevens attempted to calm Anthony down. "She's not dead," Anthony cried in disbelief. Moody decided to show Anthony the crime scene photos to prove to him that Sonya was indeed gone. As Anthony flipped through the pictures, he started to hyperventilate and get dizzy. The detectives noticed that he was about to pass out, so they quickly grabbed him and sat him down. "Are you okay buddy," Stevens asked while handing him some bottled water. Anthony accepted the water with gratitude. He drank about three quarters of it, then squirted the rest in his face to cool himself off. "Are you alright?" Ms. Hines asked while studying his every move.

"I'm okay," he responded while the tears ran down his face uncontrollably. "I just hope you find that bastard before I do," Anthony said as he wiped his face with the back of his hand.

"Mr. Moore, please don't take the law into your own hands. We'll catch this creep," Det. Moody said while adjusting his gun in his holster. "We'll catch him!"

Henry woke up with the worst hangover of his life. The pounding in his head felt like someone was beating him in the head with a bat. His body ached like he had fought a Championship Prize fight. His attempt to swallow was useless because he had what weed smokers call *cottonmouth*. He laid silently on his back trying to get his eyes to focus on his surroundings. It took a minute for him to realize that he was in his apartment. Henry had one of his *blackout episodes* and hated when he couldn't remember the previous day's events. He usually lost his keys, wallet, or ended up getting into a beef with someone at the club. "Shit," Henry screamed out loud to himself as he sat up realizing that he slept in his clothes all night. As he stood up, the room began to spin. Henry leaned on the wall for support and massaged his temples. "I swear to God, I'll never drink or get high again."

He made it to the kitchen, opened the refrigerator and grabbed a bottle of spring water to quench his thirst. After hydrating himself with almost a half gallon of water, his bladder filled beyond its capacity. Henry immediately felt the uncontrollable urge to urinate. So, he ran to the bathroom to take an 8-ball piss. For the average malt liquor drinker, the best piss of their life was the piss that came after consuming large amounts of beer. "Yeah babe! Get it all," Henry said looking at the commode with relief as he filled it with his contaminated urine.

After flushing the toilet, Henry washed his hands. Then he splashed cold water on his face to tighten up his skin before he shaved. He turned on the bathroom light and began to brush his teeth. He looked into the mirror that was adjacent to the sink and noticed that his eyes were bloodshot red. *"Damn, you look like shit,"* he said to himself as he went into the medicine cabinet to get his Visine eye drops and four 800 mg Motrin for his headache. He was about to shave when he noticed the welt and scratches on his face, neck, and arms. *"What the fuck!"* he said looking down for the first time noticing that he had blood all over his upper torso. *"Damn, I must have really fucked someone up last night,"* Henry said with a puzzled look on his face as he finished shaving and hopped his ass in the shower.

FIVE

The ongoing investigation at the 43rd precinct seemed to be at a standstill. Detectives Stevens and Moody were determined to find the person(s) that savagely beat, raped and murdered Sonya, but they had no promising leads to follow up on.

"We gotta find this cocksucker before he leaves town, or decides to murder someone else. Right now, we really don't have shit to go on. The only thing we know about this creep is that he is African-American, has a scar on his face and he's tall." Det. Stevens said to his partner.

Detective Moody rummaged through his file cabinet trying to locate his personal Rolodex. He kept it hidden because it contained the names of all the CI's (Confidential Informants) in the Bronx Jurisdiction.

"Ahh, here it is!" He said with excitement, kissing the Rolodex and holding it in the air so that his partner could see it.

"Hey Eric, I got a feeling we're going to catch this creep sooner than we think!" Detective Moody said to his partner as he flipped through his Rolodex, looking for the Bronx Parolees who were released within the last six months. "Let's see, what do we have here?" He said as he read each name one by one: "Julian *"Klondike"* Miller, Pablo *"Yirro"* Martinez, Gerald *"Twin"* Wright & the Infamous Nathaniel *"Big Nate"* Biggs". "These are the top CI's in the Borough. Oh shit!" Det. Moody said breathlessly. "I think we got something here!" He said in a slight whisper as if he didn't want anyone else but his partner to hear him.

"Whatcha got partner?" Det. Stevens asked getting noticeably excited. "Well, it says here that Nathaniel Biggs aka "Big *Nate"* just came home from Elmira Maximum Security State Prison 7 months ago".

"So what the hell does that have to do with this case?" Det. Stevens said in a dismal tone as he watched his partner go into his file cabinet and pull out a black folder with red letters labeled, *"Sensitive Material"*. "It says here, he did three years on a 1 to 3 bid for Manslaughter, and that he was convicted for Drug Manufacturing, with Intent to Distribute Heroin". "Oh never mind, this guy can't help us because he lives in Castle Hill Projects" Detective Moody said looking at his partner, trying to look serious as a smile started to form on his face.

"Come on Jim, stop jerkin' my chain, keep reading!" Det. Stevens said in a sarcastic but joking manner. "Okay, Okay, it says Nathaniel *"Big Nate"* Biggs has been assisting the authorities on a State and Federal level for the last 8 years. He has helped the Chief Prosecutor and the U.S Attorney get convictions in 17 Drug cases, 6 Homicides, and one jail house Rape Charge, a third of which he did from behind bars". "Holy shit! This Rat is something special!" Det. Stevens shouted, as his Partner continued to read further. "It also says that he is currently living in Castle Hill Projects and is on the Feds payroll". Both Detectives looked at each other and gave one another hi-fives. "All we have to do is find this guy, and I'm willing to bet the Ranch that if he doesn't know the killer, he will be able get us the 411 on him". Detective Stevens said silently thanking GOD for giving him the reassurance he desperately sought.

"Yes this is true, but what makes this guy even sweeter than deer meat is that, back in my rookie days, he was my #1 Informant. In fact, I received my first Accommodation and became a Chief Detective after being on the Force for only 18 months; because of a tip he gave me. I led the 43rd Precinct on the City's largest local bust in the Bronx's history. It was like taking candy from a baby. None of our Officers got hurt, plus we found 110 Kilos of 87% pure "Smack" (Heroin) in the basement of the strip club "Mr. Wigglers", on Hunt's Point Ave. The street value was marked at over 60 million dollars. It was such a massive bust that the Feds took over and offered me a job. But I didn't take it because of my loyalty to the Bronx Police Force, plus I can't stand those snobs with the tight ass suits." Moody said with a hardy chuckle.

"You're shittin' me!" Detective Stevens said in admiration.

"If I'm lying, I'm flying. Shit! It was his testimony that helped me take down the Kevlar Crew." Det. Moody said to his partner, reminiscing briefly. As he snapped out of his zone, he wrote down Big Nate's last known address and handed it to his partner.

"Come on buddy, let's get outta here. We got a rat to trap!" Detective Stevens said grinning as he held the door open for his partner.

Henry drove down Castle Hill Ave. and stopped on Bruckner Blvd to go into Presley's Unisex to get a haircut. Presley was an O.G. that owned the Unisex Salon, and had been cutting hair for over 40 years. He had been cutting

Henry's hair since he was 4 years old. The Unisex had 5 barber chairs in front of the shop. In the back was the women's area where the women got their hair and nails done while they gossiped, watched television, or listened to music.

When Henry arrived, it was crowded as usual, but he didn't have to wait long because he had a personal Barber that cut his hair by appointment. The celebrities, neighborhood kids, and all the major playas all came to Presley's. If you wanted to know what went on in the hood, or kick it to some fine honeys, Presley's was the place to be.

"Yo' Henry what's up kid?" Shakiem said as held his hand out to give one of his best customers some dap and a brotherly hug.

"Ain't much, just trying to get money." Henry said as he sat down in the barber's chair to get his haircut.

"So what'll it be today?" Shakiem asked while putting the neck strip on Henry's neck.

"Well, I want a skin fade on the sides and I want the top flat" Henry said while reaching for the Nintendo controller that sat on Shakiem's barber station counter."

Shakiem was one of the first Barbers to put a video game at his station for the customers to play while getting a haircut. It was a brilliant idea on his part because all of the youngsters would wait for him to cut their hair, just so they could play Nintendo while they got "hooked up". He showed all his customers love.

Henry finished getting his hair cut and paid his Barber $8 dollars, plus a $10 tip. "Good looking! I really appreciate this!" Shakiem said enthusiastically while spraying Henry's hair with some oil sheen.

"Hey Sha, hit me with three lines on my left eyebrow" Henry said leaning his head back.

As Henry was leaving the barbershop, he received a 911 page. He hated when he received emergency pages, because he knew it meant that there was a crisis of some sort occurring. He went to a payphone to call the unknown number back.

"Yo' who dis?" He asked hoping that for once, there was no major drama going on.

"Yo' Henry what's up? It's me Flip, Yo' kid, you need to come to the block right away. Five-O just hit both of our spots on the Hill". Flip said, while biting his finger-nails.

"What! What the fuck do you mean Five-O hit our spot?" Henry asked feeling a sense of dread overcome him, knowing that Flip was talking about his two Coke spots in Castle Hill Projects.

"All I know is that the Homicide Division raided all the major spots. They shut down Castle Hill, Monroe and Sound View Projects." Flip said hoping Henry would allow him to go home.

"Tell all my Lieutenants to meet me at the crib in about an hour. You can go home, because I have a stop to make first."

He didn't inform his workers that he was right down the block from them, because he was dirty. Something told Henry not to drive his jeep back up to the projects, so he decided to leave it parked in front of the Barbershop. He felt paranoid, so he decided to sit in his jeep to get his smoke on, to calm his nerves.

When Henry hopped into his Pathfinder, he reclined the driver's seat, and rolled a fat joint of some Skunk Weed mixed with Red Devil (Angel Dust), so he could get nice before he made his move. He cut on his radio, lit his joint and kicked back, singing along with Keith Sweat's song "Make it Last Forever".

After about an hour, Henry decided it was time for

him to get going. He cut his jeep off, grabbed two Kilos' of Cocaine from under the passenger seat, and wrapped it in an old black hooded sweatshirt. After putting it carefully into his knapsack, he hopped out of his jeep, placed the bag over his shoulder, then locked the door and activated the alarm.

Henry proceeded cautiously down the street, going in the opposite direction of his Projects. He glanced side to side periodically to make sure he wasn't being followed. On a whim, Henry decided to stop by to see his son's mother, so he could drop the drugs off at her crib until it was safe enough to pick it up. When he finally arrived at Parkchester, he pulled his cell phone out to let her know that he was coming by.

"Hello" Libra said as she dried her hair.

"Yo', i'm downstairs, come down now so you can put something up for me." Henry said as he walked into the parking lot of her building.

"Okay, I'll be right down." Libra said, hoping that he was dropping money off, so she could peel some off the top. Her money hungry ass would do anything for money. She loved Henry, but the only thing she loved more than him, was his money. As long as he kept her dipped in the latest fashions; she would continue to be his bitch.

"Damn! What took you so long? I told your stupid ass to be downstairs when I got there." Henry said in an irritated voice.

"Damn! I'm sorry boo, I was in the shower when you called" Libra said in her most seductive voice.

"Here, take this and put it in my safe." Henry said handing her the bag and reaching into his pocket pulling out a wad of money. "I'm giving you $700 hundred dollars to go shopping for you and my son. Make sure you get him the Forty Below Tims like I have." He said as he counted off seven 100 dollar bills.

"Thank you babe. Please come home tonight because I'm horny." Libra purred reaching into Henry's pants to caress his semi-erect dick. "Hmmm, I want you in my mouth right now." Libra said trying to get Henry to come upstairs, so they could get their "groove on." Henry knew that he had business to tend to, but the combination of being high and horny made him weak in the flesh. Henry's dick became harder than Chinese Arithmetic when he felt Libra's soft hand massaging his tool.

"If I come up, are you going to let me hit you in that fat ass too?" Henry asked, knowing that Libra would let him have his way with her.

"Yes babe! You can do whatever you want to me. This pussy, ass, and mouth belong to you and only you." Libra said as she felt her sweet juices sliding down her leg.

Henry gabbed her roughly by her hair and began to tongue kiss her. All of his plans for the day would have to be put on hold. He broke the passionate kiss and said, "Come on, Quick! Let's go upstairs; I got somewhere to be in 35 minutes.

Meanwhile on the block, the police were out in full force. All the Hustlers and Stick-up kids went back to their designated safe havens, staying far away from the drug strip. It was common for the hustlers to clear the block when the heat came. This helped to ensure their longevity on the streets. One slip up or one picture taken was all it took for them to be on some Law Enforcement Agency list. If it was the Locals, you had to worry about Sealed Indictments, and if it was the Big Boys (the Feds), you could catch a Conspiracy case just for a couple of people just mentioning your name.

Detective Moody and Stevens pulled into the parking lot of Castle Hill Projects. They noticed that there were a lot of nosey bystanders standing around watching their every move.

"Damn Partner! Did you see how these so-called tough guys scattered like roaches when we pulled up?" Stevens asked his partner as they scanned the crowd for Big Nate. While they were making their way through the projects, they noticed four teenage boys sitting on a park bench smoking marijuana and drinking Old English malt liquor.

"Hey Jim, lets ruffle these guys feathers a little". As the Detectives approached the kids, they heard one of the kids yell.

"Ouuuu-Ouuuu, Five-O's coming!" The youngest boy threw down the 40 oz bottle and took flight. Detective Stevens took off after the adolescent, while Moody held the other kids captive on the park bench.

"Don't move assholes!" he said while pointing his pistol at the biggest boy, who looked to be no older than 16 years of age.

After about 5 minutes of ducking and dodging in between cars, Detective Stevens finally caught the young man that ran away from him, bringing him back to where the others were being held. One the project's residents stood and watched, as the Detectives questioned and admonished the young men for breaking the law.

"What the hell is wrong with you guys? Do you want to be dopefiends and alcoholics before you are old enough to Vote? Huh? Answer me dammit!" Det. Moody asked as he roughly patted down each of the young men.

"Looks like, we hit the Jackpot Partner!" Stevens said as he saw Det. Moody pull out a Ziploc bag containing about two ounces of Sess and two packs of E-Z Wider rolling papers. "This shit here will get all of you five years Up-North." Stevens said trying to intimidate the young men, at the same time trying to teach them a lesson. "I'm going to give you one chance to go home. If you lie to us, we're going to haul your asses off to Rikers Island. Now, where did you get the reefer from?" Moody asked, directing his question to the kid who had the weed in his possession.

Young Petey looked at the Detectives with disgust and said, "I ain't tellin' you shit! I ain't no fucking Rat man! I want a Lawyer!"

"You want a fuckin' Lawyer? You want a fuckin' Lawyer! Well, people in hell want ice water."

"Look, either lock my ass up, or let my black ass go, you fuckin' Pig!" The young man said spitting on Moody's shoes.

"Okay, we'll see how tough you really are." Moody said as he handcuffed the young man and radioed for a squad car to take Petey down to the Precinct.

"Hold ya'll heads, don't tell them shit! I'll see ya'll down at the station." Young Petey said arrogantly, knowing that his boys wouldn't fold under the Detectives "scare tactics." He knew from this point on that the 'hood' would recognize his Possee as "*Thoroughbreds*." Little did he know that, his friends wouldn't be joining him at the Precinct. They had only one motto, Self-preservation first.

After Petey was escorted to the Precinct, his little buddies sang like "The Temptations!" "The weed wasn't ours, it was Petey's." The biggest kid out of the group said. Stevens wasn't really interest in the weed at all, but he played along.

"Where did he get it from?"

"His Uncle Nate gave it to him" the oldest boy said looking around to see if anyone saw him giving information to the Detectives.

"Is this his Uncle?" Moody asked, showing him a black and white mug shot of Big Nate.

"Yes that's him." The young man said in a whisper.
"Where can I find him?"

"He always stands in front of the Kennedy's Fried Chicken spot, selling weed." Another member of the Posse volunteered, with the rest of the crew nodding in agreement with him.

"I'm going to let you guys go, cause your two friends did the right thing. Don't let me catch you getting high or drunk ever again! Do I make myself clear?"

"Yes sir" the kids said in unison.

"Okay, now go on! Get the hell out of here!" Detective Moody said watching the kids rush up the block towards the train station.

As the detectives walked back to their car, they heard shots fired. Out of instinct, they both ducked behind the car and came up with the guns drawn, looking in all directions. They didn't see anyone shooting, but they notice a crowd running from the direction of Kennedy's Fried Chicken, They both ran toward Kennedy's, and when they arrived, they noticed a body lying stretched out on the sidewalk violently convulsing. Detective Moody was the first on the scene as he kept his gun drawn and yelled to his partner to call for backup.

"Somebody call an ambulance!" he screamed to one of the bystanders. As the blood poured out of the man's chest with every heartbeat, Detective Stevens knew that it would take a miracle for the young man to survive his gunshot wounds. As he watched the life seep out of the man's body, he wondered why this younger generation had no regard for human life. Back in his day, the kids would settle little squabbles in a fistfight. Win or lose, no matter what, they would live to see another day. He marveled at how easy it was to kill in broad daylight with the cops less than 4 blocks away.

"Hey Jim, check his pockets, so we can find out who this poor bastard is." Detective Stevens said as he approached the victim. "Well I'll be a Son of a Bitch! Damnit! I can't believe this shit!! We must have the worst fuckin' luck in the world!"

"What? What's the matter?" Moody asked with concern, walking towards his Partner. "Do you know him or something?"

"Yeah, and you know him too. Come take a look for yourself". Stevens said tossing him a black leather wallet that contained a driver's license inside.

As Detective Moody opened the wallet, his worst fears were confirmed. "Jesus Christ!" He said, shaking his head solemnly. "I guess our Rat got caught in someone else's trap!"

SIX

"Oooh babe! It feels so goood!" Libra said moaning. Henry had her legs over his shoulders, long dicking her as she dug her nails into his back. Libra was on the brink of having her third Orgasm. The sensation was becoming too much for her to bear, so she tried to slow Henry down by placing her hands on his chest. "Okay! Okay babe! You got it, it's your pussy babe!"

"I know it is!" Henry said as he began to ravish her body like a madman. He began to pound her petite 5'4" 138 pound frame hard into the bed as he ignored her cries of pain and passion. Henry picked up his pace, causing Libra to drop her hands down and frantically grab a pillow in order to muffle her screams. He knew that Libra liked it rough, so he snatched the pillow from her, pinned her legs behind her neck, and pinched her nipples hard as he sucked on her neck.

"OOH Shit! OOOH! Why are you doing this to meee? OOh! Shiiit!! I'm Cumming babe! Uuugh!" Libra screamed as Henry plunged as far as he could into her. She felt him all in her stomach. Henry was finally about to cum after 30 minutes of straight fucking.

"Whose pussy is this? Huh?" Henry asked in a ragged tone of voice as he began to explode. "Aaaagh!" "It's your pussy daddy! Uuugh! Uuugh! Don't cum yet! Please let me taste it!" Libra said as she began to cum again for the fourth time. It turned her on to watch Henry's body go into convulsions as he came inside her. As Henry's Orgasm subsided, he let her legs down so he could lie on his back. Libra watched as her man began to doze off.

"Oh no you don't niggah! I told you I want to taste you! You know I need my protein for the day" Libra said putting Henry's dick in her mouth. "Now it's my turn to make you scream!" Libra said while licking the head of Henry's dick like a lollipop. Libra gagged when she first tried to deep throat Henry. It had been awhile since she had her tonsils tickled by her man. It didn't take long for Libra to get accustomed to Henry's size. Within 5 minutes, she was handling his dick like Vanessa Del Rio. As her head bobbed up and down on Henry, she controlled her gag reflexes and deep throated him.

"Aaagh! Yeah suck this dick for daddy!" Henry screamed lifting his hips off of the bed to meet her halfway.

Libra's throat started to get sore, so she grabbed Henry's dick and started to stroke him hard as she sucked him off, concentrating on the tip of his dick. "That's right babe, suck this dick till the head pops off!" Henry said as Libra felt his body tense up. "I'm about to cummm!" Henry said grabbing Libra by the hair, forcing her to swallow all 10 inches of his dick down her throat. Libra's airway was completely blocked. She couldn't breathe, but that didn't stop her from swallowing every drop of Henry's seed. "Damn babe! You give marvelous head!" Henry said giving Libra her props.

"Thank you babe." Libra said giving Henry's dick

one final lick.

"Get me something to drink, shorty". Henry said to Libra while he rolled up 2 more joints of Skunk Weed mixed with Leaky-Leak (Angel Dust).

Libra returned with 4 Guinness Stout beers. Henry sparked up the blunt, took two tokes and passed it to Libra.

"Two puffs and pass Iron Lungs" Henry said jokingly as he watched Libra deeply inhale like she was smoking with a chalice. She had no idea that they were smoking weed laced with PCP. She had only smoked weed 4 times in her life, all of which was with Henry. Libra knew it tasted funny, and had a funny smell to it, but she figured it was some new exotic shit. "This shit tastes minty! What kind of Ganja is this?" She asked already feeling the effects of the Dust. Henry was already lighting up the next joint.

"This shit is called "*Piss Cat Ganja*," it's imported from China". Henry said laughing, because he made the story up.

Libra tried to get up, but her equilibrium was off. She couldn't walk in a straight line. Everything seemed to be moving in slow motion. She flopped down face first on the bed and began to hump the stuffed Teddy Bear that she placed between her legs. Her sexual appetite seemed to increase 10 fold. She had no sexual inhibition. "I'm horny babe," Libra said gyrating her hips, so that her clit came into contact with the beak of the oversized stuffed animal that Henry won for her at the Westchester County Fair.

Henry downed the last beer, went into the bathroom to take a piss and get the Vaseline out of the medicine cabinet. "I'mma tear that ass up tonight," He said feeling higher and hornier than usual. He knew that Angel Dust had a way of magnifying whatever mood you were in. If you're sad, you may become suicidal. If you're feeling violent, you may become homicidal. He knew Libra was horny, so he figured she would turn into his porn star for the night.

As he stepped out of the bathroom, he noticed Libra sleeping butt ass naked, lying on her side with her ass poked out. She still had the teddy bear in between her legs. "Look at this freak bitch here!" Henry said as opened the Vaseline to "grease up" before fucking Libra in the ass. Henry came up behind and snatched the stuffed animal and threw it into the corner. "What the fuck is you doing?" Henry asked while lifting Libra by her mid-section to flip her onto her stomach. Libra put her face into the pillow and pushed her ass up into the air to give Henry easy access to her asshole. He parted her butt cheeks and proceeded to lick her asshole.

"Ohh! Ummm!" Libra moaned as Henry fucked her with his tongue.

Henry stopped and stuck two fingers into the Vaseline, then stuck his pointer and middle finger into Libra's ass. He went in and out slowly to allow Libra to loosen up and adjust to the size of his fingers.

"Oh shit! That feels sooo good!" Libra said enjoying the sensation. "Put that big dick in me pleeease?" Henry took that as a sign that she was ready, so he worked the head of his dick into her ass slowly. Libra pushed her ass back onto his dick anxiously.

"Come on Derek, put it in me and fuck me hard!" Libra said in her inebriated state not realizing what she had said.

"Bitch! I know you didn't just call me Derek" Henry said with animosity. Derek was a guy that Libra cheated on Henry with while he was doing a 6 month stint on Rikers Island".

In the blink of an eye, it seemed like Libra sobered up. "I'm; I'm sorry honey". She said feeling bad that she slipped up. Her apology fell on deaf ears. The next thing she felt was the most excruciating pain she had ever felt in her life. It felt like Henry had put a hot comb in her ass. Her bowels were on fire.

"Aaagggh!! Take it out! Take it out! She screeched as Henry pulled her by her hair into the doggystyle position.

"It hurts boo! Please take it out! I'm so sorrrry!" Libra said crying. Slappp!

"Shut the fuck up you trifling bitch!" Henry screamed smacking Libra on the side of her face.

"Owww! You're hurting meeee! Get off meee!" Libra said between sobs, crying like a baby. "Stop Henry! You're hurting meeee! Please stop! I can't take it."

Henry went buck wild when Libra begged him to stop. He locked both arms around her stomach, put all his weight on her so that they would collapse and she would be lying flat on her stomach while he was on top and still inside her. He pounded her ass so hard that all Libra could do was bite into the pillow to muffle her screams. All of her struggling, and tears turned Henry on even more. As he reached the point of no return he held her tight and went as deep as he could into her ass, and just stayed there. "Oooh shit yeah!" Henry whispered into Libra's ear. He stayed inside her until every drop of nut was out of him. "If you ever play me like that again, I will kill you bitch. Do you fuckin' understand me?" Henry said grabbing her by the neck.

"Yes babe!" Libra said with fear in her eyes.

"Good, now go clean yourself up."

"Yes babe." Libra said submissively as she went into the bathroom to take a shower.

Before getting into the shower, Libra grabbed her cordless phone and took it into the bathroom with her. She locked the door and began to cry. Her asshole was on fire. When she wiped herself after using the bathroom, she noticed the blood on the tissue. "This muthafucka want to put his hands on me and fuckin' rape me?" She said talking to her reflection in the mirror. "I'm going to fix his black ass!"

Libra opened the bathroom door and peeked out to see where Henry was. She saw that Henry was sleeping like a baby. All kinds of vengeful thoughts ran through her mind. "I should boil some liquid Drano and throw it in this bastards face!" Libra said knowing she didn't have the heart to hurt anyone. She had never had a fight a day in her life, plus she was scared to death of Henry. "I know just how to fix his ass!" Libra decided to call the cops on him. *"Once they lock his ass up, I'll take all the money and drugs outta the safe and bounce."* She thought to herself as she dialed 911.

"911, what is the nature of the emergency?" The operator asked dryly, as she looked on the computer to see the name and location of the caller. She was tired of all the prank calls, so she wanted to make sure she recorded the call and identified the caller.

"My name is Libra Nichols. My boyfriend just beat me up and raped me, please help me, I'm scared" Libra said crying frantically. The operator jumped to attention realizing that this was no prank call.

"Is your boyfriend still in the house?"

"Yes"

"Where are you?"

"I'm locked inside the bathroom"

"Where is your boyfriend?"

"He's sleeping in the living room with a gun on his lap"

"I will send two officers to your home. If you can, leave your home and go downstairs to a neighbors house until the Police arrive"

"I can't, if he sees me trying to leave the house, he's going to kill me. I told you he has a gun!" Libra said in a terrified voice.

"Okay Libra, just stay in the bathroom. I will stay on the phone with you until the officers arrive"

"Thank you" Libra replied with a devious smile.

"Attention all units report 1970 East Tremont Avenue apt. 6-Z. A woman has been assaulted and raped by her boyfriend. She is being held against her will. Be careful, she says he has a gun. So consider him Armed and Dangerous!"

SEVEN

Detective Stevens and Moody had just finished interviewing the last witness, and decided to call it a night.

"Thank-you for your assistance Mrs. Lozada, I wish there were more good Samaritans like you." Detective Stevens said to the obese 70-year-old Hispanic woman.

"It's really no problem young man, I just want to be able to come out and go to the corner Bodega without having to worry about getting hit with a stray bullet. I've been living in these projects for over 40 years. Back in my day, Castle Hill Projects was a safe place to live. I don't know what happened." The elderly woman said reminiscing briefly.

"Ok, well, here's my card ma'am. Please don't hesitate to call if you remember anything else." Detective Moody said motioning his partner towards the door. "I won't. You two take care of yourselves and be safe out there." She said in a whisper, silently praying for their safety.

Detective Moody had just started the ignition when they heard the Emergency Dispatch. "Attention all Units! Attention all Units! We have a Hostage situation in progress. The victim has been raped and assaulted by her boyfriend. All units! Report to 1970 East Tremont Ave. apartment 6-Z! All units report to 1-9-7-0 East Tremont Ave. apartment 6-Zoo! Subject is an armed black male. Proceed with caution! I repeat! Subject is an armed black male! Proceed with caution!!"

"Shit!!" Detective Stevens shouted as he hit the switch, cutting the siren on.

"Here we go again," Detective Moody said to his partner while making a screeching U-turn. The Detective expertly weaved in an out of traffic. He stopped at all of the red lights, looked both ways, and then proceeded with caution. He had stopped driving recklessly when his younger brother, Officer Derek Moody was killed in a police car chase six years ago. His brother was pursuing a robbery suspect in a high-speed chase. The suspect ran red lights at speeds that exceeded 85 mph in the rain. Derek was right on his tail until a car pulled out of a parking spot at the last minute, causing him to swerve and lose control of the police cruiser. He had a head on collision with a fire truck enroute to a four-alarm fire. Derek and his partner were both killed instantly. "The Jaws of Life" had to be used to get their broken bodies out of the police car. Detective Moody was never the same after that day, so he valued life more, and refused to take it for granted.

They made it to Parkchester in 13 minutes. Their adrenalin was in overdrive, which was good considering that they hadn't slept in almost 48 hours. They were quiet during the ride, both trapped in their own thoughts.

"Come on Partner! Let's find this creep!" Detective Moody said breaking the silence as they pulled into the parking lot.

"Damn we got here quick!" Stevens said snapping out of his zone.

The Detectives were on point as they exited their vehicle. They didn't know whether the perpetrator was still in the building or lurking outside somewhere, waiting to ambush them. With their backs to one another, they quickly scanned the perimeter to make sure there were no suspicious characters in the surrounding area. The coast was clear, so they proceeded with caution.

"Hey Eddie, it's over here!" Det. Moody said to his partner while pointing to the building.

Together, they walked at a fast pace with their guns drawn. Moody noticed that there were no officers in plain view, so he figured that they had already went into the building to arrest the alleged "perpetrator". As they approached the building from the back, they saw three uniformed officers ushering out the adults and children from the vicinity of the building, across the street into the local supermarket.

"Please everyone, move as quickly and quietly as possible. If you have somewhere to go, please go there, and come back later. I am going to ask you to wait in the supermarket until we resolve this matter. Thank you for your cooperation." The Senior Officer announced earnestly. The residents followed the high ranked officer's command without incident.

"Greetings Detectives"

"Tim" Both Detectives said in unison, acknowledging their co-worker. "What do we have here?" Detective Stevens asked while he tightened the Velcro straps on his bulletproof vest.

"Well, we have a woman who has been sexually assaulted and beaten. Her deranged boyfriend is holding her against her will. The only pertinent information we were able to get from her before she hung up was that his name is Henry Anderson. He's the father of her son, 22 years of age with priors, and he's armed with a handgun. The last thing she said was not to call back, because if he caught her on the phone he would kill her." The Senior Officer said shaking his head. "This is one hell of a situation!"

Detective Moody said as he paced back and forth, glancing up to the 6th floor of the building.

"I want all the entrances and exits barricaded. Call for more back-up, something tells me we're going to need it!" Detective Stevens said as he checked his pistol, making sure there was one bullet in the chamber and the safety was off.

"Oh, one more thing, the young lady was able to unlock the door for us she says he is still asleep, but she is terrified of what he might do if he catches her trying to leave."

"All right, we are going to go upstairs and try to arrest this guy peacefully. We're going to need a few of your officers to assist us, just in case things get ugly."

"Not a problem. You take care of the inside, and I'll secure the outside." The Senior Officer in command said while rounding up the officers with the most experience. "Mahoney, Watkins and Kibler, front and center!"

"Here Sir!" The men responded enthusiastically, awaiting instruction from their Supervisor.

"I have selected you three to assist Detective Moody and Stevens in capturing this rapist. You do whatever these Detectives ask you to do. Do not take this situation lightly, each one of you are responsible for one another. I want you all back here in one piece. Keep your eyes and ears open. Are we clear on this?"

"Yes sir." The trio said trying to look serious. The plain-clothes officers were actually excited because they were looking forward to finally getting in on some "real action." "If we go in and take this guy out, we'll come out heroes." Mahoney said to his partners as they stood in their private huddle.

"Yeah, getting an accommodation for killing a nigga,

you can't beat that fellas." Officer Kibler whispered to his racist buddies laughing.

Meanwhile, up in the apartment, Henry had just finished smoking another Angel Dust joint. "Damn this shit is good as a muthafucka!" He said as he glanced at his watch to check the time. "Oh shit! I gotta bounce!" Henry said remembering that he had someplace to be. "Yo' Libra! Libra! Bitch! You better answer me!" Henry yelled as he started to get up. "If this bitch makes me call her again, I'mma beat the shit out of her!" He mumbled to himself as he walked to the bathroom. Just as he was about to turn the knob, the door opened up.

"Yes boo?" Libra asked in a passionless voice.

"You didn't hear me calling you?"

"No honey, I was in the shower." She replied as she dried her hair with a towel.

Henry calmed down when he saw Libra's nude wet body. "Yo' I gotta go shorty. Go get my bag so I can bounce."

"Okay." Libra responded walking to the bedroom to get the bag with the coke in it. "Shit!" she said to herself as she returned with the bag. She was upset because she noticed that Henry took most of the cash out of the safe, only leaving a thousand dollars in it. She knew better than to ask him about his money, so instead, she cursed him under her breath. *"Bitch ass nigga, your day is coming!"* She thought to herself, wishing she had enough heart to say those words to his face, but she knew better. Henry was a 4th Degree Black belt in Karate and knew how to use his hands well, so he definitely would have broken her jaw, if she ever came out of her mouth like that to him. So instead she kept her thoughts to herself. "Here you go honey, please be careful out there."

"Bitch pleeaase! Save that drama for your mama! The only thing your sheisty ass is concerned with is my muthafuckin' money and this pipe I be layin' on you!" He said grabbing his dick to emphasize his point. "So kill the concerned girlfriend act. You and I know that if I was one of those broke ass herb niggas, you wouldn't have given me the time of day."

"That's not true, I love youuu". She said in a childlike voice trying to hug him. He became aggravated when he thought about her calling him Derek.

"Get off me girl!" He said pushing Libra off of him, giving her the ice grill. "Just remember, don't ever cross me or play yourself like you did earlier. If you're doing something you have no business doing, you better stop. Cause I will catch you, and when I do, I swear on everything that I love, I'mma murder you!!" Henry said with so much venom in his voice that it made Libra's whole body shiver. He snatched the bag and headed for the door.

Libra looked nervous as she tried to figure out a way to keep Henry in the apartment until the Police arrived. "Are you coming back home tonight?" She asked, trying to stall for time.

"Nah, I'm going to be in the street taking care of my business. Why? You got one of your little boyfriends comin' over or somethin'?"

"Hell no! Come on boo, I'm not crazy! You know that you are the only man in my life. The only reason I asked is because my mother won't be bringing the baby back until tomorrow, and I was hoping ...."

"Yeah whatever, just remember what the fuck I said!" Henry said paying Libra no mind as he stepped out of the door into the hallway.

"I love you!" She said as she stood in the doorway,

bringing her hand to her lips to blow a kiss to Henry. "It's really the Kiss Of Death Muthafucker!" Libra thought to herself as she smiled, showing him her pearly whites.

"Yeah, I'm sure you do." Henry replied sarcastically as Libra locked the door.

As Henry turned around, he felt the cold sensation of hard steel pressed against the back of his head.

"Don't make a fuckin' move, you scumbag! Raise your fuckin' hands up slowly and put them on your head" the mystery man said in a country accent. Henry didn't recognize the voice, but he could tell it was a white man. He began to panic as he followed the instructions. All kinds of thoughts ran through his mind. He just knew it was the cops or some country ass out of town stick-up kids. He wondered who put them onto him. No one knew where Libra lived. Henry swore if he made it out of this situation alive, he would hunt each and every one of these guys down and murder them and their families. But, little did he know, he would be getting the shock of his life!!

Henry decided to draw attention to himself, hoping that Libra would hear his voice and come out blazing with his .44 magnum, but he scratched that thought, as fast as it came. He knew Libra was a punk bitch, all bark and no bite. "Listen man! I don't have any mon-neey. I'm just coming from seeing my seed, man!" Henry said talking at the top of his lungs, hoping someone would hear him.

"Shut the fuck up!" Mahoney said dragging Henry by the neck into the stairwell where his partners were waiting.

When Mahoney shoved Henry into the stairway he fell onto the floor. As Henry started to get up, Officer Kibler kicked him in the ribs.

"So you like to beat up and rape women?" Kibler said as his partners joined in on the assault. Henry grunted as the cops beat his ass. He covered his face to ward off the blows to his head. Henry decided to use his con man game. He acted like a scared puppy.

"Please don't kill me, just take the money and the drugs. I swear to God I won't call the cops!" Henry said, acting as if he didn't know that the men who were beating his ass were police officers. When Watkins heard him say, "Take the money and the drugs," his eyes lit up.

"Okay that's enough! Help this piece of shit up! Take the bag from him."

When Mahoney opened the bag, he damn near fainted. "Great Mother of Christ! Hey guys take a look at this!" He said, unable to believe that the bag held what appeared to be 2 Kilos and a shit load of cash. "How, how, much cash is in this bag boy?" He asked Henry while rummaging through the bag pulling out nothing but Grants and Benjamins.

"It's 75 G's in there and 2 kilos of Coke." Henry said playing the scared roll.

"Okay, today's your lucky day. Watkins, take the bag up to the roof and stash it someplace safe. We'll come back tonight to pick it up, when you're done, meet us on the 10th floor, so we can deal with our little situation." Officer Mahoney said winking at Officer Watkins.

"When my partner comes back, we'll let you go. Then, from here you're on your own". Mahoney said to Henry, knowing that he had no intention of letting him go. He actually planned on taking him to the roof so they could throw him off of it, making it look like he committed suicide when they came to arrest him.

Stevens and Moody were still waiting for the elevator to come. They had been waiting for the elevator for the last 10 minutes.

"Shit! These damn ghetto elevators are something else!" Stevens said pressing the button repeatedly.

As they continued to wait, they noticed a tenant

come out of her apartment and go to her mailbox. "Excuse me Miss, we are gonna have to ask you to stay in your apartment until we handle some Police business. Please go in and lock the door." Detective Moody said sternly to the young attractive woman.

"Oh, okay" The woman said taking her mail out of the box. "By the way, if you're waiting for the elevator, it's out of order. It hasn't been working for over a week now."

"Thank you very much." The Detectives said as they headed for the stairs.

After Watkins dropped the money off, he headed down to the 10th floor to meet his partners.

"Everything go alright buddy?" Mahoney asked while Kibler kept his eye on Henry, who was sitting on the steps.

"Yeah, everything went smoother than a baby's ass. We are going to celebrate after this is all over." Watkins said breathing heavily, as he thought about the expensive private school that he could afford to send his daughter to now.

"What are we going to do with this asshole?" Kibler asked Mahoney out of curiosity. Henry over heard them talking about walking him to the roof so that he could *"Fly like an Eagle."*

"Oh shit! These bastards are going to try and throw me off the fuckin' roof!" He said to himself, feeling the sudden urge to defecate.

"Alright buddy, we are going to take the steps up to the roof and leave you up there. How you get away is on you. You'll wait until we are out of your sight before you leave. Then you are free to go. Understand?"

"Yeah, I understand". Henry said realizing that he had one last chance to get away.

"Okay, let's move out!"

As the three officers escorted Henry up to the next floor, he froze. "Keep going boy, New York's finest will be swarming the building soon." He said trying to rush Henry to his death. But Henry wouldn't budge. Mahoney slapped the shit out of him.

"Move it nigga!"

When Henry tasted the salty blood in his mouth, he flipped. "Muthafuckaaa's!!" He screamed as he chopped Mahoney in his throat knocking him unconscious. He grabbed Kibler and threw him down a whole flight of stairs headfirst. His forehead split open like a cantaloupe. The Angel Dust made him feel like superman. It magnified his strength and rage. All he saw was a red hue. He wanted to kill these people that tried to do him harm, fuck the fact that they were cops. Fat ass Watkins scrambled as he tried to back up the next flight of stairs away from Henry, forgetting about his partners. He just saw this man exhibit superhuman strength, and it scared the shit outta him! Henry saw him tugging at his holster trying to get his gun loose. He pulled him down the stairs by his legs and pounced on him like a cat does when it has a rat trapped. As he jumped, Watkins fired his service revolver. "POW!" The first shot hit Henry in his left shoulder. The force of the chrome .38 Police Special threw Henry into the side of the staircase wall, but he kept coming. When Watkins second shot missed, his body shook with fear. Henry took that opportunity to rush and attack him like a wild savage, wrestling the gun away from him.

"Please don't kill me! I have four children!" He said crying like a bitch. Henry showed no mercy as he pistol-whipped the officer with his own gun.

"Somebody help meee!! Please!!! The officer said squealing like a pig in a slaughterhouse.

"Shut up! You bitch!!" Henry screamed, breaking the officers jaw, and knocking him out cold.

Detective Moody and Stevens had just made it to the 6th floor when they heard a commotion coming from above them.

"Come on partner let's go!" Moody said leading the way up the stairwell. They walked quietly up the steps, taking two steps at a time. The further they went up, the louder the voices became.

"Bitch ass faggot! You come into my muthafuckin' building tryin' to extort and murder me? I'm Hen Dog! You can't kill me!" Henry said as he repeatedly stomped Watkins head into the steps. Just as he lifted his leg to kick him in the mouth again, he heard someone scream.

"Freeeze! Drop the gun! Drop the gun right now!"

Henry immediately raised the gun up, firing a shot at the Detectives. The bullet struck Detective Stevens in his chest. He dropped instantly. Out of instinct, Moody dropped into a crouching position and fired two shots. The first shot missed its target; the second one hit him in the thigh. Henry dropped the gun, fell onto the steps and held on to the rail for support. Moody ran to Henry and kicked the gun out of reach. He put his gun in the holster so he could handcuff Henry. As soon as he grabbed Henry's arm, he realized that he had made a terrible mistake. He felt Henry's vise like grip grab him and pull him down onto the steps with him. Henry jumped and twisted Moody's arm until he heard the bones crack.

"Aaaagh!!!!!!" The Detective cried out as he felt his right arm break.

"You can't kill me." Henry roared like a crazed lunatic, foaming at the mouth. He took his gun from him and aimed it at his head. A tear came out of Moody's left eye as he looked down the barrel of the pistol. He closed his eyes to say a prayer as he prepared to meet his maker.

"Go to hell Muthafucker."

"Pow! Pow!"

Henry's eyes got wide when he felt the hot slug rip

through his back. He turned and dropped, falling flat on his face.

A squad of officers came rushing up the steps a few minutes after they heard the gunshots.

"What the hell happened in here? Are you guys alright?" The senior officer said as he called for an ambulance.

"Yeah, I'll live. See about the others, and make sure that the bastard is cuffed." Moody said as he watched the *"Boys in Blue"* come in and tend to the other injured officers.

"Hey partner, I thought you left us." Moody said to Stevens, thanking God that all of them made it through the ordeal.

"Nah, that slug knocked the wind out of me when it hit me in the chest." Moody said wincing as two officers helped him take off his vest.

"All units, this is Senior Officer McNeil from the 43rd precinct, I have five officers and one suspect that needs immediate medical assistance! Location is 1970 East Tremont Avenue; we are on the 10th floor. I am requesting backup and medical assistance!" "Ten-four McNeil, Help is on the way!"

Libra walked up to the 10th floor with the rest of the neighbors to be nosey and see what was going on. When she opened the stairway door and saw Henry lying on the floor unconscious. A grin formed on her face, but she quickly wiped it away before anyone could notice it.

"Ms. You can't go in there." The officer said trying to restrain her.

"Get, get off me!" Libra said going into her actress mode. She pulled away from the young officer, ran to Henry and dropped to the floor next to him, cradling his head in her lap. As the officers tried to pull her away from Henry she screamed.

"Why! Why! Why did you do this to him? Nooooo! Oh Goddd noooo! You killed my Baby's Daddy!!"

EIGHT

Myah grabbed her books from off the bed and ran down the flight of stairs to the foyer. When she opened the coat closet, she looked at herself in the full length mirror that was on the opposite side of the door. "Ah-ight, this will work" she said to no one in particular as she picked out a lightweight jacket that matched her outfit.

A powder blue windbreaker was appropriate enough since it wasn't too cold outside that morning. "I love this weather!" she added as she slipped on the jacket and took another glance in the mirror to make sure that it looked right. As Myah was about to close the closet door, she heard a car horn beep three quick times indicating that it was her best friend Nikki. She opened the front door and motioned for Nikki to hold on a minute.

Myah's Uncle John was about to leave for work when he almost ran into her since he had his head buried in his Wall Street Journal newspaper.

"Oh, I'm sorry! I thought you left already".

"No, I forgot to get my money from Aunt Mary. Is she still upstairs?" Myah asked as she headed towards the stairs.

"No, she's in the kitchen getting ready for school". Myah

made a detour and headed to the kitchen. Her uncle looked at her as she walked down the hallway and loudly cleared his throat. "Ummmm! Are we forgetting something?" he said hoping that Myah would get the message.

"Oh my God! I'm sorry Uncle John", she walked back towards him, gave him a hug and kiss on the cheek. "Good morning. Have a good day". With that said, she turned back around and headed back to catch her aunt.

They were a close knit family, especially ever since Myah came into their life. She was only five when they adopted her, but it was as if they were her birth parents. John and Mary Dial were Myah's aunt and uncle. Mary was Myah's mother's older sister that hit it big when she married John Dial fifteen years ago. As an up and coming Stock Broker at the time of their wedding, he was now one of the major partners of the Brokerage Firm St. Range, Perry, and Barrow. They lived in the affluent suburbs of Dix Hills, Long Island where their neighbors were millionaires. It was a very big change from where Myah was born, but this was all that she knew since coming there twelve years ago.

When Myah reached the kitchen, her aunt was sitting at the table looking over some test papers she had to grade the night before. Her aunt was a petite woman in her mid-forties, but could easily pass for someone thirty-five. She was a high-school biology teacher at the local high-school and has been there for about ten years.

"Aunt Mary, can I get ten dollars for lunch today?" Myah asked fluttering her eyes as if she was a little kid again. It wasn't unusual for Myah to ask for money for school since she went to one of the wealthiest high-schools on Long Island. "Plus, I could use the extra money for gas" Myah added to assure that her aunt would give it to her knowing that Nikki drove her to school everyday.

"Sure Myah. Just go up in my room and grab my purse. It should be on the dresser next to the door." Myah raced up to her aunt's bedroom, found the purse and raced back down trying to be as quick as possible knowing that she had Nikki waiting in the driveway. Her Aunt took out her wallet, opened it up and pulled out a twenty dollar bill. She handed it to Myah and continued to finish her grading of the papers she had in front of her.

Myah thanked her, kissed her on the cheek and said good bye as she headed for the front door. Before she could make it out, her aunt screamed, "Be careful and don't be late for my class this afternoon Myah Ann!"

All Myah could say was, "I won't!" and with that, opened the front door and left.

"Damn gurl! What took you so long?" Nikki asked as Myah got into the passenger side of her car.

"I just had to get some money from my aunt. What's up girlfriend?"

"Nothing much." My dad let me take his car since he had to use my Jeep to pick up some furniture from his Farmingdale store.

"So, we're rolling in style today huh?" Myah said as she got comfortable in the plush butter tan leather seat. The car was definitely something to bestow. A Mercedes Benz 560 SEC Class. It was hunter green with the butter leather interior. The windows were tinted with 5% limo tint, which was legal in the state of New York. Myah had seen Nikki's dad's car plenty of times, but never had the opportunity to ever ride in it. So as she looked around at the interior, she was amazed at how luxurious the car was.

Nikki's family was very rich. They lived in a gated community and owned a huge house. The garage alone held six cars. Her father owned one of the largest furniture stores on Long Island. Anything that Nikki wanted, she got. So as they drove down Barrington Rd. towards Half Hollow Hills High School East, Myah turned the radio station to 107.5 WBLS to listen to her favorite morning radio personalities.

"What are we going to do today Nik?" Myah asked as she leaned back in the seat, resting her head on the headrest and closing her eyes.

"I thought that we'll head to Walt Whitman Mall after class and pick out some out outfits."

"You know I don't have the loot for that!" Myah yelled giving Nikki one of those looks as if to say "Yeah Right!"

"Since when did you worry about money Myah?" Nikki replied.

Myah knew that she was right, but she felt bad that Nikki spent her money on her whenever they hung out together. But by the same token, Myah knew that Nikki could afford it, so she just played the role. "If you get me then I'll get you later ah-ight?"

"No pro-ble-mo. You know I gotcha!" Nikki responded as she made a right onto Vanderbilt Pkwy passing some people that were walking since they lived close enough to the school, or they didn't have parking permits that allowed them to drive on school property.

"Look! There's Kiesha" Myah screamed as she pressed the button for her window to roll down. "Hey girl. What's up?" Myah asked leaning her head out the window.

"Whoa! I see ya'll. Yeah, I see how ya rolling" Kiesha answered as she realized who it was that was calling her. Nikki gave her a fake ass greeting, but she really didn't care too much for Kiesha and her friends.

"Hey Kiesha. You want a ride?"

"Nah, I'm alright. I'm waiting for Mimi. She should be coming soon. Thanks anyway. I'll see ya in homeroom." Nikki hit the gas and headed straight for the school's parking lot, passing a security guard who waved her through after seeing the parking permit hanging on her rearview mirror.

"You know what? I received another letter yesterday." Myah said while grabbing for her books that were in the backseat.

"Oh yeah? What's he saying now?" Nikki asked as she parked the car next to a black two door BMW 325i.

"I'll let you read it during your homeroom. You tell me what you think he's saying."

"Alright. How long have you been writing this guy now?" Nikki asked trying to prolong getting out of the car.

"About a year or so, why?"

"I was just wondering, why you put yourself through that if you have no intentions of ever being with him."

Myah opened the passenger side door, stuck her foot out and said, "Just something to do," But in the back of her mind she had her reasons.

"Well, you do you. Who am I to judge right?"

Nikki stepped out of the car and after making sure that she had everything, she pressed the alarm on the key chain to activate the car's security system.

They walked towards the side doors that lead into the school. The school was huge. It resembled a college campus. As they stepped through the door, they were greeted by a slew of students that were roaming the hallways. Even though the school started from tenth to twelve grade, it was crowded as if it contained K-12th. The official student count was two-thousand plus. It was one of the biggest, if not the biggest high school on Long Island.

Nikki and Myah looked around in the crowd to see if they saw anyone that they hung out with, but saw no one.

"Are you gonna send him a picture this time?" Nikki asked while leading the way through the congested hallway.

Myah had no intentions of sending him a picture. She

wanted him to be surprised when they finally did meet, but it didn't stop him from sending plenty of pictures of himself in various poses. Henry even wrote poems describing what he would do to Myah once they met.

At first, it was sort of difficult to get him to confide in her, but after a while, he felt comfortable enough to open up and share little things about himself with her. After the first year, he let his guard down and started trusting Myah. Finally, he felt like he had met someone special.

In Nikki's mind, it was strange that Myah would keep this game going on for so long, but then again, it didn't matter since the person she was writing to was in prison and would be there for a long time. Myah usually told Nikki everything, but her true motives for writing was something that she had to keep to herself.

The school bell rung and once again, Myah was late to her homeroom class. After giving Nikki the latest letter, she tried to make it to class, but was distracted and lost track of time. As Ms. Desmond scolded her for the umpteenth time that month for her tardiness, Myah slid past the students and went to her desk that was situated between Tanya and Keisha.

"What's up Myah? That was a nice ass ride ya'll were riding in. That bitch Nikki got plenty of loot huh?" Keisha said in her wanna-be-ghetto lingo. She was no more ghetto then Myah, but if you heard her talk, you would have thought that she was straight out of the hood.

"Yeah, that was her dad's car. That shit is so comfortable. You should of got in, and yo, stop calling her a 'Bitch!' Keisha."

"My bad, my bad. I didn't mean to upset ya." Keisha said mocking a fake sounding apology to Myah.

"Ayo Myah, you're sure looking good today." Danny bellowed from a few seats away. He has had a crush on

Myah since he first layed eyes on her in Junior High.

"Not now Danny. I'm trying to get my thoughts together. I appreciate the compliment and believe me, it's got nothing to do with what you said or done, but please, let me be!" Myah replied in a nasty tone. After being told a thousand times the same thing over and over by the same guy, one starts to feel like it's annoying beyond belief.

"Damn! I was just trying to be nice. I'm sorry for being alive." Danny responded as he walked to the back of the classroom towards his desk.

"Hey girl, why you bark on poor Danny like that?" Tanya asked Myah sounding too concerned for some odd reason.

"A person gets tired of hearing the same shit over and over again. Plus, he should know that he ain't got a chance in hell with me anyway. I've been dissin' his ass since Junior High. When is he gonna realize that I'm not interested?" Myah said not knowing that she was talking loud enough for everyone to hear. She was sure that Danny heard every word, but she didn't care.

Ms. Desmond quieted the class down long enough to take attendance. Once she was done, everyone was allowed to talk until the bell rung for their first period class. Nikki was in another homeroom class, so Myah was forced to listen to Keisha go on about her night of sex with Johnny Simmons.

"....Yeah, I was making him sweat with what I was putting on his ass. He didn't even have a chance to recuperate after he bust that first nut. I was trying to get mines, but I'll give him his props, his sex was the bomb girl."

Now, Myah knew for a fact that Johnny couldn't stand her ass, but she didn't put it past him to give up the dick for kicks. Just for something to talk about in the locker room. Keisha's sex chronicles were something

Myah didn't want to know about. Everyone already knew how easy she was in bed. A couple of beers transformed her into a raging sex addict, but she was still one of the girls, so Myah had her back no matter what.

As soon as the bell rung, Myah ran out of the classroom into the hallway looking for Nikki. Once she found her coming from the water fountain, Myah called for her. "Nik-kki!"

Nikki looked up and started walking towards Myah shaking her head as if saying "Oh man!" When they were close enough to talk without anyone hearing them Myah asked what she thought about the letter.

"So whatcha think?"

"Gurrrrl, what did you tell this poor man? He's obviously in love with you, and he's not trying to hide it either! He hasn't even seen a picture of you, and he's getting all serious."

"I know. What should I do?" Myah asked trying to figure out what she was going to write back in her next letter.

"I don't know, but it looks like you're handling your business." Nikki replied

"Come on Nikki, I need some guidance!" Myah expressed sounding like she was a little girl. "Myah, I know that you can handle this situation, so I don't know why you're asking me. Yo..." Before Nikki could finish what she saying, the bell ending the ten minute move to get to your next class had rung. "Oh shit!" Nikki and Myah both screamed as they started to run to their classes.

"I'll holler atcha later!" Myah yelled as she turned the corner and sprinted to her Language Arts class with Mrs. Camera. Of course, Myah was late arriving to class, but the teacher was just starting. Myah walked to her desk next to her friend Tasha and placed her books in the basket that was attached to the bottom of the chair, leaving her

Language Arts book on top.

"Pisss! Pisss!" Tasha whispered while the teacher's back was facing them. Myah turned around to look at her, but before she could respond, Mrs. Camera turned around to start class.

"Alrighty, now that we are all settled and ready to go, let's start by opening our books to the last chapter we covered yesterday. You all had an assignment to do pertaining to the chapter, so if there aren't any questions, let's go over it."

Everyone started opening their books and pulling out their assignments which Myah didn't have. "Damn! I forgot all about that shit." she said to herself, but almost everyone heard her.

"Ms. Johnson, do you have a question for me?" Mrs. Camera asked in a sarcastic voice trying to make Myah feel uncomfortable.

"Huh, nah. I mean, no Mrs. Camera." She quickly corrected herself knowing that Mrs. Camera didn't approve of slang in her classroom. "Okay then, since there isn't any further interruptions, let's start with John."

John Singletary sat in the first row towards the door on the left. He was one of those geeks that loved all of his classes. He always came prepared and was always on time. He was obviously the teacher's pet and she let it be known.

"Yes Mrs. Camera. The answer to number one is C. Since the sentence doesn't have a comma to break up the two complete thoughts, it's considered a run-on sentence."

"That's Correct. Now, does everyone understand what John said?" Mrs. Camera asked waiting to see if anyone looked confused or raised their hand. When no one did, she went on to the next question. Tatianna, take number two."

Myah realized that Mrs. Camera was going from the

front of the class to the back and figured that she had time to think of something before she got to her.

"Good job Tatianna. Now for number three..." As Mrs. Camera was about to call on George, Myah raised her hand to get Mrs. Camera's attention.

"Yes Myah."

"May I go to the bathroom?"

"You just got here. I'm sure you can wait until after class." Just as Mrs. Camera was about to turn her attention back to George, Myah stood up and walked towards the front. "Ms. Johnson, where do you think you're going?" Mrs. Camera asked in a stern voice.

"I really have to go to the bathroom. It won't take long." With that, Myah walked out the door and headed towards the girl's bathroom down the empty hallway, leaving Mrs. Camera standing in front of the class fuming with her hands folded across her chest.

As she stepped through the bathroom door, she saw that Michelle was fixing her makeup in front of the mirror situated above one of the sinks. Once Michelle recognized who it was, she greeted Myah with a smile and said, "Heyyy Myah."

"What's going on?"

"I had to get out of Mrs. Camera's class for a few."

"Ahh, I know that's right. She's a bitch isn't she?" Michelle replied looking at Myah through the mirror.

"You ain't say nothing wrong." Michelle finally turns around to face Myah and comments on her outfit.

"Girrrl, that outfit is the bomb!"

"Yeah?" Myah asks as she looks at herself in the mirror.

"Hell yeah! I love those jeans especially with that blouse. You gotta tell me where you got it from. I'm a gonna go ri..." Before she could finish, the bathroom door opens up making both girls turn abruptly to see if it was a teacher or another student. A girl about five-seven with long straight strawberry blond hair walks in and greets Myah and Michelle with a smile and walks to the second stall, closing the door behind her. Myah turned back around to face Michelle only to find that she was back in the mirror applying mascara to her eyelashes. Sensing that Myah was looking at her, she turned her head and says, "Some of us aren't as fortunate as you to be blessed with natural beauty."

At seventeen, Myah was starting to fill out in all the right places. Her Hersey complexion was flawless as was her glistening white teeth. Myah's thick black hair was shiny and long. It came to the middle of her back. She had the body of a grown woman.

Standing at five-nine and a half, she could have easily been a model, but Myah wasn't into that glamorous look. She loved to wear tight jeans with a pair of boots or sneakers. She wasn't into skirts or dress shoes. Myah would down play her beauty as much as possible, but with all the curves she had, it was hard for her not to be noticed.

All the guys in her school saw only a pretty face, thick hips and voluptuous ass. They didn't care that she was smart, funny and caring. They just wanted to get in her pants. Most of the girls at school envied her. Others secretly admired her. No one had a bad thing to say about her. Myah didn't date or mingle with the people from her school other than Nikki, Keisha, and occasionally Mimi and Tanya. Some of the guys thought that she was a lesbian since no one could get close to her enough to find out, but the girls that were into that lifestyle quickly dispelled that rumor. It was as if Myah was saving herself for that someone special, and guys at school wished it was them that she was waiting for.

After spending about fifteen minutes just kicking it

with Michelle, Myah decided that she'd missed enough of Mrs. Camera's class. She said good bye to Michelle and headed back hoping that the assignment that they had to do was now over and they were now onto something new.

Just before she turned into the classroom, she heard someone call her name.

"Piss! Myah" the voice sounded distant, but just loud enough for her to hear. As she turned towards the sound to see who it was, Danny suddenly appeared from around the corner.

"Hey Myah. It's always a pleasure running into you like this."

Myah looked at him, curled her lip in disgust and says, "What!"

Danny took a step back after seeing the look on her face and realized that she wasn't to happy to see him. "Damn girl, I was just speaking to you. You don't have to look at me like that!" In the back of his mind as he looked at her, all the sexual fantasies that he's had of Myah were now playing out one by one. He looked her up and down and wondered what color panties she was wearing. Nothing she said or did ever turned him off, it just excited him even more. He was convinced that eventually, she would come around and see that she should be with him.

As he was standing there in deep thought, Myah must have said something that warranted a response because he was snapped out of his trance when she called his name, "Danny, Danny! What the fuck's wrong with you? You weird muthafucka!" He shook his head and watched as Myah turned around and disappeared into Mrs. Camera's classroom. All he could do was look at the closed door and wonder what it would be like to just hold her the way that he wanted to.

Once she stepped through the door and tried to head

to her desk without disturbing the class, all eyes were on her. Mrs. Camera called her name out loud so that everyone that wasn't paying attention looked up.

"Ms. Johnson! Nice of you to join our class minutes before the class is about to be over." Myah didn't break stride as she kept walking towards the back of the class knowing that Mrs. Camera was waiting for a response.

She sat down, looked up and simply said, "Sorry."

With that, Mrs. Camera tried to be calm, she said, "See me after class!" But it came out harshly as she spoke through gritted teeth.

After seeing that Mrs. Camera had turned her back to the board, Tasha looked over at Myah and handed her a small folded piece of paper which Myah quickly took. Trying to conceal it in her hand, she opened it up and read, *"I tried to cover for you. I told Mrs. Camera that you weren't feeling well, you know, cramps and all."* It was signed by her with a smiley face next to her name.

Myah looked over at her, smiled then whispered, "Thanks." Tasha was one of those girls that even though she wasn't in Myah's circle of friends, she just wanted to be known as one. That little move definitely earned her some extra points in Myah's eyes.

As soon as the bell rung for the class to dismiss, Myah already had a story prepared. She stayed at her desk and waited for everyone to leave before she attempted to get up. Mrs. Camera was at her desk looking over some papers, but as soon as everyone was gone, she looked up and gave Myah a hard stare.

"I don't know what's going on with you Myah, but you're on the verge of failing this class if you don't put forth some effort. I'm sure you don't want me to discuss this matter with your Aunt because if I don't see some improvement. I will!" Myah swallowed hard and pretended that she was concerned about Mrs. Camera's threat, but the fact was, this class would neither make or break her GPA since she already took the SAT and received a twelve forty. Her college options were plentiful, but she didn't want Mrs. Camera to know that.

"I understand Mrs. Camera. I do appreciate the fact that you are being patient with me, but I just had a lot on my mind. Plus, you know how it can be when you are having your period, right?" Myah look at Mrs. Camera and knew that she had gotten over once again.

"Well, I'm sure you will act accordingly in the future. You are free to go to your next class."

Myah gathered her books, thanked Mrs. Camera and headed out the door.

Dear Myah,

> *Hey love. I just received your letter today and I must say I'm really feeling you. This shit is really strange because I have never even seen a picture of you. Our bond seems to be growing stronger everyday. It doesn't even matter to me what you look like. I am convinced that we are soul-mates.*

> *I have never felt this way about anyone in my life. You have demonstrated to me what true love really is. I promise you that when I get out of here, it is going to be all about us.*

> *All I ask of you is to be real with me at all cost, and I will do the same. I would never play with your emotions or mind. Just keep returning the love to me. I won't let you down. And please, don't ever cross me.*

> *Can you please send me a picture of you? I would like to put a face to your beautiful letters. Well, I'm going*

to go now. There's something very important I want to talk to you about, but I'll save it for another time. Write back soon!

Love Always,
Hendrick

Myah walked down the hallway that was now congested with students trying to make it to their next class. As she made her way towards her locker, she met up with her crew of girlfriends. "Myah, come here girrl!" Keisha screamed motioning with her hand for Myah to hurry up. Myah walked over quickly thinking that something was about to go down, but then again, she knew better after looking around and seeing Mimi and Tanya standing nearby. They were all huddled up whispering about God-knows-what.

When she poked her head inside of their little circle, she heard Keisha talking, so she thought about what she had told her in homeroom about Johnny Simmons.

"Yeah Myah, do I got some shit to tell you." *Here we go with the rumors again.* Myah thought to herself.

"What is it Keisha?" Myah asked sounding like she really could care less.

"Well, since it's about you, I kinda figured you might want to know Miss. Bitch!"

"Oh no you didn't just call me a Bitch! You know that this Bitch will also fuck your ass up in a heart beat, so don't be trying to get all ghetto hood rat on me." Myah knew that she had to straighten Keisha's ass out in order to make sure her crew knew that she was still that bitch if they had forgotten.

"Calm down Myah. Good morning to you too! Can't a person even joke with you anymore, or are you in such a foul mood that you have to take it out on us?" Tanya jumped in sensing that Keisha wouldn't know how to take Myah's word play.

"Nah, if the Bitch got something to say then tell her to say it, if not, then I'm outta here." Myah replied making sure that her words were understood.

Keisha's pride was hurt, but Myah was too popular for her to leave alone, so she had to bite her tongue and apologize even though she wanted to kick Myah's ass.

"I was just kidding girl." As she was saying that, she embraced Myah around her neck and pulled her close. Tanya and Mimi followed suit.

"Girl, you know we love you. Stop tripping on your homies." Tanya responded while they were still embracing. Just then, Nikki walked up, saw the girls hugging and quickly jumped in.

"Wow! Isn't this cute. The gangs all here." Myah started to smile because now she knew that the one person she did have respect for out of the bunch was there. The rest of them, Myah didn't really give a damn about, but a leader had to have followers.

"So, what the news Keisha?" Myah asked pulling away from the group hug.

"Oh yeah, I almost forgot. Well you know, I overheard some people talking during my Biology class that a special someone is going to ask you out on Friday to go with them to Commack to see that new movie "Friday" with Ice Cube. I know you ain't gonna pass that up now are you?"

Keisha smiled at Myah knowing damn well she knew who that special someone was.

"Hell No! If he comes at a girl correct, you know your girl is gonna represent. Shit! I would be a fool not to go." Myah replied in her Ghetto Slang trying to make Keisha and the rest laugh a little. Nikki was smiling, but on the inside, she was heated. She was wondering if Myah really was gonna go with Tommy James. Friday nights were usually their hang-out night and since both of them didn't have steady boyfriends, it was like their "Girl's Night Out." Nikki knew that Myah was feeling Tommy a little more than she led on, but now hearing it from her own mouth made Nikki a little jealous.

"Hey Myah, I thought we were going to Sunrise Mall Friday." Everyone turned in Nikki's direction and stared at her in disbelief. They couldn't believe that she had said some stupid shit like that. Keisha was the first to respond.

"Girlfriend, ya'll can go to the mall another day. It's not like Tommy does this shit on a regular. Let the girl breathe Nikki damn!"

"Yeah Nikki, you act like Myah's your man or some..." before Tanya could finish her sentence, Myah jumped in to check the bitches before they went too far.

"Naw hold up! Ya ain't gonna diss my girl like that. Don't be coming at her like that cause it's like ya coming at me." As Myah was screaming on them, Tanya, Mimi and Keisha looked at each other and couldn't believe that Myah was taking up for the white bitch.

They didn't like Nikki's "Rich Cracker Ass," but they tolerated her only because she was Myah's friend. Every once in a while, they would throw in little sly remarks about her, but always made it seem as if they were just joking. This time, their hate of Nikki came through loud and clear, and Myah felt it.

Nikki was loving the fact that Myah was sticking up for her. She really didn't like Keisha much, but knew better not to start any shit with her because of the tough group of girls she hung with from Wyandanch. Keisha thought that her shit didn't stink. Myah was the only one out the group that stood up to her whenever she got out of hand. Just because

Myah lived in an upscale community, she still had that N.Y.C mentality and every once in a while, it would surface.

That was the last straw for Keisha. She wasn't going to be screamed on by anyone, especially by Myah. She decided it was time to say something and whatever happens happen.

"So you think that what she said was kosher huh?" Keisha gave Myah a hard stare as if daring her to say the wrong thing.

"It doesn't matter what I think. Nikki can say what the fuck she wanna say. Who's you to put someone down with your trifling ass!"

"Oh, that's how it is now?" Keisha asked standing her ground ready for whatever.

"It is what it is!" Myah replied looking straight into Keisha's eyes. Keisha saw that Myah wasn't backing down like some of the girls she screamed on in the past, so she opted for the easy way out before it got out of hand.

"I'm outta here. Fuck you and that white trash bitch!" With that, Keisha started walking down the corridor towards her next class.

Tanya and Mimi couldn't believe what just went down, so instead of choosing sides, they just waited then excused themselves claiming that they had to get to class. At that moment, the bell rung for everyone to clear the hallways leaving Myah and Nikki standing by the lockers watching everyone scramble to get to their class on time.

"Thanks Myah. You didn't have to...."

"Fuck that bitch! I should of smacked the shit out of her. She'll get hers, don't worry. This shit isn't over by far. Let's go!" Myah said in a tone that startled Nikki. Myah started walking off with Nikki following closely behind her.

That whole day, Myah wasn't too happy about what went down earlier, but she wasn't going to just stand by while her best friend got belittled right in front of her. Nikki has been there for her since day one. They were best friends and the only thing that separated them, or made them different was the fact that Myah was black and Nikki was white. The racial difference wasn't what bothered Myah, it was the fact that no matter who her friends were, they never understood Myah and Nikki's relationship.

Myah was about to meet Nikki in the parking lot since she didn't see her during lunch and that was only because Myah was trying to avoid everyone. She was still a little heated about the shit that Keisha pulled and didn't want to take it out on Nikki. Now that school was letting out for the day, she was going to meet Nikki at her car so they could go to the mall. Myah really didn't feel like shopping. All she wanted to do was head home. She wanted to lay down in her bed and forget about everything that had happened, but she knew that once she did fall asleep, her sleep would be interrupted by the nightmare that constantly invaded her dreams. *That was a chance she was willing to take* she thought to herself as she watched Nikki coming out of the side door with her head down walking in her direction.

NINE

Det. Williamson was sitting at his desk looking at a picture of his family that was in a small gold picture frame. It seemed like it was just yesterday he was fresh out of the Academy, a rookie that was let loose on the streets of New York. He was a good honest cop that kept his nose clean of all the bullshit that was out there.

While he watched some of his fellow officers take the wrong road, he opted for the road less traveled. Hard work and determination landed him a Detective position within the same precinct that he started his career at twelve years ago. He was proud of his accomplishments. The officers that he graduated with were either still patrolmen, desk cops, suspended for inappropriate conduct, or died in the line of duty. He was fortunate to be in the position that he was in, and Detective Williamson knew it.

His wife was very understanding of his job. It hasn't always been good times, but the good times far out weighed the bad ones. After nine years of marriage, two kids that simply adored him and a job that he loved, he couldn't have asked for anything more. As Det. Williamson reminisced, he found himself drawn back to his second day on the job when the call came over his car radio to respond to a 911 dispatched call. He was by himself that particular day, patrolling in the Castle Hill section of the Bronx.

His mind was racing as he looked at everything and one in sight. He wanted to do a good job and had these great expectations of stopping crime all by himself. When he responded to the call, he had no idea what he was in store for. Hoping that the call was just a domestic dispute, which he really wouldn't have much to do, but in his mind, he really wanted it to be something big. He had no idea that the call was going to lead him to a homicide case.

That day changed his views a little about criminals and just how brutal they could be. After finding that poor little girl in the closet shaking uncontrollably, the only thing on his mind was finding the bastard, or bastards that left that little girl motherless.

"Well, I guess she's not a little girl anymore." he said to himself as he picked up his phone book from off of his desk. "I wonder what she's up to these days." It's been a while, almost three years, since the last time he called her Aunt to see how she was doing. Ever since he found out that Myah was living with the Dials out on Long Island, he's been in contact with them throughout the years. But when he was promoted to Detective, his workload had been a little too full for him to continue to call like he wanted.

The good thing about it all was that the Dials had kept their promise of not telling Myah about him, so he wanted to keep it that way. He didn't want her to feel like she owed him anything, or that she had to thank him. So far, it's been good for the both of them.

The Dials had asked him to come out and visit, which he did once when Myah was twelve. They introduced him as their good friend from the Bronx. When he finally did get to see her, he couldn't believe how much she looked like her mother. He was just happy that she was doing well. The Dials were doing a great job of raising her. He could tell that they were a happy family.

Detective Williamson snapped out of his trance and opened up his phone book to look up the Dial's home number. He flipped through the D section and ran his finger down the page until he found what he was looking for. "O.K, here it is. 631-784-5555." He picked up the phone and dialed their number. As he waited for someone to answer the phone, he looked up at the clock on the wall in front of him and noticed that it was going on four o'clock, then he remembered that Mary was a school teacher and probably wouldn't be home at that time of the day. Just as he was about to hang up, a young girl's voice came through the receiver.

"Hello!" Williamson froze for about ten seconds before he said something. "Hello, is Mrs. Dial in this afternoon?" Det. Williamson knew that the young voice belonged to Myah, but he was amazed at how grown she sounded.

"No. She's still at work."

"Can I take a message?"

"Yeah. Can you tell her that Det. Williamson called just to say hello."

"Sure Detective. Is there something wrong?" Myah asked with a little concern in her voice.

"No, no. I was just calling to see how they were doing. How are you Myah?"

Myah was taken back when he said her name. "I'm fine. How did you kn..."

Before she could finish asking her question, Det. Williamson cut in and said, "Well, I have to get going, but give your Aunt my message. Thank you. Bye!" With that, he hung up and held the phone in his hand and thought about how he almost fucked up.

Myah was still holding the phone in her hand when the dial tone came on. She hung up thinking about how the Detective knew her name and why did he ask for her Aunt.

When the phone rang, Myah was watching T.V. in the family room drinking a Pepsi from the can and snacking on some Wise plain potato chips. She couldn't sleep after Nikki dropped her off from school, so she decided to relax on the couch and catch her favorite show. She was just getting into it when she heard the phone ring which disrupted her comfort zone.

After she found the phone that was underneath some throw pillows on the floor, she quickly thought it was Nikki trying to convince her to go with her to the mall like she did the whole ride home, but instead, she was confronted by silence.

Thinking it was someone playing games on the phone, she was about to hang up when she heard a male's voice say, "Hello" At that point, she then thought that it might be Tommy James calling about the movies, but as the person continued to talk, she was quickly disappointed.

"...This is Detective Williamson, is Mrs. Dial in this afternoon?"

Myah was thinking back at how strange that phone call was when the phone rang once more startling her. This time, she grabbed, it quickly.

"Hello!" she said in an excited tone as if she was an-ticipating someone's call.

"Hey Myah, I thought you were trying to sleep." Nikki questioned trying to sound upset.

"Oh, it's you." Myah responded in a disappointed voice.

"Well thanks! I can feel the love. I guess since you're not sleeping, you can go to the mall with me now, right?"

"I don't feel like going anywhere Nik. I'm tired."

"I'll get you those shoes we saw the other day, pleasssse." she said trying to persuade Myah.

"Damn ho! You really want some company huh?"

"I'm bored to death. Plus, I want to spend some money. What do you say, we go now, so we can make it back by nine."

"A-ight! A-ight! I'll go with you." Myah finally said giving in to Nikki's pestering. "I'll be there in five minutes!" Before Myah had a chance to respond, Nikki had hung up the phone.

"Damn! That's the second time someone hung up on me. What the fuck's going on?" She said out loud as she hung up the receiver and walked up the stairs to her room to get dressed.

With everything that had gone on throughout the day, Myah totally forgot about Henry's letter. She told herself that she would respond to his latest letter when she gets home. After getting back from the mall with Nikki, which was about ten o'clock, when Myah walked through the side door of her house and saw her Aunt in the kitchen sitting at the table drinking a cup of juice. She remembered the phone call she received earlier and decided to inquire further once she gave her Aunt the message.

"Hey Aunt Mary!"

"Hey sugar. Hanging with Nikki again huh?"

"Yeah, we went to the mall to get her an outfit. Look! She bought me some shoes just for going with her." Myah lifted the bag that the shoes were in to show her Aunt as evidence.

"That girl just wants to spend money. Her poor father would go broke if he left it up to her to manage their money." Her Aunt said as she raised her cup to her lips to take a sip.

"Oh yeah. You had a phone earlier from someone name Det. Williamson."

With the mention of his name, Mary's eyebrows raised up and she almost choked on her juice. She started to cough which made Myah rush to her side and pat her on her back.

"You alright Aunt Mary?" Myah asked in a concerned voice.

"Yeah." she managed to say as she tried to clear her throat and wiped her mouth. She looked at Myah to make sure she didn't look too worried. "Det. Williamson called today! What did he want?"

"He said he was just calling to say hello, but the funny thing about it was that he knew my name as well. Have I ever met him before?"

"Yeah. You met him about five years. Remember, he was my friend from the Bronx?" As Myah tried to remember, Mary walked over to the counter to put her cup in the sink.

"Oh yeah! It's been so long ago, I totally forgot. Well, I'm gonna go up to my room. Where's Uncle John at!"

"He's in the bedroom reading some reports he brought back from the office. Why don't you go up there and say hello."

"I will. You sure you're alright?" Myah asked as she started to leave out the kitchen.

"Yeah, I'm sure. That juice just went down the wrong pipe that's all. I'll be okay."

Once Mary heard Myah going up the stairs, Mary thought about why would Det. Williamson call now after three years of silence, and why would he let Myah know who he was after trying for so long to be unknown. After cleaning off the table, Mary cut off the light and went straight to her bedroom to inform her husband of what Myah had just told her.

TEN

Once Myah reached her room and got settled, she sat on her bed and thought about her Aunt's reaction when she gave her the message that Det. Williamson left for her. It was as if she was scared that he called. "Is Aunt Mary and Uncle John in trouble? Did I do something wrong?" All types of questions were running through Myah's mind. Then she thought about what her Aunt had said, "You met him about five years ago." She did remember an older guy coming to the house introducing himself as a friend of the family, but what Myah didn't know was that, he was a Detective from the Bronx. As far as she knew, her Aunt and Uncle has always lived on Long Island, but she also knew that her mother had moved to the Bronx after she met her father. *"Could there be a connection between the Detective and my mother's death?"* Myah said out loud to herself. Before Myah went to bed that night, she had her mind made up. She was going to pay a visit to this Detective Williamson from the Bronx.

Dear Hendrick,

I received your letter yesterday, and I must admit, I was a little surprised by your confession of love. I too feel as if our relationship has progressed to a new plateau. Even though you have never seem me in person or in a picture and still feel the way you do flatter's me, but I think that we should wait until you are released and able to spend time with one another before you make a decision of that caliber.

Don't get me wrong, I do appreciate the fact that you feel like you do, it's just that I want it to be for the right reasons. I want you to love me physically just as much as you love me mentally.

I'm going to end this for now, but I hope to hear from you A.S.A.P after receiving this letter. Until then...

Love Always,
Myah

p.s. I will be sending you some pictures soon!

The rest of the week went as quickly as it came. With minor excitement here and there, it was a normal week for Myah. She had to convince Nikki to take her up to the Bronx, if she was going to find out who this mysterious friend of the family truly was.

During the week, Myah managed to find out exactly what precinct Det. Williamson worked at in the Bronx. She narrowed the field of her search to precincts that were situated with the Castle Hill section since that's where her Aunt told her only after being tricked into it during casual conversation.

Myah made a list, sat down on the couch and started dialing each one looking for a Det. Williamson. She didn't know his first name or what department he worked in, but as long as she knew that he was a Detective, she knew that she would find him.

After countless unsuccessful calls, Myah final found what she was looking for. She called the 43rd Precinct and heard the officer that she was talking to say, "Yes, Det. Williamson just walked in. Can you hold for a minute while I get him?"

"No, No!" Myah said as she grabbed for a pen with her right hand and asked the Officer for Det. Williamson's office number. "Can you just give me his office number?"

"Sure" the officer replied. "It's 555-3572 Ext. 222."

"Thank you." Myah read the number to herself then folded the paper up and shoved it into her back pocket.

Now, that Myah knew exactly where Det. Williamson worked, she had to convince Nikki to take her there without her knowing exactly who she was going to see. But, there was one problem, Nikki didn't like to drive in the ghetto. She hated to even drive in Wyandanch, which was like a country club compared to Castle Hill projects. Myah would have to think of something since Nikki was her only transportation.

Myah thought about what she was going to say, and once she was sure that Nikki would cooperate, she then picked up the phone and proceeded to dial her cell phone. "Damn! She has to do this for me." Myah said out loud, as she waited for Nikki to answer her phone. On the third ring, Nikki's voice bellowed in her ear.

"Hello" Nikki said in her up-beat tone of voice

"Hey girl, whatcha up to?"

"Heyyy Myah. I was just thinking', What the hell

am I going to do?' then I heard my cell ringing. Whatcha getting into?'"

"Nothing. That's why I was calling you. I'm bored as shit sitting in this house. You know my Aunt and Uncle are home bodies." Myah was just setting Nikki up knowing damn well Nikki would take the bait.

"You want to go to that new club in Farmingdale, off of Old Country Road?" Nikki asked as she grabbed her stereo remote to turn on the CD player.

"Nah, I gotta get up early tomorrow and go into the Bronx to see a friend of the family. I really don't want to, but I promised him that I would, so..."

"You're going out there by yourself?" Nikki asked in a surprised tone.

"I was, but I'm having second thoughts." Myah wondered how long will it take before Nikki bit the bait that she was dangling in front of her.

"You want me to come with you?" There it was, the offer that Myah was waiting for.

"If you want. I know how you feel about driving around the projects and all, but if yo..." before Myah could finish her sentence, Nikki jumped in.

"If you're going out there, then I'll go with you. You want me to drive or are you taking your Uncle's truck?"

"You know that I can't drive that big ass car around there. I hate parking it as it is." Myah's Uncle had a 1999 Cadillac Escalade that Myah hated to drive because it was too high up and too much trouble to park.

"Well, we could go in my car if you don't feel like driving." Nikki responded.

"You sure it's not gonna bother you to drive in the Bronx?"

"Nah. While we're there, we could visit your old neighborhood. Are there any malls around to shop at?"

Nikki always found a way to get in some shopping no matter where she went.

"I'm sure there is. Let's head out by ten in the morning, so we can get back by at least three or four." Myah said trying to cut the phone conversation short.

"Ah-ight. Sounds good to me. I'll be at your house by nine forty-five, so be ready young lady!" Nikki started to laugh because she knew that it was usually her that was late.

"Yeah right." With that, they both said their good-byes and hung up the phone. Myah now had to figure out how she was going to approach Det. Williamson when she finally did get to confront him face to face.

The next morning, Myah woke up around seven twenty-five. After she finished taking a shower, she went to her closet to find something to wear. She decided to wear something out of the ordinary, well out of the ordinary for her.

"Hmmm, maybe I should wear something that will show off my legs. I know how guys tend to be more helpful when a girl is showing a little skin," she said out loud to herself as she picked out a short light blue D&G skirt that would come above the knees to show her smooth unblemished thighs and legs every time she would sit down. Next, she had to basically flip a coin to see if she would wear shoes or sneakers to compliment the shirt. Myah went with a pair of pink Manolo Blanink sandals, "I'll get to show off my toes!" she thought as she began to search her closet for a shirt. "Here we go!" she quickly said as she grabbed her pink D&G short sleeve body shirt off the rack. "Now, I'm ready."

After getting herself together and looking in the mirror for the umpteenth time, Myah liked what she saw. Her body shirt accented her 36C-cups perfectly while at the same time, letting her flat stomach show through the clinging thin material. Her skirt was form fitting to let people see her Serena Williams' type hips and thighs. She looked down at her feet and liked the way her sandals let her toes breathe while at the same time, admiring the pedicure that she had gotten a few days ago. Her hair was wrapped over to her right side to give that Aliyah look. Just as she was about to apply her favorite Victoria Secret Green Apple body lotion, she heard a car horn in her driveway.

"Beep! Beep"

"Damn! She early like a muthafucker!" Myah said out loud as she made her way towards her bedroom window that over looked the front of the house. Once she saw it was Nikki, she lifted up the window and yelled, "Hold on!"

Nikki sat in her 1998 snow white four door Ford Expedition that her parents had bought for her sixteenth birthday. She was listening to her latest Alanis Morrisette CD, trying to sing along with the song while Myah went into her Aunt and Uncle's bedroom to tell them she was about to leave. She had lied to them earlier, which she rarely ever did. "Wow! Now that's how you should be dressing young lady." Her Uncle told her once she entered the bedroom.

"Yeah, I like that a lot better than those other outfits that you usually wear. Ensembles like that suit you better. Don't you think?" Her Aunt questioned.

"You know I can't wear these types of outfits all the time. The only reason I'm wearing this is so I can change up from the ordinary, but I'm glad that ya'll like. You better take a picture because this is probably the last time you'll see me like this." Myah jokingly said as she was about to turn to walk out.

"Hey! Do you need some money?" Her Uncle asked

as he got out his wallet.

"Sure." Myah replied.

So her Uncle pulled out five twenty dollar bills and handed them to her.

"Thanks. I'll be back around three or four, that's if Nikki doesn't want to buy out the mall."

After they enjoyed their moment of bonding, Myah said her goodbyes and headed down the stairs. But, before she walked out the front door, she opened the coat closet and looked at herself in the mirror just one more time to make sure she still had that "Girl Next Door" look. Once she was satisfied with what she saw, she closed the closet door, opened the front door and walked out.

When Nikki saw Myah walking towards her truck, she had to do a double take just to make sure she wasn't seeing things. "Oh my God!" Nikki mumbled under her breath when she finally realized that it was really Myah dressed like that. Myah was wearing an outfit that looked to be illegal in public. Nikki always knew that Myah had a body to die for, but to actually see her showing it was something totally different.

Myah was walking so seductively towards her, Nikki had to turn away just in order to stop staring so hard. Nikki's mind was thinking a million and one things as she continued to take glances at Myah's voluptuous body. Her own body began to tingle as she started to feel a little hot. Myah opened the passenger side door and climbed in after greeting Nikki, whose mouth was opened slightly from the shock of what she was looking at.

"What's up girl? Kinda early huh?" Myah said once the door was closed.

"Yeah. I thought that we would get an early start with traffic." Nikki replied as she watched Myah adjusting her seat belt to get comfortable. Myah was twisting and turning trying to fix the seat belt so that it didn't have to cross over her chest. Nikki's eyes went down to Myah's thighs, which were visible since the skirt she was wearing barely covered them, as she moved about. Just as she was letting her eyes roam up and down Myah's body, Myah looked at her and noticed that she was staring hard between her legs. Myah looked down at herself and saw that her skirt was showing more thigh than she wanted to show, but instead of Nikki telling her, she was staring as if she was a guy in heat.

"Ayo, what's wrong with you girl? You ah-ight?" Myah asked feeling a little uncomfortable with Nikki looking like she wanted to fuck her or something.

Myah usually had that feeling whenever she was around guys and certain girls, but not Nikki.

"I'mmm sorry." Nikki stuttered trying to come up with some kind of excuse for her behavior. "I was just into this new CD. I was trying to figure out one of the verses she was saying. My mind was totally someplace else." Nikki knew damn well she was lying her ass off, but hoping Myah would buy it.

"Damn! You was looking kind of hard." Myah managed to say as she pulled her skirt down some.

"Yeah, I can't believe that you're dressing like that. That outfit is banging Myah! I thought you didn't like to wear clothes like that. What's up?" Nikki asked as she adjusted her seat belt.

"I know. I just figure I'll surprise my friend and dress sort of girlish for him." Myah replied hoping that Nikki would buy it.

Nikki started the engine, put the transmission in reverse and pulled out of the driveway. Once they were on the Southern State Parkway heading north, Nikki turned down the volume on the CD player and tried to make small talk to find out exactly who this family friend really was that made Myah want to dress the way she was. Myah was just staring out the window, letting the air blow on her face when she heard the music go low. She turned to face Nikki who was trying to drive, but sneaking glances in her direction. When they locked eyes on each other, Nikki smiled and said.

"So, how old is this friend of the family?" She was stressing the words a little too much that it made Myah think that Nikki thought she was lying about visiting this mysterious friend of the family.

"He's about thirty-something." Myah really didn't have a clue as to exactly how old Det. Williamson actually was, even though she could care less.

"Is he married with kids, what?" Nikki asked pressing the issue a little too much for Myah, but she had to play along until she could accomplish what she came to do.

"You know what, it's been so long since I've been out there that I hope I can recognize anything. Let's swing by my old projects before we go visit my friend." Myah said trying to change the subject.

"How far is it from your friend's house, or does he live in an apartment?" Nikki sarcastically asked trying to get Myah to admit that she wasn't going to visit a friend of the family.

"It's not that far, if I remember correctly."

Nikki gave Myah a look that made her think she should come clean and truly confide in her best friend. So, Myah decided that it was best that she did and proceeded to tell Nikki everything as they drove over the Throgs Neck Bridge into the Bronx.

"I knew you weren't going to visit no family friend, once I seen you in that outfit!" Nikki said excitedly.

Myah had finished telling Nikki the truth and was feeling better about it. It was like a giant boulder was lifted off her shoulders.

"I figure, if I wear an outfit like this, they would help me a little more knowing how guys think with their little head more than their big heads." They both laughed after realizing how that sounded.

"You saw how you was looking at me and you're a girl, so you can imagine how they will react, right?" Myah looked at Nikki after asking that question and saw that she wasn't smiling back like she was before the question.

"What's wrong Nik?" Myah asked in a concerned voice.

"Ah nothing. I was just, ah it's nothing" Nikki couldn't explain what she wanted to do to Myah without feeling a-shamed about it. She didn't think it was the right time, but then again, when was it the right time?' Nikki thought to herself.

As they were nearing Joe's Pizzeria on Castle Hill Ave. Nikki saw the sign and felt her stomach starting to growl.

"Let's get some pizza Myah!" Nikki said trying to get her mind off of what was really bothering her.

"Ah-ight. I am kinda hungry myself." Myah answered after seeing the sign and smelling the pizza in the air. The closer they got, the hungrier they became.

Nikki made a right into the parking spot in front of the small pizzeria, they both stepped out of Nikki's truck at the same time and headed for the front door. Nikki was wearing a tight pair of Frankie B Jeans that showed her small figure well along with a canary yellow Fendi tank top that covered her 34B-cups, which looked larger than they really were. As they made their way into the pizza shop, heads definitely turned to look at the two dime pieces that were walking through.

Even though Nikki was white, she was a beautiful white girl. Her dark curly blond hair, hazel green eyes and golden tan gave her that "Pop Star" appearance. Her five foot six, a hundred and ten pound frame made her look compact with the curves in the right places. Next to Myah, Nikki looked small, but nonetheless, beautiful. The few guys that were seated in the booths eating their pizzas and drinking sodas looked at them as they made their way towards the counter. All conversations stopped as they watched them pass by, no doubt, trying to figure out who they were.

Myah was the first to notice the looks that her and Nikki were getting, but she wasn't fazed by it one bit. On the other hand, Nikki was aware of it, but she was too afraid to turn around and look. She didn't want any confrontations, while they were there. Myah held her head high and walked as if she didn't notice a thing. Once, they were at the counter, a older woman with a white stained apron greeted them and asked if they were ready to order. Myah was the first to speak.

"Yes, I would like two slices of pizza with extra cheese and a large Cherry Coke please."

The older woman wrote down her order then looked at Nikki. "And you miss?"

"Ummm, I would like the same thing she just ordered, if you don't mind." Nikki added trying not to look to nervous.

"Okay, so that's four slices with extra cheese and two Cherry Cokes right?"

"That's two large Cherry Cokes." Myah reiterated to the older woman.

The older woman corrected the error and said, "Have a seat and I'll be there in a few minutes." With that she ripped off the ticked she was writing on and disappeared into the back.

Myah then tuned around to view the room and saw that all eyes were on them. She located an empty booth in the corner, tapped Nikki on the shoulder and started to walk towards it with Nikki following behind her.

ELEVEN

Irk's attention was on the two young ladies from the moment that they walked into the pizzeria. His homie Sadell, who was sitting across from him, was too busy trying to explain to Irk why he was short with his paper. He knew Irk would be pissed, because he fronted him three keys of Crack months ago. "...And you know, Premo has been having problem with those niggas, I told you about from up the way trying to jack his skinny ass. I'm seriously thinking that he's been dipping in his own shit and coming to me with that weak-ass excuse na-mean son?" Irk wasn't even paying attention to a thing that Sadell was saying. He was too occupied with trying to figure out if he had ever seen the thick dark skinned honey that was sitting two booths down facing him.

"Yo Dell," Irk whispered cutting him off hoping that he was being quiet enough so that no one heard him.

"What's up?" Sadell answered nervously. He knew that Irk didn't take no shit when it came to his paper. He seen his work personally, when he smashed that nigga Jo-Jo for coming up short Fifty G's, so it wasn't nothing for him to smash a nigga over Fifteen G's just to prove a point.

"Did you see that honey that just walked in?"

"Yeah. Why, what's up?" Sadell turned around in the booth to get a better look at her, since he really didn't get that good of a look before.

"Don't turn around you fucking idiot!" Irk whispered in an aggravated tone of voice. "I gots to holla yo. She gonna be my future baby's mama by the end of the night, that's my word son!" Sadell was feeling a little relieved hearing how Irk was more into those bitches than him, so he went along with it trying to keep him interested in them.

"Yeah kid, she's definitely wifey material, but what about the white chick that's with her?"

"You kick it with her, while I kick it with shorty ah-ight?" Irk demanded more than asked knowing that Sadell would go along with anything he said right about now, since his ass was still in the doghouse with him.

"Ah-ight. I'm with it!" Sadell said trying to slide out of the booth to step to them.

Irk got up and walked towards them, eyeing Myah the whole time, since she was facing him. Sadell was right behind him wishing that he was the one hollering at her instead, but once they reached the booth, he changed his mind when he got the chance to finally see Nikki up close. The first thing he noticed were her hazel green eyes and golden tanned skin, not to mention the way she was sucking on that straw.

Myah noticed that one of the guys that was sitting two booths ahead of them was definitely sweating a bitch hard, but she kept her poker face and pretended to pay him no mind. When she glanced at them again, she noticed that they were walking in her direction. She gave Nikki a slight kick in the leg under the table and whispered, "Two guys are walking our way and I think they're coming over here." Nikki didn't want to turn around and look for fear that she would look too nervous, so she just waited until they made their way to their booth to look.

Irk wasn't trying to hide the fact that a brotha was looking. His confident attitude and swagger made him look invincible. As he walked up along side of Myah, she had her head down sipping on her large cup of soda. She looked up a gave him that, "What the fuck do you want!" look, but as he got closer look at her, something in his mind told him that he knew this girl from somewhere, but he couldn't figure out where he knew her from. He just couldn't put his finger on it.

"Excuse me! Can I help you?" Myah finally asked noticing that he was just staring at her like he was star struck or something.

"Oh my bad ma. It's just that you look mad familiar to me. Where you from ma?"

"First of all, my name is not 'Ma,' my name is Myah and this here is my friend Nikki. Secondly, who's you?" Myah asked with an attitude tryin' to sound ghetto.

"My bad ma, I mean Myah." Irk finally said backing up a little, as if what she said made him stumble. "My name's Irk and this is my homie Sadell." Sadell looked in Myah's direction and smiled a greeting then turned his attention towards Nikki.

While Sadell was trying to kick it with Nikki, Nikki was trying to see if Myah was going to give Irk some play. Just watching Myah go through that tough girl routine made her jealous. She knew that Myah was feeling him. As she turned back around to face Sadell, she realized that he was asking her a question.

"So Nikki, where ya'll from?"

She didn't know if she should answer that, thinking that she wasn't going to tell this guy where she's from, so he could rob her ass. She looked at Myah silently asking for help.

Myah caught the look that Nikki was giving and came to her aid. "Ya'll from around here?" she asked trying to divert the question back on them.

"Yeah, we're from Castle Hill Projects, right up the street." Irk answered still trying to figure out who Myah reminded him of.

"Well, we're from Long Island." Myah added not wanting to give them too much information, since she didn't know them that well.

"Damn! You two are far from home princess." Myah smiled at Irk after he called her "Princess" which made her feel kind of special.

"I know. We're out here trying to find my old projects that I grew up in."

"Word!" Irk said excitedly. "Where's that?"

"Uh, not far from here. See, I moved when I was five years old, so I don't remember a whole lot about them. I wa..." Before she could finish, Irk's eyes lit up as if he had just gotten hit with something hard.

"Myah, Myah, Myah, ohhh shittt!!!" Irk shouted as he finally figured out why Myah looked so familiar. "Ayo' Myah, is your last name Johnson, Myah Johnson?"

Myah's face frowned from hearing her last name. "How tha fuck do you know, I mean, how do you know my last name?" she asked dumbfoundedly.

"No, hell no! It can't be!" Irk said in a excited whisper as he sat down in the empty booth right behind her.

Nikki was in total shock that this total stranger knew Myah's last name. Just like Myah, she too was curious to find out how he knew about her. Sadell was lost between the conversation but he didn't try to interrupt their reminiscing, so he to waited for the answer that everyone else was waiting to hear.

"Ayo' Myah?" Irk finally said after about a minute of being silent. "I need to holla at you in private, if you don't mind.

Myah looked at him and decided to go in order to find out how he knew her last name. "Ah-ight." So Myah slid out the booth, looked at Nikki, who was looking at her and said "I'll be right back!"

Nikki wanted to go also but she played her position and stayed seated as Sadell slid into Myah's spot once she was up and walking towards the door with Irk. Myah and Irk walked out the front door and went by Nikki's truck, so that Irk could give her the 411...

TWELVE

Now, that they were alone outside, Myah turned around to face Irk who was walking behind her with his head down.

"How do you know my name?" Myah shot the question at Irk as he came to an abrupt stop in front of her. Irk was trying his best to find a way to explain everything to her, but couldn't find the right words, or the best approach to use.

"Hel-loo" Myah said trying to get Irk's attention.

"Yeah, yeah I hear ya'." Irk replied as he looked at her and tried to get the picture of Sonya, Myah's mother, out of his mind. Myah definitely was her mother's twin, Irk thought to himself. Even her hair was like hers. He couldn't believe it, even though he was seeing it for himself.

Myah and Irk were standing in front of the Pizzeria talking, but to Nikki, it looked like they were arguing. Her eyes were glued to them. Her and Sadell were trying to see what was going on even though they couldn't hear them.

"That's some weird shit that just went down huh?" Sadell said trying to get Nikki's attention.

He was really feeling Nikki. The whole look that she

was sporting intrigued him. He never been with a white girl before, but secretly, he's been fantasizing about it since he saw Catherine Zeta-Jones in the movie Entrapment a couple of weeks ago. As Sadell looked at Nikki's curly blond hair, he started thinking about how she would be in bed. He heard stories about how freaky they got behind closed doors, so he wanted to find out if the stories were true.

Nikki's mind wasn't even on Sadell, she couldn't care less if he was there or not. She was so focused on Myah, that nothing else seemed to matter. Her obsession with Myah ran deep, ever since they first met. Not only was Myah her best-friend, but secretly, Nikki wanted so desperately to tell Myah exactly how she felt about her. Everyday that went past was an opportunity lost. Now, as she sat in the booth watching her through the window, all she could think about was how Irk was all up on Myah.

"Myah, I knew your parents very well." Irk explained as he leaned against Nikki's Expedition facing Myah, who had her arms folded across her chest and tapping her foot waiting to hear his explanation.

"Your father and I were partners a long time ago. He taught me so much about the game that I looked up to him as a role model. When he died, it was as if my best-friend was taken from me, so I vowed that you and your mother would be taken care of as long as I was around. I would send your moms five hundred dollars every month to make sure ya'll didn't want for nothing. The day that I heard about your mother's death, I was just coming back from upstate, and all I saw were cops everywhere. At first, I thought my spot was being raided, but I saw a few of my homies still in front of our building, I knew it had to be something else. So I walked up and saw that they were all in your apartment. My heart stopped for a moment because, I didn't know the exact reason, but it had to be something bad the way they were all around, so I crept up to your door and looked in. That's when I saw your face." At that moment, Irk looked into Myah's eyes and saw tears welling up in them. As he reached out to her, she walked into his arms and for the first time in years, Myah cried, cried like she never cried before, because as Irk was telling her the story; visions of that day flooded her mind. She was reliving that day all over again.

As Irk held her close to him, tears also formed in his eyes. He had been looking for her ever since that day and now here it was, twelve years later, she found him. There were so many questions that he wanted to ask her, and vice-versa, but as they held each other close, comfort was what both of them needed the most.

Sadell and Nikki watched through the window and neither of them said a word. Sadell was impressed with the way Irk was laying his mack game down to the young honey. He knew he would have to step his game up if he was going to get into Nikki's pants.

Nikki's mind was racing with confusion and anger. She couldn't believe that Myah was falling for that clown Irk. She knew she would have to say something if she wanted to get Myah away from Irk. Nikki jumped up out of the booth and walked towards the door.

"Hey, what's up Boo?" Sadell screamed just before Nikki opened the front door.

Without saying a word, she walked out and headed straight for her truck to confront them.

The only thing on Nikki's mind was getting Myah and going back to Long Island where things were a lot safer and less complicated. As soon as she saw Myah's face, she immediately rushed to her side.

"What's wrong, you alright? What did he do to you?" Nikki held Myah's arm trying to turn her away from Irk, who was standing next to her looking down as if he was ashamed of something. Before Myah could say anything, Nikki turned towards Irk and in a vicious stern voice said, "Get away from us now!"

Irk couldn't believe how quickly Nikki had flipped on him. Myah couldn't believe that she just heard Nikki talk like that. As long as she has known her, she's never once heard her use that type of tone with anyone. Irk looked at Nikki and before he could say a word, Sadell came out of the pizza shop and said in a humorous voice, "Party's over herrre! Party's over therrre!" Everyone turned towards him and if looks could kill, he would have died three times already.

"Damn! My bad." he said as he turned back towards the door of the pizza shop and headed back in. When he was out of sight, Irk and Myah turned their attention back to Nikki who was still holding Myah's arm looking at Irk.

Myah wiped her face with the back of her free hand and yanked her arm away from Nikki with an attitude. Irk was the first one to say something since he felt that he had to explain to Myah's overprotective friend what the situation was.

"Yo Nikki, it's not what you're think it is Boo. I wa..." Before he could finish, Nikki interjected.

"I don't care what it is. All I know is that my friend is standing here with tears in her eyes, and you're trying to console her. For what? I don't know what's going on, but I do know that I'm taking her home before I slap the sh..."

"Hold tha fuck up! Who tha fuck you think you're talking to like that *BITCH!* Myah, you better check this ho' before I do, that's my word!" Irk was visibly angry at Nikki for coming at him like that.

Myah felt like she should explain the situation to Nikki since it was all about her. She looked at her as

Irk walked back inside the pizza shop to sit with Sadell, leaving Myah alone with Nikki to handle her business. "Nik, what the fuck is wrong with you?"

"What you mean what the fuck is wrong with me. What the fuck is up with you! I come out here and, see you crying, and you're asking me what's wrong?" Nikki replied as she stared into Myah's eyes.

"He didn't do anything to me. I just found out that he knew my parents and was there when my mom died, but before I could find out anything else, you came charging out here like you're Madam-save-a-bitch or something! Irk is alright, believe me, he's not trying to hurt me. You don't have to worry, I know how to take care of myself." When Myah finished explaining to Nikki, Nikki felt like the biggest jackass imaginable. Not only did she have Myah upset with her, Irk probably couldn't stand her as well. She had to make it right. Nikki didn't want to lose what she had with Myah, nor did she want to get herself killed while she was in the Bronx.

"I'm sorry. I was just making sure that..." Nikki couldn't even finish what she wanted to say before she started to cry.

"Don't worry about it." Myah said as she grabbed her and pulled her close to her giving Nikki a hug to comfort her. "I think you better save that apology for Irk since it's him that you really pissed off."

"Yeah, I know, but what should I do?" Nikki asked as she put her fingernail in her mouth showing her nervousness. "Let's go back in there and make it right. I'm sure he'll understand plus, I'll be with you, okay?"

"Okay." With that, they both went back into the pizza shop and sat at the same booth as Irk and Sadell.

Nikki apologized to Irk for acting the way she did and for jumping to conclusions, but she still harbored strong feelings about what Myah did. Sadell was just happy to be out of the doghouse with Irk since he was more focused on Myah. Irk was excited over the fact that he finally found Myah. He was already planning to make sure that she was well taken care of. He was going to treat her like she was his own daughter, or at least family since both of her parents were deceased.

Myah looked at her watch and realized that she had to get going if she was going to catch Det. Williamson at the precinct. "Hey Nikki, we have to get going. I still have to meet that friend of the family soon," she said trying to talk in code, so she didn't have to explain anything. Nikki caught on quick and played it off like a vet.

"Yeah, I was just thinking the same thing." Nikki was glad that they were about to leave. She didn't really feel comfortable just sitting there. She didn't really want to apologize either. In her eyes, she felt she did nothing wrong, but she didn't want Myah upset with her.

As they were about to get up from the booth that all of them were sitting at, Irk stood up and said, "Yo Princess, let's exchange numbers, so we can keep in touch." Irk pulled out his Palm V from his pocket and waited for Myah to recite her number for him.

At first, Myah was hesitant about giving her number to him, but after realizing that he could be of use to her, she gave him her beeper and cell phone number. She took his as well.

"You know Princess, your father would have been very proud of the way that you turned out."

When Irk said that, Myah looked at him and thought of what her mother use to tell her about her father. *"Your father would have been spoiling you like crazy if he were still here. You were his whole world. I use to think he loved you more than he did me...."* tears welled up in Myah's eyes as she thought about all the pictures her mom would show her of her father.

"Ayo Princess, you ah-ight?" Irk asked snapping her back to the present. "Yeah, yeah I'm ah-ight." Myah responded as she wiped the tears away from her eyes with the napkin she had in her hand. She turned to face Irk after getting herself together and said, "Try giving me a call tomorrow at around five-thirty ah-ight?"

"Sure Princess. I'll do that." With that said, Irk and Sadell gave Nikki and Myah a hug and watched as they walked out the door of the pizza shop, hopped into Nikki's truck and left.

"Ayo Irk, Myah one fine bitch. Word is bond son!" Sadell said once he saw them leave the parking lot, but the way Irk looked at him, he knew he had fucked up.

"What the fuck did you just say?" Irk asked him to make sure that he heard him right.

"I was just saying that shorty is the one." Sadell replied stepping back a little from Irk.

"First of all, she ain't a bitch! And if I ever hear you calling her that again, I'm a bust a cap in your ass myself. Matter-of-fact, where's my fuckin' paper nigga? You thought I forgot that shit Son?"

Sadell swallowed hard as he tried to look around to see if there was anybody watching.

"If I don't have my shit in the next twenty-four hours, on everything I love, your ass will be history!"

Sadell didn't say a word. His heart was racing a mile a minute. "You got it Irk! You got that!" After he said that, Sadell got up and made his way to the door leaving Irk still seated in the booth alone.

Once he was gone, Irk thought about Myah and what had transpired earlier between them. *"Don't worry Princess, I got you. No one will ever disrespect you as long as*

I'm around." he said to himself as he grabbed his keys from his jacket and placed his empty cup on the table before he walked out.

He pressed his remote on his keychain to start his midnight blue S-600 four door Mercedes Benz. As it came to life, he admired the fine detailing that the car had. He had just taken it to the car wash earlier and as the afternoon sun hit the 22"chromed Enkei rims, they looked like giant mirrors. The wood grain, with the soft butter interior, and automatic tinted windows accented the car perfectly as he opened the door and hopped in.

Irk pressed the play button on his steering wheel, which controlled his multi-disc CD player, and waited for his favorite song to come on. DMX came blaring through the speakers. Irk pressed the volume up to level seven and leaned back to absorb the music before he drove off. "Stop! Drop! Shut em' down open up shop, ohhh, nooo, that's how Rough Riders roll. Stop! Drop! Shut em' down open up shop, ohhh, nooo, that's how Rough Riders roll...." Irk looked at his platinum diamond bezeled Cartier watch and saw that it was twelve twenty two. "Damn! I gots to get the fuck outta here if I'm gonna meet Lil' D at the spot." Irk put his car in reverse and pulled out of his spot, switched the transmission into drive and blended into the traffic on Castle Hill Avenue heading west towards his destination.

THIRTEEN

Elmira, New York (State Penitentiary March '99)

"Good morning young man," the Parole Commissioner said in a jovial tone.

"Good morning" the nervous young man said looking at the floor.

"You may be seated. Today you are up before the Parole Committee. I would like to introduce to you the Parole Board Members. This is Mr. Chambers, Mrs. Saunders, and I am Mr. Thornton." Mr. Thornton said cutting on a recording device to tape the entire parole hearing.

"Please state your full name."

"My name is Henry Shelawn Anderson."

"Alrighty Mr. Anderson, it says here that you have been convicted of the following offenses:

Assault & Battery on Police Officers, Attempted Abduction, Reckless Endangerment, Resisting Arrest, Aggravated Sexual Assault, and Threatening a Witness. Can you explain to us why you performed such heinous acts?"

"Yes sir." Henry said humbly.

"As far as the police are concerned, they were dirty

cops that tried to rob me and take my life. I was just defending myself and fighting for my life. I was high on PCP at the time of my arrest, so I didn't realize the extent of my actions until after it was all said and done."

"I see here in your Psychological Evaluation that you said being high is definitely what saved your life." Mrs. Saunders said as she read her copy of the report.

"Yes, I did say that ma'am." Henry said trying to exemplify his reverence for her.

"How so?" Mr. Thornton asked Henry inquisitively.

"They said that the drug slowed my heart rate down, which stopped me from bleeding to death when I got shot. I was left in the stairwell to die. I wasn't taken to the hospital until 45 minutes after the injured officers. After I got shot, I was in a coma for two months, stayed in Intensive Care for 5 months, and I was in a wheelchair for 18 months. I was paralyzed from the waist down. They said I'd never walk again, but by the will of God and Aggressive Rehab Therapy, I am able to walk, run, and play sports like I use to."

"How long have you been back to normal Mr. Anderson?" Mr. Chambers asked.

"I have been back to normal for a little over seven years." Henry said proudly,

"Tell me about the Rape and Sodomy of Ms. Libra Nichols. According to our records, it states here that she is the mother of your son Henry Jr.?" Mrs. Saunders asked incredulously while looking Henry up and down with disgust.

Henry's whole demeanor changed when he heard Libra's name mentioned.

"First of all, there was no rape. We had sex like we always did, that's all. That trifling chick set me up to die.

It was all out of greed."

"What about the threats on her life?"

Well, I'll admit I was upset; it was very hard for me to understand how she could betray me like that. She literally tried to get me killed. She called 911 and told them that I raped her, I was holding her against her will, and that I had a gun, all of which was a lie. She wrote me first, so I responded, telling her not to ever write me again, and that she was dead to me now. I told her that GOD didn't like ugly, and she would have to someday pay for her actions. But I didn't threaten her. I would never hurt her." Henry said trying to look sincere. He knew if he had ever seen her again he wouldn't hesitate to murder her, but he kept those feelings to himself. "Then shortly after that, she killed my son." Henry said fighting the urge to breakdown.

"What do you mean she killed your son?" Mrs. Saunders asked in disbelief.

"Well, after I got arrested, she started to treat my little man like shit. Please excuse my language." Henry said apologetically. "She would beat him for little things and curse at him because he reminded her so much of me. Her sister told me that every time she came to visit, he always had a new bruise or scratch on his body. She also said whenever she questioned her sister concerning the bruises, it was always the same story, he was playing, and he fell. She called Social Services to report the neglect, but they never followed up with an investigation. I have the police report to prove it." Henry said while searching though his folder.

"There's no need, please continue" Mrs. Saunders said impatiently.

"Anyway, to make a long story short, she left my son alone in the living room by himself while she was entertaining her boyfriend in the bedroom. Henry Jr. found an opened bottle of beer and drank almost half of a 40 oz. Bottle of Old English malt liquor, then took the two grams of cocaine that these bastards left on the table and swallowed it. My son stood there helpless, choking and suffocating until he passed out. He didn't know any better, he was only 2 years old! He was trying to emulate what he saw his mother do so many times. His mother didn't even come to check on him until two hours later. By that time it was too late, he was dead!" Henry said as he wiped his tears away with his handkerchief.

"I'm sorry for your loss Mr. Anderson," Mr. Thornton said speaking on behalf of himself and his colleagues without a hint of remorse in his voice. "But, we must continue discussing the matter at hand, which is whether you have been rehabilitated or not. So let me ask you this question because perhaps, I may have missed something. Are you guilty of anything? I mean, not once have I heard you say anything about your guilt, nor have you shown the slightest penitence for the crimes you have committed and been convicted of." Mr. Thornton said giving Henry the opportunity to speak.

"I am not guilty of anything but being black and being with the wrong person at the wrong time. If I were a white man, things would have never gotten out of hand like they did. I would have never been forced to take a plea for something I didn't do. I only took a plea because my lawyer advised me to. He said if I went to trial I would be railroaded and would receive a minimum of 40 years to Life." I was tried and convicted before I took that plea. So I did what my lawyer recommended that I do, which was plead guilty." Henry said getting noticeably agitated.

"So you're telling me that the sexual assault never happened at all?"

"Yes, that is exactly what I am telling you." Henry

said looking directly into the eyes of each of the Parole Board members.

Well Mrs. Nichols' statement says otherwise!" Mrs. Saunders states boldly as she prepares to read Libra's statement.

"Okay, I am going to read to you Ms. Nichols' statement."

"Henry came to my home in the early afternoon and we got into an argument because I didn't want to have sex with him. He started acting crazy and out of nowhere accused me of not wanting to have sex with him, because I had just slept with someone else. I tried to explain to him that I was not in the mood and that the baby was awake, but he slapped me and told me to shut up. He dragged me into the bedroom and made me perform oral sex on him until my nose bled. He ripped my clothes off, when I started to cry he slapped me in my mouth and grabbed me by the neck and choked me. As I started losing consciousness I heard him saying "Shut up! You know you like it rough." When I came to, he was on top of me raping me vaginally. Then he sodomized me. I cried into a pillow because I didn't want my son to hear us and come in to see what his father was doing to me, plus I didn't know if he would harm my son as well. But when I looked up, I saw our son standing there watching. He began to cry, but Henry didn't pay him any mind. He continued to rape me in front of our son. When he was finally done, I stayed there until I was sure that he was asleep. I eased out of bed, grabbed the cordless phone, locked myself in the bathroom and dialed 911. I am petrified of him. He told me that when he gets out he's going to kill me. He is an animal! Please don't let him out. He hasn't changed one bit. If you decide to release him, please give me sufficient notice so that I can take my children and move out of New York State."

"She's a fuckin' liar! I didn't rape her! My fuckin' son

wasn't even there!" Henry screamed slamming his hand on the desk and standing up.

The two officer's posted outside of the room ran in to see what the commotion was about.

"Everything ok?"

"No it's not. We would appreciate it if you stayed in here to monitor Mr. Anderson while he is in our presence." Mrs. Saunders said in an uncertain tone as she gave Henry the evil eye and admonished him.

"Mr. Anderson, sit down! These loud outbursts will not be tolerated. You are in a Parole Board Hearing, not a zoo! Do you understand?"

"Yeah, whatever." Henry said under his breath, knowing that he just killed his chances of making his first Parole Board.

"Excuse me? What did you say young man?" Mr. Thorton said coming to his co-workers aide.

"I said yeah, I understand!" he said in a nasty tone.

"Good. Let's continue. "What have you done while you have been incarcerated?"

Henry took the time to pull out his folder with all of his Certificates in it. "I have received my G.E.D, a Bachelor's Degree from Thomas Edison's Correspondence College Program, completed the ASAT Drug Program, and took the AVP (Alternative Violence Program) with the Quakers. I also have 80 other certificates, and two Apprenticeships."

"That's pretty impressive." Mr. Chambers said as he wrote something down in his notepad.

"What are your plans if we grant you parole? And why should we grant you parole?"

"My plans are to start my own van service, and work with troubled teens. I want to help children because they are our future. I wouldn't wish this hell on my worst enemy. It's oppression and genocide. I feel you should grant me parole because I have never received any tickets (write-ups), and I regret ever getting high. I am a changed man, and I hope that I will not be judged solely by my past."

"Excuse me for a minute." Mrs. Saunders said to Henry as a Correction Officer came into the room and whispered something into her ear.

"Oh, okay. Send them right in."

Henry had a confused look on his face as he tried to figure out who else could be coming into his Parole Hearing. As soon as he saw the African-American and Caucasian men walk in and sit down, he knew exactly who they were. It was Detective's Stevens and Moody, two of the officers that he went to war with.

"Mr. Anderson, I'd like to introduce you to your arresting officers: Detective Moody and Stevens. They would like to address the Parole Board before we come to a decision on whether you are a candidate for Parole at this time."

"Thank you Mrs. Saunders." Detective Moody said as he stood up. "First of all, I am speaking on the behalf of the 43rd Precinct, and I would like to make it known that we vehemently oppose the release of Henry Anderson. He is a menace to society, and a violent sexual predator. He attempted to kill 5 officers with no regard or respect for the law, or our lives. We have reason to believe that he has been involved in numerous homicides. At this point, we can't prove it, but as soon as we can get a witness, or some tangible evidence, we will present it the Grand Jury to try and get an indictment. This is a guy who we feel beat the system. He has no conscience and feels that he has been dealt with unjustly. It is very likely that he will be a repeat offender, so our recommendation is that he isn't considered for parole at this time."

"Thank you Mr. Moody." Mr. Chambers said standing up to shake their hands as they exited the room.

"Do you have anything else to say Mr. Anderson?"

"No I don't!" Henry said as he waited for them to finish so that he could return back to the depths of hell, his cell!

"Okay, this concludes our hearing for Henry Shelawn Anderson # 87-D-2197." Mr. Thornton said into the recorder before shutting it off.

"We will send you a notice of our decision in the mail within 72 hrs. You have 30 days to appeal our decision. Do you have any questions or anything else you'd like to add?"

"No sir. I would just like to thank you for your time. Have a good day!" Henry said sarcastically as he stood up to go into the hall to let the next convict know that it was their turn to get judged.

"Hey Walker!"

"What's up?

"They want you up in there now playa." Henry said giving his man some dap.

"How'd it go?" Walker asked trying to get some indication whether the Parole Board was in a good mood or not. Usually the parole board predetermines the inmate's fate before they arrive to the prison for the hearing. They have a quota to meet. A small percentage make their first parole board, the rest aren't as fortunate. They are considered "the bottom of the barrel."

"They shitted on me son, I know those devils are going to hit me with 2 more years." Henry said accepting his fate.

"Damn, that's fucked up son, hold ya head! I'll see you on the other side." Walker said as he went into the room to try his luck with the Devil.

FOURTEEN

While Myah and Nikki were just blocks from the 43rd Precinct to question Det. Williamson, he was in his office receiving a call from Myah's Aunt.

"Michael, you called the other day?" she asked as she stood in front of the bay window in the kitchen that over looked their Olympic size in ground swimming pool and Koi pond with the stone waterfall.

"Yes I did Mary. I just wanted to see how things were going since I've been so tied up with work and all."

"It's been awhile Michael. It was nice of you to think of us, but I really don't think it was a good idea with Myah getting older and more inquisitive. She asked me who you were and all I could say was that you were a friend of the family. I really don't think she bought that after she saw the way I reacted when she mentioned your name."

Det. Williamson leaned back in his soft worn leather chair behind his desk and looked at the ceiling. "I'm sorry about that. I didn't mean for it to cause you any problems. After I hung up with her, I knew that I messed up somehow. I even slipped and said her name which caused her to ask me some questions. She really has become a mature young lady Mary." Det. Williamson stated as he thought back to the conversation he had with Myah.

"Well, let's hope that she doesn't get too curious and wants to know more then what John and I have already told her. We tried to keep those memories suppressed by not mentioning anything about that day. When she turned thirteen, she wanted to know about that night because she was having nightmares, so we told her the watered down version. She found newspaper clippings about the trial that I kept in a box in the basement and wanted to know about the guy that was accused of it, and why no one was convicted of the murder. What could we tell her?"

"You could of told her the truth Mary! She has a right to know the truth."

"I couldn't! I don't even know the truth! All I know is that someone raped and killed my sister and left a little girl mentally scarred because of it. So for twelve years we tried to keep Myah from being hurt any more than she has been already."

"I understand. Believe me, it won't happen again. I wish you and John the best and thanks for allowing me to be a part of Myah's life as long as you have." Det. Williamson was starting to feel bad for causing so much trouble for John and Mary.

"You're more than welcome. Please, give my regards to that beautiful wife of yours." "Will do," the detective replied.

"And you take care of yourself, you hear?" Mary said before she hung up the phone and walked out of the kitchen.

Det. Williamson didn't hang up until he heard the dial tone. He placed the receiver back on the base, looked at his watch and remembered that he had to meet Det. Moody and Stevens in an hour. He gathered his personal effects from off his cluttered desk, put on his sports jacket and walked out of his office closing the door behind him.

He walked down the corridor towards the front door and just as he was about to approach the front desk of the police station, two beautiful young ladies were walking towards him.

Nikki had just found a parking spot across from the Precinct. The building looked old, but it was buzzing with activity. They passed a few officers that were either coming or going from the building. As soon as they entered the front door, Myah was taken back a little when she saw an officer behind a maple brown colored desk that was positioned on a raised platform in the front lobby.

The officers, that were moving around inside, looked in their direction and eyed them suspiciously from afar. Most of them were young black officers that looked at Myah with a lustful eye. Nikki held her Fendi bag tightly under her left arm not knowing what to expect as she followed Myah up to the front desk. This was her first time ever inside of a police station and from what she saw, it was nothing like what she was used to seeing on T.V.

An officer passed by them with a young black male in handcuffs, they stepped to the side allowing the officer to converse with the desk Sergeant.

"And what do we have here Joe?" he asked as he stopped what he was doing to look up.

"Oh just Jimmy Morris again. This time for a DUI charge."

Myah and Nikki could smell the alcohol emanating from the young man's pores as he tried to speak without slurring his words. "But I wasssn't dooiing anything off-icerrr."

"Yeah, yeah, yeah. You weren't doing anything, but driving down a one way street right?" the officer asked sarcastically.

"Whattt'ss wronggg with thatt?" the young man

asked as he struggled for balance. "Oh nothing if you were going in the right direction."

"Take him to detox Joe. I'll sign you in." The desk Sergeant said as he wrote in a thick green book.

After he was finished, he looked in Myah and Nikki's direction, smiled and asked, "May I help you?"

Myah stepped up to the desk when she realized that he was talking to her. "Yes, I'm looking for Det. Williamson."

"Ahh, the great Detective Williamson, who isn't looking for him! You'll find him in room 228 young lady." The Sergeant was in his mid-forties. His neatly cut and trimmed beard was sprinkled with gray, and as he looked Myah up and down, noticing her perky breast and thick thighs, he licked his lips and thought to himself, "If I was a little younger, I would knock bottom out that young black thang!" When he looked back up at her, he noticed the way that she was looking at him, with a look of disgust, so he looked back down at his ledger, hoping that she didn't notice the lust in his eyes and said, "If you go down that corridor." using his right hand to indicate which way. "You'll find the room that you're looking for, but please knock before you enter."

"Thank you." Myah replied as her and Nikki made their way towards the direction that he gave. Myah noticed the way that he was looking at her.

Even though she was grossed out by the fact that an old man was getting his look on, she wasn't mad at him. That was the reason she wore the outfit that she did. "At least I know its working," she thought to herself as she led the way down the long hallway.

After they walked away from his desk, the Sergeant snuck a peek at their asses before they could disappear from the lobby. "Damn!" was all he could say as he caught

Nikki's ass in her tight fitted jeans just before she turned the corner.

As they moved further along down the long hallway, passing officers in uniforms and Detectives in civilian clothes, Myah saw a familiar face walking towards her. At first, she didn't recognize the older gentleman since his head was down and he was fumbling in his pockets, but as soon as he looked straight ahead, his face became visible. She knew that she had seen him someplace before, but she couldn't place where.

Myah stopped abruptly when they made eye contact which caused Nikki, who was following closely behind her and not paying attention, to bump into her.

'I'm sorry!" she said stepping back a little. Myah was too distracted by the stranger to even notice what Nikki was saying.

Once Det. Williamson found his keys to his unmarked police car, he looked straight ahead and saw two young ladies just standing off to the side of the hallway about ten steps ahead of him. The way they were looking at him, especially the tall dark skinned one, made him think that something was wrong. He looked down at himself first, to make sure that everything was alright, then he turned his head around to see if there was anyone behind him. When he was sure that it wasn't anything wrong with him and that no one was behind him, he turned back around towards the young ladies once again. He started to walk forward, but as he took two steps in their direction, he too thought that he recognized the dark skinned young girl from somewhere. With the type of job that he has, he comes in contact with numerous individuals on a daily bases, so it was nothing for him to think that he may have seen a person before, but something told him that this one was different.

"Damn! Who's that? You know him Myah?" Nikki asked when she noticed the way that the two were looking at each other. Myah heard Nikki, but couldn't say anything because she was in shock that she was finally coming face to face with the person that found her on that awful day. As Det. Williamson moved closer towards them, Nikki broke Myah's train of thought when she tapped her on her shoulder, which startled her, causing her to divert her eyes away from him.

"What's wrong with you girl?" Nikki asked as she looked into Myah's eyes when she turned around.

"Nothing!" Myah snapped answering Nikki's question.

"Well if it's nothing wrong, why are you looking like you just seen a ghost?" Before Myah could give a reply, Det. Williamson was upon them.

"Excuse me, may I help you?"

Det. Williamson was thirty-seven years old and had been on the job for over twelve years. He was 6'3" and weighed 220 lbs. He was still fit from the work-outs he did every week, other than a few gray strands, he basically looked the same. Now that he was a Detective, he was able to dress in civilian clothes that truly accentuated his athletic build.

All of his superiors called him "Mr. G.Q." because of the way he looked and dressed. The suits he wore were all tailor made for him, and his shoes were all made from designer Italian leather. Det. Williamson's dark brown hair was cut short on the sides with the top curly, which gave him that Denzel Washington appearance. Women always complimented him because of his light brown eyes, which had a hypnotizing effect on people. Overall, Det. Williamson was a good looking guy, and he knew it.

Myah was now face to face with him. They both stood there frozen not wanting to be the first to make a move, or the first to say something. The frightened little girl that he met twelve years ago was now a strikingly attractive mature young woman. Myah knew exactly who he was as she studied his soft features. Her mind went back in time to when she first laid eyes on him with his uniform on. The man that had helped her many years ago was now standing in front of her. "Are you Det. Williamson?" was all that she could manage to utter.

"Yes, I am. How may I help you?" Det. Williamson said trying to act as if he didn't know her, hoping she wouldn't ask him any questions. He was never a good actor and the truth was, he was interested in why she was there.

"Are you the same Det. Williamson that called my house a couple of days ago?"

"That depends. May I ask what your name is?"

Myah looked directly in his eyes and knew that he knew exactly who she was. "My name is Myah Johnson. You called my Aunt, Mary Dial, a few days ago."

As Nikki listened to them go through a thousand and one questions, something just didn't seem right, so she stepped around Myah and asked, "Is this that friend of the family that you were talking about?"

Myah turned towards her and simply said with an attitude, "Yeah, that's him."

Det. Williamson's eyes gave him away, he couldn't keep up the charades any longer. "Listen Myah, I know you know who I am, and yes, I did call your house to talk to your aunt." He looked at Nikki, extended his hand towards her and said, "And who is your lovely friend?"

Nikki smiled, took his hand and said, "I'm sorry. I'm her friend Nicole Seaman. It's nice to finally meet you." Det. Williamson looked sort of puzzled by the statement "It's nice to finally meet you." He wondered just how much she knew of him. "Seaman, Seaman, is that like

Seaman's furniture stores?" he asked since that last name wasn't a common one.

"Yes it is. Matter-of-fact, that's my father's furniture chain." Nikki replied proudly.

"I see Myah keeps good company. It's a pleasure meeting you." He turned his attention back to Myah and smiled. He was finally able to see her up close without hiding his identity. "It's nice to see you again Myah." he said in a soft voice.

Myah wanted to bombard him with a million questions that's been on her mind ever since her aunt told her about her mother's death, but she didn't want to ask any questions while Nikki was there. "Is there someplace we can go, so we can talk in private?"

Det. Williamson was so taken back by how beautiful Myah had become that he just stood there staring at her as she talked. When he realized that she was asking him a question, he blinked his eyes a couple of times and cleared his throat which gave him time to gather his thoughts. But before he could respond to her question, a couple of young officers in uniform walked by them and greeted him with a nod of their heads. They looked at Myah, then Nikki and smiled. Once they had passed them, the young officers glanced back over their shoulder trying to sneak a peek at the young ladies' asses. Det. Williamson caught them and shook his head indicating his disapproval, which made them quickly turn their head back around.

Williamson waited until they were gone before he answered Myah's question. "Yes, we can go to my office." He looked at his 14k gold Seiko watch as he started to turn around to head back in the direction from which he had just came from. He still had forty-five minutes before he had to meet the two Detectives.

Myah looked at Nikki and asked her to wait in the

truck, so she could talk to the Detective in private.

Nikki didn't feel comfortable leaving Myah alone, but she also didn't want to be inside of the precinct any longer than she had to. She was sort of relieved that Myah gave her a way out.

"You sure you'll be alright?" she asked.

Det. Williamson turned around to face them after hearing the concern in Nikki's voice and said, "She's in good hands, believe me."

Nikki smiled at him, "Okay! I'll just finish listening to the rest of my new CD." With that, she turned and headed back towards the front door. Myah watched Nikki clutch her Fendi bag under her right arm tightly and disappeared around the corner. Det. Williamson was also watching her, but he was wondering how she was able to walk in those tight fitted jeans. They looked as if they were painted on the way they were hugging her small waist and wide hips.

Myah caught him staring just a little longer than he should have and thought to herself, "Men are all the same. All they care about is a big butt and a smile."

Once he had his fill of watching Nikki's ass, he then told Myah to follow him. He led the way with Myah behind him. Now it was her turn to admire what he was working with and the smile on her face proved that she liked what she saw.

Once they stepped into his cluttered office, Det. Williamson directed Myah to have a seat in one of the two hard looking metal chairs that were situated directly in front of a wooden desk. As Myah passed by him, he could smell the faint scent of green apples which made him smile. He always loved a woman that smelled good.

After she was seated, Det. Williamson closed the door and walked around to the chair behind his desk. Myah tried to make herself comfortable, but the chairs were obviously not designed for that purpose. Det. Williamson looked at her and tried to think of the possible reason why she would come all this way from Long Island to just ask if he was the one that called her aunt. He could see the resemblance of her mother in her. It was no mistaking it, she was definitely a beautiful young lady.

"Now that we are alone, you can start calling me Michael." Det. Williamson said while he looked into her eyes.

"Okay Michael, I have so many questions I want to ask you, but where do I start?" While Myah was trying to figure out what she wanted to ask first.

He leaned back in his chair said, "Let's just take it slow and eventually you'll know everything that I know."

Myah finally looked at him and asked the one question that's been on her mind ever since her aunt and uncle had told her the story of what happened that night to her mother.

At first, it was a little awkward for Det. Williamson to talk to her about that day and what he remembered of it, but as they spoke further, he felt compelled to let her know everything, even his theories about who he thought did it. "Well, that's all that I can tell you concerning that day Myah. If you want to know more, you will have to ask Det. Moody and Stevens, they were the ones who handled the case.

"Are they still here?" Myah asked as she uncrossed her legs to stand up. Myah knew that he found her attractive, so she knew that it wouldn't be hard for her to manipulate him down the road in order to get what she wanted. There was no need to entice him any further, her charm and looks were all she needed.

The Detective watched as she got up from the chair and straightened out her skirt. He swallowed hard then said "They still work here, if that's what you mean, but they are not available at this time." He looked at the clock on the wall behind her and noticed that they've been talking for over twenty minutes. He would have to get going if he was going to make it on time to meet with Det. Moody and Stevens. He stood up and came from behind his desk, gave her a hug then added, "If there's anything else I can help you with, please don't hesitate to call." He took out a card from his jacket and gave it to her. It had his office and cell phone number on it. "I'm sorry that I had to cut this short, but I'm already running late for the meeting I have with the two Detectives I've told you about." Det. Williamson wasn't sure if he should mention the Parole hearing of Anderson until he found out the status, then he thought about what he said to her aunt earlier, "....Tell her the truth!" He realized that she was entitled to know, so he told her all about it.

They were standing by his office door about to go out when Myah grabbed his hand and hugged him once more as tears rolled down her face.

"Thanks for everything that you have done for me and for telling me the truth. I'll always consider you my guardian angel." Det. Williamson wiped the tears from her face with his right thumb and looked into her eyes and smiled,

"That's my job. Look at how you turned out. You are a beautiful young lady that has a lot going for herself. I will never stop protecting you. If it's up to me, I'll make sure that he never gets out. I know that he was the one responsible for your mother's death and there is no statue of limitation for murder."

When he let her go, she regained her composure. He opened the door and they both stepped into the hallway. Det. Williamson locked the door behind him and turned to head for the lobby. The officers that were walking by them made it their business to check her out, especially since she was wearing a revealing outfit.

Once they reached the lobby, the same Desk Sergeant that she had met earlier, was still sweating her. She looked at him, smiled and kept it moving. She went to the glass doors, turned to thank the Detective once again and walked out. Myah crossed the street to a white SUV and climbed in on the passenger side. The girl that Det. Williamson met earlier was sitting in the driver seat. As they pulled into traffic, he watched and thought to himself, "Damn! She's gonna break a lot of hearts."

FIFTEEN

Henry had been in a bad mood ever since he came from the parole board. He didn't speak to any of the nosey inmates waiting in line to question him about the previous day's events. He had insomnia, so in the last 72 hours he had only slept about 12 hours, which averaged to about 4 hours a day. Today was judgment day. Henry was restless as he waited for 3:00 pm to come so he could be at mail call. It seemed like time stood still and everything went in slow motion as he waited for the CO (Correction Officer) to call out his name.

"Mail call! Mail calllll!" The CO shouted at the top of his lungs. All of the inmates in I-block stopped what they were doing when they heard the call. They piled up by the CO's office and hoped that their name would be called. Mail call was the most important time of the day to anyone that had someone on the outside. One thing you didn't mess with was a person's mail; even the racist CO's, as much as they would abuse and harass the convicts knew that tampering with their mail was a sure way to get killed. So most of them just gave out the mail without a problem because they didn't need the drama.

"Rodriquez, Jones, Hawkins, Rodgers, and Anderson".
"Right here, pass it back!" Henry said as he reached
out to grab his mail.

Three letters were passed back to him; he stuffed the
letters in his pocket and made his way back to his cell.

When he got back to his cell, he went into his locker
to get his Newports. As he lit his cigarette, he pulled the
envelopes out of his pockets to see who had written him.
The first two envelopes were from Libra and Myah; the third
one was from the "Parole Board." He placed the letters on the
bed and picked up the letter from the Parole Board. Henry
stared at the envelope for a few seconds, then felt it to see
if the envelope was thick. "Shit! I knew these muthafuckin'
bastards were going to hit me!" Henry said knowing that he
didn't get parole without even opening the letter. Anyone
that has did time in New York State prison knows that if
your envelope is thick it means that it has appeal papers in it,
which means you have to do more time. But if it is thin, you
have no reason to appeal because you were being granted
parole. Since Henry knew that he was hit, he decided to read
the letter to see how much more time he had to do.

> "Mr. Henry Shelawn Anderson, We, the
> parole board feel that it would be a grave travesty of
> justice to consider you for parole at this time. You
> are a Violent Felony Offender that seems to have no
> remorse for the heinous acts you have committed.
> We recommend that you serve another 24 months.
> During which we'd like you to complete more
> **Anger Management** classes, and to be a part of
> the "**Scared Straight Program**." You stated that
> you want to work with troubled teens, so this
> should help give you the experience you need as
> well as be a positive role model and mentor for the

*children. We have scheduled you to come back for
reconsideration on March 17th 2001. Stay out of
trouble and don't receive any write-ups and take
the programs we have recommended and we will
critically assess if you are a candidate for Parole at
that time. "*

Sincerely,
Mr. Thornton
(Senior Parole Commissioner)

Henry threw the letter on the floor and cursed out loud. "Fuck the Parole Board! One thing for sure and two things for certain, they can't keep me forever!" Henry said picking up Myah's letter. Just as Henry was about to open up the letter, his right hand man Ed Ski rolled up to holler at him. "What's up kid? How'd it go?"

"They slammed me with 2 more muthafuckin' years!" Henry said pissed off.

"Let me tell you something dawg, that little two year hit ain't shit! They really doing you a favor because that's less time you'll have on paper, plus when you step out of these gates you'll be sharper than you were before. You won't make the same mistakes. Shit, look at me, I've been down since '84, and they have hit me with two years for the last four parole boards. But since they hit me until my "C.R. date" (Conditional Release Date), I'll only have 18 months on paper instead of nine and a half years. So hold your head, cause it gets greater later!"

Henry thought about what his homey said and started to feel better. He realized that he wasn't the only one who wanted to go home, and that there were people who weren't as fortunate as him. The parole commission could not hit him with two more years at his next board, the most he could be hit with the next time would be one year, and then they would have to let him go. "Yeah, you're right Ed Ski, they can't hold us forever."

"You damn right they can't, one day we are going to laugh about this shit! We're going to get them tender young thangs, get the best weed in the world and live life to the fullest! So hold ya head my brother, and I will holler at you later. Oh! I almost forgot, come to the yard later so we can blaze and I can hit you off with this Dro'. My little CO broad brought me two onions (Ounces) of that Head Banger Boogie! One is for you the other is for me."

"Word?"

"Word is born son!"

"Ah-ight, You know I'll be there. Yo' my bitch "Luscious" is suppose to hit me off this weekend at the Family Day Festival. I told her to bring me a half-ounce of that Purple and five bags of that Leaky-leak. So we'll be more than alright." Henry said while thinking about fuckin' his light skin Puerto Rican hood rat at the festival.

"No doubt. Well, I'll meet you tonight after chow."

"Okay, Peace!"

"Peace!" Ed Ski said giving Henry some dap as he exited his cell.

The next letter Henry opened was Libra's. He knew that she was going to say something slick that would make him want to kill her, but he lit another Newport, inhaled deeply and exhaled slowly to calm his nerves. He opened the letter and was shocked with what he was reading.

Dear Hendrick:

> *I know that I am the last one that you would want to hear from, but I want you to listen to me closely and understand where I am coming from.*

Henry I have never stopped loving you, and you have always been on my mind. I have felt so lonely without you and Henry Jr. I think about you two every day, and I just wanted to say I'm sorry about everything. I am pregnant again with my third child (a girl) and I'm not with her father Derek anymore. He started beating my ass because I didn't want to get an abortion. He didn't want me to have another baby, but I couldn't kill my child. After Henry Jr. passed away, I couldn't function. I thought another baby would fill the void I felt in my heart, but it didn't. Anyway, one day Derek came home drunk and we had an argument, he told me that he couldn't stand Henry Jr. or you. He said he was glad that he got rid of little Henry and when he caught you, he would send you to be with him. When I asked him what he meant by that, he told me that he had purposely left that shit on the table to shut little Henry's crying ass up. I punched him in the mouth for saying that, we fought like wild animals, but he beat me down and stomped me unconscious. When I woke up he was gone. I waited for him to come home, cooked him a steak dinner, and had on nothing but a thong and a see through bra. We ate and made love. When I was sure he was asleep, I took the aluminum bat and broke his kneecaps, then I tried to bash his skull in for killing our son, I thought I was in love with him, but he tricked me. He's the one who made me set you up! He told me how you were cheating on me and that you didn't care about me. And the crazy thing is I believed him. Anyway, I'm not telling you all this to make you feel sorry for me. Ha, ha, ha, Gatcha!! Nigga, I was just messing with you. Derek and me are happily married now, and we are having our third child. Oh! I'm glad the parole board gave you another two years; you deserve it! I heard that you are messin' with that cokehead bitch Luscious. How could you fuck with my best friend? I hate you! If I ever catch her, I'm going to cut her ass up. As long as I'm alive, I'm going to make sure that your life is miserable. If it were up to me, you would be doing a life sentence without parole. But believe me, I got something for your ass when you get out in 2001. Have a lovely life you bastard! I'll tell Henry Jr. you said Hello! Ha, Ha, Ha, Ha!!

> *Sincerely,*
> *Your worst fuckin' Nightmare!*
> *Libra*

Henry wasn't surprised at how ignorant his son's mother could be. What he couldn't believe was that she could be so coldhearted and vicious when it came to the death of their son. It was like she didn't care about little Henry. Her letter really put him on edge. He knew in his heart that the first chance he had, he was going to murder Libra. He took her letter and placed it in the same folder that contained all of the previous letters she wrote to him over the years.

The more he thought about her words, the more it made him think of his son. He picked up his picture off of his desk and began to talk to his son as if he was right there with him.

"Hey little man, how are you doing?" Henry said kissing the picture that he took with Henry Jr. at the Bronx Zoo. "Oh, you're fine? That's good, but daddy misses you so much? I am so sorry that I left you alone with your mother. I swear to you, I will find out what happened to you. And when I do, that person is going to be sorry for taking you away from me. Trust me son, you will always be with me in my heart and mind. I will never forget you! We will be together some day. Take care, and I will see you when I get there little man." Henry said laying the eight by ten picture of his son carefully at the head of his bed. As he wiped the tears away with his handkerchief, he made a vow to GOD that he would turn his life around after he took care of some unfinished business.

Henry pulled out a pair of his Nike sneakers from under the bed, took the sole out of the sneaker and pulled out a fat jailhouse joint of skunk (weed) mixed with a twenty-dollar bag of Angel dust. He lit an incense to camouflage the weed smell so the "law", or one of the many prison informants wouldn't get a whiff of the chronic he was smoking. After Henry got his puff on, he layed back on his bed enjoying his high. Then he just went into a zone. By the time Henry finished smoking, he noticed that he had about seven minutes before the recreation move would be called. He flushed the drug paraphernalia, put on some prayer oil to kill the weed scent in his clothes, and grabbed his sunglasses. He knew that Ed-Ski would be waiting for him by their normal meeting place. Just as he was about to leave his cell, he noticed Myah's letter sitting on the bed. Henry picked it up and sniffed it. "Damn! This letter smells good!" Henry said wondering if Myah wore this scent often. It was a very common practice for women to put some sort of fragrance on letters to their husband or boyfriend. For many convicts it was the closest that they could get to smelling a woman, other than the stuck up nasty CO's who poured on perfume trying to get attention, because no one looked at them in the "Free World." So the men treasured those feminine smells. "I can't wait to turn her young ass out!" Henry said as he placed Myah's letter into his locker.

"10 minute move! 10 minute move!" The recreation move was announced so Henry grabbed his jacket and walked to the library to meet his man, Ed-Ski.

SIXTEEN

It's has been a week since Myah met Irk, and reunited with Det. Williamson. She had been in contact with Irk at least three times since then. They made plans to meet up again for her birthday, which was in less than two weeks. She was about to turn eighteen and graduation was another two months away.

Myah was going to attend the prom then after the summer, it was off to college. She decided to attend Clarkson University since it had a good engineering program, plus it was situated high in the Adirondack Mountains in upstate New York. She always wanted to major in something that she was good at. She also wanted to be far away from everyone to establish her independence, but still be close enough to her family in case of an emergency.

Henry had responded to her last letter, and she planned on keeping her promise of sending him some pictures to satisfy his curiosity, she didn't want him to get discouraged and stop writing. "No more excuses!" she told herself when she read his last letter. She asked Nikki if she would take them since she knew the purpose of it all, or what Myah wanted her to know. And now that Irk and Det. Williamson was on board, her goals were now within reach.

Her Aunt and Uncle were planning to surprise her with a new car for her birthday, but she already knew about it. Myah had her heart set on a 1999 candy apple red Mustang GT convertible ever since she saw one of Nikki's spoiled rich friends with one. She let it be known to her Aunt that she would love to have one for her birthday. Her Aunt always wanted her to have what she wanted since Myah never asked for much. She knew that her Aunt would convince her Uncle to buy it as both a birthday and graduation present.

At school, her and Keisha had decided to make up, or better yet, Keisha decided to make up with Myah since she didn't like being alienated. Myah accepted her back into the circle not because she had love for her, but because she might prove to be a valuable asset to her in the future *"Watch for phonies. Keep your enemies close, and nigga, watch your homies."* Was one of the sayings she remembered from listening to one of Tupac's songs, *"Blasphemy."*

Myah was obsessed with books that dealt with manipulation, and the power of persuasion, but one of her favorite books was "The Art of War", which she read religiously every night before she went to bed. She was quickly leaning how to control those around her. Myah was smart and she knew it. She learned that her beauty would make men do just about anything. Men were simply weak mined individuals. "All they do is think with their dicks instead of their brains." She would say to herself from time to time. Knowing this gave Myah the ultimate advantage over them. Not only was she beautiful, she was leaning how to manipulate those around her. The combination of beauty and brains was something that Myah really didn't have to work at.

Myah knew that she had to surround herself with soldiers that would protect her at all costs. All she had to do was move accordingly and everything would fall into place for her. So, as she was brushing her hair in front of her vanity mirror in her bedroom contemplating her next move, her cell phone started ringing. She got up and walked over to her dresser near the bed, picked it up. "Hello."

"Hey Princess, what you up to?" She knew exactly who it was.

"Hey Irk. I thought you said you were going to call this weekend. Is something wrong?"

"Nah. Ain't nothing wrong. I was just calling to let you know that I have a surprise for you." Irk was sitting in his 1998 white on white Yukon Denali parked in front of one of his girls cribs in Brooklyn, waiting for her to come out. They had just finished fucking when her moms came home early and started fussing about how the house smelled of weed smoke and stank pussy. So instead of hearing the bullshit, he decided to take her to a motel around his way and let her finish what they started. Since he was waiting, he decided to call Myah and tell her what his man Lex did for him. "Ayo Princess, my man just hit me on the cell about an hour ago and told me that he had copped some tickets to that concert on the sixteenth. So, I thought maybe you would like to bring some of your friends and hang with us for your birthday."

Myah couldn't believe what she was hearing. She had been trying to get tickets for the "Hard Knock Life Tour" for weeks and no matter how much she was willing to pay, nobody was willing to come off of them. Here it was, she just met Irk last week and he was able to cop them. Not just for her, but for her friends too. She had to calm herself down before she responded. She held her hand over the receiver of her cell and screamed, "OH MY GOD!!!" Her Aunt was sure to come up to her room to see what was wrong, but she couldn't contain her excitement.

"Hello! Hello!" Irk screamed into the phone after hearing Myah covering it. As she gathered herself, she put the phone back to her ear and calmly said, "Yeah, I'm here. Now how many tickets did you say he got?"

"I never did. He copped eight for me. You can invite three of your friends if you want. I got them for your birthday, so whatever you want to do, it's up to you Princess." The girl that he was waiting for opened the passenger side door of his truck and climbed in.

She closed the door and said, "I'm ready whenever you are." She looked at him while he was still on the phone, rubbed her hand over the crotch of his jeans and found the zipper. After opening them up and pulling them down, she bent over and took all of him into her mouth and proceeded to suck him off, a reward for having him wait so long. If it wasn't for her mother bitching about having niggas in the house, she would have been out. But, since she was only eighteen and still in school, she was forced to listen to her mother's bullshit.

Irk watched as the young girl did her best to get him back in the mood like he was before her mother came in trippin'. As she concentrated on him, he was still trying to sound normal on the phone, but it wasn't easy the way the young girl was slobbing his knob.

"Ahh yeah, ahh, so Princess, umm, when you figure out what you wanna dooo, holla at me on the cell a-iiight?"

Myah heard the girl slurping away in the background and knew what was going on. Irk wasn't her man, but it was something about it that got her pissed. So when she responded, it was with an attitude that Irk would feel. "A-ight. Whatever. Bye!" She knew that he would call back later, probably after he finished what he was doing. She knew that she shouldn't be mad about it, but she was and that bothered her.

Just as she expected, her Aunt came knocking on her door. "Come in!" Myah yelled from her bed.

The door opened up and her Aunt came walking in looking around, making sure there was no one other than Myah in the room. When she realized that Myah was alone, she walked over towards her and asked, "What's wrong? Why you scream like that?" Myah simply smiled and said.

"You won't believe what just happened! A friend of mine just called to tell me he just got tickets to that concert that I've been trying to go see." Her Aunt knew what she was talking about since she over heard Myah and Nikki talking about it a few days ago.

"That's great honey." As she was about to walk out the door, she turned around and told Myah, "Just try to keep it down some. Your uncle is trying to sleep."

Myah waited until her door was closed before she grabbed her cell phone to call Nikki. The phone rang about three times before Nikki answered.

"Hello!"

"Hey girl, you won't believe what just happened."

"What!" Nikki asked with excitement in her voice. "Irk just called me and told me that he got his hands on some tickets for "**The Hard Knock Life Tour**." Can you believe that?"

Nikki stared at her bedroom door in shock. She didn't say a word for about five seconds.

"Hello! Hel-looo!" Myah shouted into the mouthpiece of her cell until she heard Nikki's voice again.

"Yeah. He did what?" Nikki was just as speechless as Myah was when she heard the news. "He told me that his

man Lex copped eight tickets, and Irk asked me if I wanted to go with them, and if so, I could bring three friends.
It'll be my birthday present."

"And what did you say?"

"I didn't say anything. He was with some bitch when he called me. I heard her in the background. From the way he sounded on the phone, I assume she was sucking his dick or something."

"Whaaat!" Nikki asked surprised by how calm Myah sounded.

"That was so disrespectful. I couldn't believe he called me while she was doing that."

"What did you say?"

"Call me back when you finish!" Myah said knowing that she was telling lie.

"I can't believe he did that! Who the fuck does he think he is?" Nikki replied thinking that Myah was pissed and would agree with her.

"He's the one that got those tickets that we couldn't get. Now do you know who he is?" Myah replied with sarcasm in her voice.

When they had finished talking on the phone, Myah hung up and laid on her bed thinking about what Nikki had asked. "Who are you going to take as the third person?" She fell asleep with that question on her mind.

SEVENTEEN

On the 6:00pm recreational move, Ed Ski returned with Henry back to his unit with the "*Product*" without incident. They came into Henry's cell laughing and joking.

"Ayo', you want something to munch on?" Henry asked reaching into his locker to get some chips and a 6 pk. of Snickers.

"Hell yeah! What the hell do you think? I want to get my grub on too!"

"Then go in my locker and get whatever you need cause I'm eating with you."

"How many sandwiches do you want?" Ed Ski asked going into Henry's locker pulling out the bread, cheese, mayonnaise and tuna.

"Make me four of them thangs playa."

"Damn! You're a greedy muthafuckah! Yo', your locker is like a supermarket! Is there anything that you don't have in here?"

"I got whatever you need baby boy, I'm like Pathmark when it comes to getting' your grub on! I'm the "*King of Grub*" Henry said laughing as he raised his hands in the air like the "*Heavyweight Champion of The World*" defending his title.

"Hey Henry, roll the Blunts while I make the sand-wiches."

"Ah-ight" Henry said as he removed the zip lock bag full of Dro' from his boxers. He rolled up two fat blunts and placed it on the table until Ed Ski finished making the sandwiches. Once he was finished, Henry lit his blunt and tossed the lighter to his man so he could get his smoke on too.

"Damn, this shit is the bomb!" Ed Ski whispered in disbelief as he inhaled the smoke deep into his lungs, holding it in as long as he could, before he started choking. He could not believe that taking a few pulls on the blunt could get him so high!

"I told you playa, that's all I mess with! This shit is Chronic!!" Henry said reaching into his locker to get the letter that Myah wrote. While they continued to smoke, Henry opened the letter and saw that Myah had finally sent some pictures of herself along with a money order.

"Oh shit!" Henry cried out excitedly as he slowly admired each picture he pulled out.

"What's up partner? You sound happy like you just made parole or something." Ed Ski said looking at Henry as if he was losing his mind.

"You remember the young honey I met awhile back that I was telling you about that never sent a picture, who you said must be a man or something?"

"Yeah, what about her?"

"Well, not only did she send me pictures and her phone number, she also broke me off wit' two hundred dollars! And I must say, she is far from being a man."

"Man, get the fuck outta here! Let me see those flicks." Ed Ski said in disbelief.

"Who's da muthafuckin' man? Huh?" Henry said

sliding five pictures out of the envelope, before handing the pictures and M.O. receipt to Ed Ski so he could see Myah's name on it.

"Damnit man!!! This sister is fine! Look at those thick legs and fat ass! She really set it out for you homey. She's beautiful! I love them chocolate girls, and what makes her even more beautiful are those chinky eyes. You definitely caught one! You are the muthafuckin' man!" he said giving Henry his props and some dap. Henry was feeling himself, so he imitated his favorite character "Sho'Nuff" from the movie "**The Last Dragon**"

"Ed Skiii! Am I, the meanest and baddest when it comes to baggin' the finest honeys?"

"Sho' nuff!" Ed Ski responded remembering the movie.

"Do I know how to get that mon-neeey?"

"Sho' nuff!"

"Who's that pimp that don't mess with no suckaaa's?"

"Sho' Nuff!"

"Why is that?" Henry asked wondering what he would say.

"Cause you're a baaaaad muthafuckaaa!!" He replied causing both of them to erupt into hysterical laughter.

"Man, you're crazy!" Ed Ski said still laughing as he rolled up another two blunts from his personal stash. "What's up with her? What she talkin' bout?" He asked interested in what Myah had to say.

"Yo' kick back and relax. I'm going to read her scribe to you and we'll politic about her afterwards. I wanna see what you think about this whole situation." Henry said lighting up the blunt that Ed Ski handed to him.

Dear Hendrick, (oops I mean) Henry -smile-

How are you doing baby? I am sorry it took me a little longer than usual to respond, but I've been busy preparing for my B-Day party. You know I graduate soon, so hopefully I will get up there to see you if I can get a ride. I hope you like the pics. I had my best friend Nikki take them for me. I told her I wanted to have pictures of my body to put into my photo album, so when I am an old woman, I can look back at them and remember how I looked when I was in H.S. So, do you like them? I used a whole roll of film to take panty, bra and thong shots. I even sent you five pictures of me naked. This way you can see what will be waiting for you when you come home. Enjoy! Please do not show, trade, or sell my pictures to anyone. They are 4 your eyes only!

I really enjoy your letters and I can't wait for us to be together. You seem so sincere in every way. Guess what, I just bought my own cell phone. I'm moving up in the world!☺ You can call me at any time, as long as it is after 7:00 pm because my minutes are free after seven p.m. and on weekends, okay? My number is (347) 555-1212. I know that you don't like taking money from people because you say you don't need anything, but I'm not "people", I'm Myah! The woman you are going to build a future with, so you better take the money punk!☺ If I have it, you have it! That's how I do; LOVE IS LOVE!!

Speaking of love, I can't wait for you to make love to me. I got so wet taking those pictures for you that I had to take a cold shower to cool off. I look at your pictures on my wall and nightstand *everyday, and I feel like the luckiest woman alive to have you in my life. I know those bitches are going to swarm you when you get out, but they better recognize. You better tell them who the queen bee is! -smile- All that I ask is that you keep it 100% real, and stay true. If you can do that for me, I will do **anything** for you.*

Well I'm going to go so I can mail this letter out to you. Please send me some pictures of you in your sweatpants and with your wife beater on. I want to see that chiseled frame of yours.

Oh! I'll be taking pictures at my graduation, and when I do, I will be sending copies to you. I wish you were here so you could take me to my prom. But don't worry; when you come home we are going to make up for the lost time.

Call me ASAP. Until next time....................

Love Always,
Myah

"Damn kid, how the hell did you get her open like that?"

"Well, just being who I am, she couldn't help but to fall hard for me. Let me tell you something, on the bricks, I wasn't a cruddy ass nigga. I was good to people that were good to me. I never crossed anyone that didn't deserve it, or had it comin'. My motto is: **Cross me, I will crush you**, plain and simple. I'm on some Eye 4 an Eye, a Tooth 4 a Tooth shit. Everything in life is **Tit 4 Tat**, ya feel me?" Henry replied in his comatose state. The weed had them both in a philosophical state of mind, it had them building like two scientists analyzing and building a bomb.

"Yeah I feel you, that's what I mean, some people are

just born with the gift. I never had the gift of gab like you, but I still had some bad bitches back in the days." Ed Ski said finishing off the last of his tuna sandwich. "Check this out, on some real shit, from everything you have told me about her and from what you've read to me, stay on point." Ed Ski said playing with the hairs on his chin.

"Why in the hell would you say that?" Henry asked in a perplexed tone. "I say that because somethin' just ain't right. Everything seems like it is too good to be true. Here's a girl that is 17 years old getting ready to graduate and go to college. She has no boyfriend, and now all of a sudden, she's waiting for you to come home? Come on son, give me a break! There is something going on, I can't put my finger on it, but my gut tells me that whatever it is, it's bigger than *"Henry S. Anderson."* She could be a man in disguise that had a sex change, a psychopath, or for all we know, an undercover agent. Trust me, she's not your average young freak. I'll tell you one thing, don't sleep on her, and don't trust her until she really proves herself. Look at the pictures she sent you, these joints are the bomb for sure. But don't you find it strange that it took her over a year to send you some pictures? Now all of a sudden she's setting it out like a stripper at Mr. Al's Wedge. You don't even really know this broad. Look at her eyes in all the pictures, they tell a serious story. She has a look in her eyes that says she's had a rough life. Her eyes tell me she has an old soul. I'd bet my left nut that she's very bitter about something. She has been betrayed or hurt really bad by someone before. So all I'm saying is be careful! Don't fall for the banana in the tailpipe. If she happens to be a sweetheart that's *"Wifey material"*, don't break that poor girls heart."

"Niggah you buggin'!" Henry said laughing at Ed Ski's *"Psychic Psychoanalysis"* of his girl Myah, a girl he didn't even know. "Trust me kid, I know what I'm doing. But thanks for the advice *Dr. Ed Ski*. Yo', hold that thought, I'll be right back. I'm going to call my girl Luscious to see if she still is coming to the Festival this weekend. Roll up so we can blaze again when I get back." Henry said as he opened the door to go down to the phone room.

"Ah-ight, I'll be here listening to your walkman."

Henry went down two flights of the stairs and snatched up the first available phone he saw.

"Hello?"

"Ma'am you have a collect call from: sir, please state your name."

"Henry"

"Will you accept the charges Ma'am?"

"Yes I will. Hi sweetheart!" Luscious said happy to hear from Henry.

"Hey Ma, what's the deal? I just wanted to find out if you were still coming to the *Family Day Festival,* and if you got everything I told you I needed you to get."

"Yes, I took care of everything and I'm definitely still coming. I wouldn't miss coming to see you for the world. Are we going to get our groove on like we did at last year's Festival?" Luscious asked already knowing the answer, but just wanting to hear Henry talk dirty to her.

"You know it! I'mma tear that ass up! But hey, I'll call you later because they just called chow, and I don't have any food in my locker." Henry said cutting the conversation short after finding out what he wanted to know.

"Okay, make sure you call me back please. Also, you'll be getting the money I sent you probably tomorrow."

"Good looking, I love you baby."

"I love you too. Bye."

"Bye." Henry said as he walked back to his cell thinking about Luscious.

Luscious was a twenty nine year old Dime piece. Her mother was Black and her father was Puerto Rican, so she came out exceptionally beautiful. She had two kids, one son was by a guy who was doing a 40 year prison sentence for robbery, the other was by an African guy that she thought was single with a lot of money. She didn't find out that he was married with seven kids until she was in her six month of pregnancy, by then it was too late. It was her idea to try and get pregnant so that he would marry and move her out of the ghetto, but it didn't work out like she planned. When her African boyfriend Kujufu found out she was pregnant, he left her to raise another child alone.

Henry knew that she was actually a good girl, but she involved herself with the wrong people and looked for love in the wrong places. Her situation hasn't changed the whole 12 years he's been in prison. She's a drama queen in denial. She still lives in the ghetto, she's bi-sexual, (but in the closet), a cokehead (but fronts like she only smokes weed), and she's a habitual liar! She cheated on him on three separate occasions when he was in the street, but he didn't care because she was just a piece of ass to him. Luscious was really a slut, but she was his slut for now. Henry was always attracted to stuck up women who had serious issues and drama in their lives. For some strange reason, drama and hood rats still turned him on. Henry was always up for a good challenge, he loved defying the odds and overcoming obstacles. Henry couldn't figure out if it was because her brain game was on one thousand, or because she was a ride or die chick. Either way, he figured he would use her until he came home. Then he would dump her, and start a new fresh life with Myah. As he made it back to his cell, he saw his man Ed Ski in a zone enjoying his high.

"Yo' Son, "Roll that shit up! It's time to celebrate!"

EIGHTEEN

"Myah, can you go to the garage and get me the blue cooler from off of the work bench? I hope I cleaned it out from the last time we used it." John stated as he pretended to busy himself at the sink in the kitchen.

"Okay, but what are you going to put in it?" Myah asked as she got up from the table. "Oh, I was thinking we would get some steaks and cook-out for your birthday. What do you think?"

Myah made a confused facial expression and said, "Whatever." It was too early in the morning to be thinking about cooking out, especially for her birthday. Myah had other plans for the day and staying home cooking out with her aunt and uncle was not one of them.

She knew that they were up to something, they had been acting strange all morning. It was only nine-thirty two, and her uncle was asking for a cooler. When Myah headed for the stairs that lead to the garage, John motioned for his wife to come with him and together they followed Myah down the stairs. When they heard the door open up and saw the lights come on, they waited for Myah's scream to come next.

Myah opened the door, flipped the light switch on and immediately noticed the bright candy apple red, 1999 two-door Mustang GT convertible sitting in the middle of the garage floor. The surprised look on Myah face said it all. When John and Mary finally heard her scream, they ran to the door and watched as Myah read the sign that was attached to the passenger window. "HAPPY BIRTHDAY MYAH!" The car was wrapped with a red ribbon tied into a bow and with the garage lights shining off of it, the car sparkled.

Myah started to cry. Even though she knew her Aunt and Uncle were going to get it for her, just seeing it physically was something totally different. Once she noticed that they were behind her, she immediately ran over to her Uncle and jumped into his arms. "Thank you! Thank you! Oh my God! Thank you!" was all that Myah could say as she hugged him tightly.

John could only smile as he tried to keep his balance and hold on until she let him go. Mary was so overwhelmed with joy from the sight of Myah and John embracing that she started to cry.

Myah let her uncle go, ran to Mary and they too began to hug each other. "Thank you sooo much Aunt Mary. Thank you!"

Mary gathered herself, looked into Myah's eyes and said, "You deserve it honey. You deserve it. Happy Birthday!" and they continued to hold one another.

After all was said and done, John turns to Myah and tells her, "You know, I was tempted to take it for myself and give you my car, but somehow, I don't think I would look half as good in it as you would." They laughed at his poor excuse of a joke then Myah went up to him, kissed him on the cheek and replied, "Somehow, I don't think red is your color." Her aunt wanted to make sure that Myah knew the rules before she accepted the car. She got herself under control, wiped the tears of joy away and laid down the rules that her and her husband had agreed upon when they bought the car.

"Okay young lady. Your Uncle and I have just a few rules that you have to follow." Myah looked at the both of them as her Uncle stood next to her and put his arm around her. When she saw that she had Myah's attention, she then continued. "Since this is your car, you are going to have to be responsible. No drinking and driving. No speeding! Even though this is a sports car, we don't need to be worrying about you getting into an accident because you wanted to test the car's speed." Myah let out a sigh which made her uncle wonder if he made the right decision in buying a sports car instead of that Honda Accord that he wanted to get. When her Aunt was finished and her Uncle said his peace, he handed Myah the keys to her brand new car and told her to enjoy, which Myah definitely intended to do.

The first place that Myah wanted to go in her new car was to Nikki's house. When she hopped inside, that new car smell was the first thing that hit her nose. "I have to get an air freshener quick!" Myah said to herself not liking the smell as she looked around at the interior of the car. "Whoa!" Myah surprisely said as she sunk back into the plush beige leather when she sat down in the driver seat. Everything was power. The power windows were already tinted by the factory. The seats were adjustable with a press of a button, so she quickly adjusted her seat since her Aunt was the last one who drove it. When everything was to her liking, Myah placed the key into the ignition and started the car. The engine roared to life and idled off to a purring sound. She noticed that the car's stereo system was from the factory. "I definitely have to buy a

new system tomorrow! But at least it has a CD changer."
Looking around, Myah saw that the car was fully loaded.
Everything was in it. She put the radio station to 107.5
WBLS and listened to how clear it came in. Myah adjusted
the rear view mirror, put the transmission into reverse and
backed out of the garage. Her Uncle gave her a garage door
opener, so she used it to close the door after she was clear
and placed it on the visor above her head. Myah put the
car in park, pressed the button for the convertible top and
watched as the top folded and slid into the space behind
the backseat.

"Damn! Now that's what I'm talking about. Let a
bitch breathe." Myah said out loud as she continued to
back out of the driveway. Myah pulled out her cell phone,
dialed Nikki's number and told her she would be there
in about five minutes. Myah wanted to make a grand
entrance when she pulled up to Nikki's enormous house.

Nikki, as expected, was waiting for her in front of
her circular driveway. Myah pulled into Nikki's long
driveway and drove another minute until she reached the
main house. She saw Nikki standing on the steps with her
hands over her mouth and a surprised look on her face.
Myah turned into the circular driveway and pulled up to
the front of the house, she parked and stepped out of the
car smiling. Nikki ran over to her and stopped to admire
the Mustang.

"Oh my God! Girrrrl, you are terrible!"

"They got it for you huh? You said they would!"
Nikki said excitedly as she walked around the front of the
car to give Myah a hug. "Happy Birthday girlfriend."

Myah was all smiles, you couldn't tell that she wasn't
that bitch. "Shit! Ain't nothing to hold us back now. It's
straight ahead for now on. Let me show you everything
that this car has Nik."

"Somehow, this one looks different from Brooke's car." Nikki quickly stated while she walked around to the passenger side door to get in. "It is! Brooke's isn't fully loaded. Look!" As they went over all the features of the car and even some that Myah didn't know about, Nikki's father came to the door and whistled his approval of Myah's car.

"Wow! Now that's nice!" Nikki's father was about six-one or six-two with a full head of hair that was starting to grey on the sides, and a body that was in better shape than a lot of men his age. Mr. Seaman was one of the most friendliest men that Myah has ever met. No matter who came over to their house, he would try to make them feel at home. He was hip to the younger generation's style and very well versed in their lingo. He was the type of father that every daughter wanted.

Mr. Seaman walked over towards Myah and gave her a hug and kiss then said, "Happy Birthday Myah! You have to come inside so that Kathy can see you. I think that she has something for you anyway." Mr. Seaman winked at Nikki and knew that Myah had caught it.

"You know I was coming to see ya'll. I just had to let my best friend see what my Uncle and Aunt bought me." Myah was so happy her face glowed. She was radiating with energy, Nikki and her father could feel it.

After they finished looking at the car, they all headed up the front steps and disappeared into the house. No matter how many times Myah has been in their house, it still amazed her when she looked around at all of the nice furniture and expensive paintings that hung on the walls and the fancy oriental rugs that laid throughout the house. Each room was decorated differently, but the feel was still the same, comfortable.

Myah and Nikki followed Mr. Seaman into his library

where Mrs. Seaman was sitting in a chair that was situated next to a picture window overlooking a flower garden. She was looking through a magazine before they came and as soon as she saw them, Mrs. Seaman jumped up, walked over and gave Myah a hug, kiss and said. "Happy Birthday Myah! Let me look at you. Oh how I wish I was eighteen all over again. You girls are so young and beautiful that I can't wait to see the both of you on prom night." Myah smiled and reminded Mrs. Seaman that her and Nikki hadn't found dates yet for the big day.

Nikki's father jumped in and stated, "That's only because you girls are so picky. Whatever happened to that nice boy Michael that use to come over here looking for you pumpkin?" Nikki was embarrassed that her father still called her pumpkin, and to know that Myah had heard it made her even more embarrassed.

"Dad! Don't call me that." Nikki said through clenched teeth.

"What? What did I say honey?" Mr. Seaman asked knowing all along he was guilty of slipping with the pumpkin name.

"Noth-thing, forget it." Nikki said as she turned towards her mom to let her know that she was embarrassed. Her father tried to justify his mistake after seeing that his daughter was upset by saying, "Nik, Myah's family."

Myah looked at Nikki and smiled, because she knew she would tease her the first chance she got.

Mr. Seaman walked over to his desk and pulled out a medium size gift wrapped box from underneath then walked back over to Myah and handed it to her. Everyone was smiling, waiting for Myah to open it. Myah thanked them all and commenced to tearing the neatly wrapped paper from the box. Once the box was free of wrapping, only then did she open it. Inside was lots of pink tissue paper, but just under a sheet of it was a card inside an envelope. Myah read the front which said "Happy Birthday Myah" in red ink. Myah looked up at all three of them a smiled. She then slid her fingernail along the seam to open it. She pulled out the card and inside was ten brand new one hundred dollar bills.

Myah was so happy about the money that she didn't even bother to look in the box any further. She jumped up to thank Nikki's parents, but before she had the chance to take a step, Nikki's father said.

"Whoa! Whoa! Whoa! There's something else inside there Myah." Myah pick the box back up and dug some more until she found another smaller box inside. She flipped open the top and was shocked to discover a pair of diamond earrings and a matching gold and diamond necklace. "Oh My God! They're beautiful! Thank you." Myah was so surprised by the gift that she started to cry.

Nikki came over to her and hugged her tightly pulling her close to her. Since Myah was sitting down, it wasn't hard for Nikki to wrap her arms around her shoulders and pull her close. She could smell Myah's strawberry scented shampoo as her head rested on her shoulder. Nikki rubbed her hands up and down Myah's arms and gave her a gentle squeeze to comfort her. Mr. and Mrs. Seaman looked on as the two girls sat on the couch and cried.

Myah stood up, walked over to Nikki's parents and gave each one a hug and kiss to thank them.

"You're part of the family Myah, you know that. We treat you like you're our own." Mr. Seaman said as he held Myah. Mrs. Seaman came up from behind as Myah was saying thank you and said, "You're welcome. I wanted to give you more, but Billy over here said that we should just give you the money and let you buy whatever you wanted. It was my idea to get the earrings and necklace. Every girl should have a nice pair of earrings." Myah thanked them once again then her and Nikki went up to Nikki's room to get ready to go shopping.

After the shopping spree, the beauty salon, and visiting with family and friends, Myah was exhausted. It was only five-twenty in the afternoon and a lot still had to be done before she had to leave to meet Irk. The concert started at eight, so she had to meet him in the Bronx by 7:00 pm. Irk was renting a stretch Escalade limo that would fit fifteen comfortably. Myah still had to pick up Keisha and her cousin Sherida that came up from Alabama to visit for a week since college was out for the summer.

Myah went straight to her room, took off her clothes and ran the water for her bath. She wanted to relax in the tub for at least an hour before getting dressed. The outfit that she bought earlier that day was definitely going to turn heads in the "Garden." All the girls were going to be looking their best, but Myah wanted to be the one that stood out the most.

Even though she wasn't into the "girlie-girl" look, Nikki convinced Myah, while they were shopping, to buy an outfit that was bangin'. When Myah was finished with her bath, she went to her room to get prepared. She sat at her vanity and put eyeliner on her eyes and did her hair. Myah then went to her lingerie drawer and picked a peach lace push-up bra and thong set from her Victoria Secret's collection. Myah wanted her cleavage to be defined in the black tank-top shirt that she planned on wearing with the platinum letters A|X along with the Parasuso jean mini-skirt. The six inch platinum stilettos that she picked to wear would show off her pedicure that she had done earlier in the day.

Myah smiled in the mirror when she was finished dressing and said out loud to herself, "Damn! Niggas are gonna go crazy when they see me!" Ever since she's been getting compliments about her figure, Myah has been dressing and buying clothes that showed off her body more. She was actually starting to like wearing the girlie girl outfits. She looked at her clock on the dresser and realized that she better get going if she was going to make it to Nikki's house on time. Myah grabbed her cell from off of the bed, dialed Nikki's number and waited for her to answer.

"Hello!" Nikki yelled into the phone trying to talk over the loud music that was blaring in the background.

"Bitch, turn down that shit!" Myah screamed, holding the phone away from her ear.

Nikki turned it down, came back on the phone and said, "I'm sorry about that, I was trying to get ready."

"Bitch! it's 6:10 pm, I'm about to leave now. Be ready in five minutes."

Before Nikki could say another word, Myah hung up.

NINETEEN

Myah picked up Nikki, who was sporting a teal green Gucci short set that showed off her tanned, thick thighs and shapely legs. The Gucci slip-ons that she was wearing matched the belt around her waist perfectly.

"Hey Nik. You're looking cute tonight." Myah said as Nikki opened the car door to get in. When she was settled, she smiled and replied.

"Thanks! You're not looking too bad yourself girlfriend."

"Well you know, I try to work with what I have." Myah said laughing as she drove out of Nikki's driveway. They were on their way to pick up Keisha and her cousin on Sunset Blvd, which was only a five minute drive from Nikki's.

As soon as Myah beeped the horn, Keisha came to the door and waved for her to hold on. While Myah and Nikki waited, Keisha was adding the finishing touches to her hair.

"Hey Keisha, should I wear a jacket with this?" her cousin Sherida asked as she looked in the mirror trying to make sure everything was right. She was wearing a loose fitting D&G light blue see through blouse that let her black lace bra show underneath. Her D&G blue capri jeans were tight around her hips and thighs, but loose at the calves. In fact they were so tight, they looked as if they were painted on. They showed every contour of her shapely ass and thighs as she walked, which left nothing to the imagination.

"I would think so, unless you want every nigga in the *Garden* following you." Keisha said as she looked at her cousin turning right to left trying to look at her ass in the mirror. Sherida's complexion was that of a rich cup of hot chocolate. Her hair was jet black and cut in a Cleopatra type style. As she thought about Keisha's response, she turned around to face her and said in a low voice.

"That's exactly what I want." then walked towards the front door.

Keisha looked at her, smiled and replied, "You conniving Bitch! Now I see where I get it from." They both laughed out loud as they made their way out the door.

Nikki noticed them coming first and made a comment to Myah. "Damn! I guess I'm inappropriately dressed for this concert huh? I thought we were supposed to be ladies not hoochie mamas."

Myah turned to see what Nikki was talking about. What she saw made her say "Damn!" also. Keisha was wearing a tight fitting dress that stopped mid-thigh and hugged every curve of her curvaceous body. Her 36C's were barely being contained inside of the small cups that encased each tit. Keisha had on the "Come fuck-me pumps" that added an extra four inches to her five-foot-five frame. Since Myah's car was only a two door, Nikki had to open her door and step out in order for Keisha and Sherida to get in.

"Damn girlfriend! You're wearing the hell outta that dress." Myah said in a sarcastic tone of voice. Keisha didn't know how she should respond to that comment, so instead of saying something wrong, she simply asked as she got comfortable behind Myah,

"This your car Myah?"

"Yeah, I got it for my birthday." Myah said smiling as she looked in the rearview mirror at Keisha.

"It's nice. I'm loving the color girl." Keisha added as she waited for Sherida to get in. Once Sherida was inside and Nikki closed the door, Myah put the car in drive, stepped on the gas and let the car jerk forward, so the girls could feel the power that the car had.

"Whoa!" was all they could say as Myah raced down the block heading towards Main Street, which would take them to the L.I.E (Long Island Expressway).

As soon as they crossed over the Throgs Neck Bridge into the Bronx, Myah saw the sign that read "Gun Hill Rd. 1/2 mile." Her stereo was playing **Dru Hill's** new song *"Somebody sleeping in my bed..."* and everyone in the car was singing along as **Sisco** broke it down. As the song was going off, Sherida asked everyone if they had seen the video for that particular song.

"Hell yeah!" Myah said as she pressed the button on the CD player for **Eve's** CD to play next.

"I just love me some Sisco." Sherida said excitedly. "That boy can dance his ass off, not to mention that the nigga's gorgeous!" Everyone was quite for a minute then busted out laughing. Keisha was the first to reply to her cousin's assessment of **Sisco**.

"That boy is fruitier than a damn fruit cake?" Myah and Nikki both laughed again which caused Keisha to do the same.

Sherida looked disappointed by the news, but tried to defend his name. It was obvious to everyone that he was special to her by the way she reacted so they stopped laughing and listened as Sherida tried to play it off. "I knew that! I was just saying that he was good looking that's all."

Myah pulled on to Castle Hill Avenue and drove another five blocks until she reached the projects that Irk had told her to meet him at. She looked at the clock on the dashboard and saw that it was 7:34 pm. They made it there a little later than she wanted to, but nevertheless, they were still ahead of schedule. "Wow!" was what everyone said when they saw the white super stretched Escalade limo parked in front.

Myah saw Irk standing on the side of it talking to three guys that were blinged out and dressed to impress. The girls were all going crazy knowing that they were going to the Garden in style, but Myah wanted to put on a show. She pulled up behind the limo and parked making sure that she had Irk's attention. Irk walked over to the car as Myah was cutting the engine off. She opened the door, got out and bent over to lift the seat up for Keisha.

Irk stopped in his tracks when he saw Myah bend over in her short jean skirt which rose high on her hips causing him to get a glimpse of her ass cheeks and the peach lace thong she was wearing.

"Damn it man!" was all he could say as he stopped in his tracks, shaking his head as if something was in his eye. After he regained his composure, he then continued to walk in her direction. "Hey Princess." Irk said once he was close enough to her.

"Hey Irk. Sorry we're late. Traffic was thick tonight." Myah said as she turned around to give him a hug and a kiss on the cheek. Myah knew that he was clockin' her hard and knowing that he was, excited her.

"I bet! Everyone trying to get to the Garden tonight. Who's your peeps?" He asked as he looked at Keisha

adjusting her dress. "Oh, this is Keisha. Keisha this is Irk."
"Nice to meet you Irk." Keisha said, coming up close
enough to give him a friendly hug.

"A-ight, I see now my boys are gonna go crazy over
you, Keisha." She smiled and stepped back allowing Irk to
see the rest of Myah's crew.

"Irk you already know Nikki and this is Keisha's
cousin Sherida. She's visiting from Alabama." Irk gave
them all a head nod and told Myah that they were running
late. He motioned for everyone to get into the limo so that
they could get moving.

"Is my car gonna be safe right here?" Myah asked not
sure if she should leave it sitting in the open. Irk assured
her that it'll be alright.

"It's cool Princess. I got some peeps looking out for it.
Plus, me and my peoples left ours here too." As he said that,
he looked over and motioned for Myah to look across the
street. She saw four expensive European cars all lined up.

Keisha's eyes lit up once she stuck her head inside
the limo. The first thing that she noticed was the three
fine brothas sitting up in there looking like male models
modeling Pelle Pelle. They were spread out in the limo,
so no matter where she sat, she would have to sit next to
someone. As she was being careful to make sure she didn't
trip getting into the truck, one of the guys gave her his
hand. When she looked up, he was smiling and said, "Let
me help Boo." Just as she was getting pulled into the truck,
Sherida, Nikki, Myah and Irk were coming right behind
her. Irk was the last to jump in and when he was seated
next to Myah, he ordered the driver to roll out.

The ride to Madison Square Garden took forty-five
minutes since traffic was heavy going into Manhattan.
They arrived on 34th St at 8:50 pm. They were almost an
hour late for the show, but the real fun was to start after

the concert was over. Irk had rented out club "**Speed**" that was located in the lower east side of Manhattan. He wanted to make sure that Myah's birthday was something that she would never forget. He invited everybody that was somebody in the industry. The guess list included people like: **Jay Z, Damon Dash, Eve, DMX** and the whole **Roc-a-fella** crew including their managers and promoters. He was cool with a lot of people, so they wanted to show him love. Irk also wanted them to be able to chill without fans harassing them.

Irk had his own peoples as security so everyone would feel safe. He came a long way from where he started to where he was now, and people respected that. When they entered the Garden through the garage, their entourage was quickly escorted to their seats by the security of Madison Square Garden. Myah and her friends were overwhelmed by it all. The V.I.P. treatment they were getting was definitely earning Irk some points in her crew's eyes. So much in fact that Keisha couldn't stop talking about him whenever her and Myah were alone.

"Oh my God Myah! Irk's really got this town on lock. Everyone knows him. Look! There's **Jay Z** and **Memphis Bleek**. I wonder if he'll introduce me to them at the club later."

Myah wasn't feeling the groupie act at all, in fact, she wished that she would have left her trifling ass back in Long Island. Myah saw the way that she was flirting with Irk whenever they made eye contact. If it wasn't for the fact that she had an extra ticket, Myah wouldn't have even told her about it. Her cousin was cool though. Sherida was nothing like Keisha. Myah could see herself being friends and hanging with her if she lived on Long Island. To get Keisha off her back, Myah simply said, "I'll see if he can." They were sitting in one of the sky boxes over looking the

Garden. There were two 52' flat screen TVs' set up in the corners of the room, so no matter where someone sat, they would be able to see one. A waiter came in to serve them champagne and whatever else they wanted. Everyone was basically paired off. Sherida was with Big Zo, a tall dark skinned brother that Irk said was his lieutenant. He had to be at least six-seven if not taller with muscles everywhere. You could tell Sherida was feeling him the way she was all over him. Nikki was sitting on the lap of Hass, a short light skinned brother that Myah said was too pretty for her. He was clean cut with hazel eyes and looked like he stayed in the mirror more than she did. Keisha was with Quadel "Q" for short, another dark skinned brother that was part of Irk's security team. He wasn't good looking at all, but to Keisha, he was all that. Irk and Myah were just sitting back enjoying the show and having fun watching their people mingle.

The concert was just about to end and Irk wanted to leave after seeing **Jay Z** tear the stage up, but Myah wanted to see The **Ruff Rider's** routine, so since it was her day, they stayed the extra fifteen minutes. Everyone was ready to go once it was over, especially since they wanted to get to the club before the crowd came. As they all filed back into the limo to head to the club, someone called out Irk's name.

"Ayo Irk! Irk!" Irk looked back and saw that it was his man Tony. Myah looked out of the window she was sitting at and saw Irk and this guy talking. Something looked familiar about him that made Myah wonder if she had seen him someplace before. She couldn't hear their conversation, but their body language told her that they were good friends.

"What's up Tony?" Irk asked wondering why he was chasing him down.

"I just wanted to know if it was alright if I bring my group "The Potheadz" with me to the club, so they could meet some of the Big Willies in the Industry." Tone asked after they embraced.

"How many are there?" Irk questioned as he looked around the parking garage.

"Oh, it's just three of them."

"A-ight. It shouldn't be no problem. I'll just tell my man "Q" to be on the look-out fo.. Matter-of-fact," Irk held his hand up for Tone to hold on a minute while he called for Quadel to step out of the limo.

"Yo Quadel! Let me holla atcha. Quadel stepped out of the limo thinking that it might be some trouble he would have to handle, but once he saw who it was, he knew everything was cool. "Yeah, what's up Irk?"

"Make sure that Tone and his peeps get into the club with no problems a-ight?"

Q looked at Tone, who he knew from the streets, nodded his head and said, "No problem. I'll handle it." Tone thanked Irk then headed back into the Garden. Myah watched as he walked away, hoping that she would get the chance to see him again. Once Irk and "Q" were in the limo, the driver pulled out of the garage and into traffic heading east towards club "**Speed**."

In the limo, Myah waited until Irk was settled before she asked him about the guy that he was talking to in the parking garage. "Hey Irk, thank you for making this one of the best birthdays ever." Myah knew that if she was going to get any information out him, she would have to play to his ego. So like a good little girl, she played the role of daughter since she knew that he so desperately wanted to be a father figure.

"Princess, it ain't over yet. The night is still young. I got another surprise for you when we get to the club, so save the thanks 'til later."

Myah smiled and thought to herself, "What else could he possibly have in store for her tonight." "Irk, that guy you were talking to in the garage, what's his name?" Irk looked at Myah as if trying to figure out why she was all up in his business, until she said, "He looks familiar." Myah saw the look that Irk gave her, so she had to play it off. "I was just thinking that I seen him someplace before."

"Tone! Nah, he's just a nigga from around the way. He's the manager of that group that was on right after Bleek's song. He just wanted to make sure that his peoples could get into the club since they weren't invited. He'll be at the club tonight if you wanna holla at him. He's good peoples." As Irk was talking, Myah was thinking about how to approach Tone later to find out if he was who she thought he was.

Irk's mouth was feeling dry, so he looked around to find that bottle of Cris he had earlier and realized Zo had it sitting in the ice bucket next to him. "Ayo Zo, Zo! pass that muthafuckin' bottle of Cris nigga!" Zo stopped what he was doing with Sherida, reached over and grabbed the bottle of Cristal from out the bucket of ice and handed it to him. Myah looked at Sherida, who was damn near ready to pass out from the shots of rum she was doing with Zo that she didn't even notice that he was feeling up her tits.

"My bad Irk. This girl's all up in my ear and shit! I didn't even hear ya" Keisha was so much into "Q" that she too didn't notice that her cousin was drunk as hell and was basically getting taken advantage of. Myah saw that Zo's left hand was on Sherida's right tit as he caressed it through her blouse. Her shirt was hanging halfway off her shoulder, partially exposing her black bra.

Nikki was too busy watching Myah's every move to notice anything. It was as if she was clockin' Myah more then trying to enjoy herself. Myah noticed it and made a mental note to herself to inquire about that later when they were alone.

Hass was trying his best to get Nikki to dig him, but being that he was drunk, he didn't notice that Nikki wasn't drinking. She only pretended to be. She didn't trust the crowd they were with, plus, Nikki wanted to make sure that no one took advantage of her or Myah. At first, she was pissed that Myah was all up on Irk, but after seeing how Irk treated her, Nikki quickly dismissed the thought that he was trying to fuck her. She knew that nothing intimate was gonna happen between them. She couldn't wait until they were alone in the hotel and away from everyone. She wanted to give Myah something that she's been dying to give her all night.

TWENTY

Henry woke up at 7:30 am to prepare for the *"big day."* He hoped that Luscious rented a car instead of driving her beat up '89 Subaru. He figured he had two hours to get ready because whenever she came to visit him it was usually around 9:30 am. If she didn't make it around that time it meant that she was stuck in that piece of shit car of hers someplace on the side of the road or highway. Henry had plenty of time to kill before the Festival started, so he decided to smoke a joint and hop into the shower.

Forty-five minutes later Henry came out of the shower twisted! He fired up a Newport and began to get dressed. He put on his green prison uniform pants, black Timberland boots and a black silk shirt. He stood in the mirror admiring his waves as he brushed his hair.

Out of nowhere, Ed Ski slid into the cell unannounced while Henry's back was turned and screamed; "Freeze! Put the brush down! You pretty muthafuckah!" Ed Ski roared causing Henry to jump, drop the brush and turn around abruptly.

"Nigga you scared the shit out of me! I thought you were Five-O or something!" Henry said as he left the top two buttons of his shirt unbuttoned to show off the platinum chain with the medallion that sat on his muscular chest. Once Henry was satisfied with his appearance, he grabbed the Green African Musk prayer oil and put a few dabs on his neck and beard. "If you need some smell good to put on, look in the medicine cabinet and get what you need." Henry said allowing Ed Ski to choose any scent he wanted out of about 70 fragrances.

"Damn, this one here smells good!" Ed Ski said as he chose the Coco-Mango oil to put on. "You wanna blaze one before they call us so we can go down there right?"

"Nah, I'd rather wait until we get back. If we weren't going down to make moves, I would smoke wit you, but I have to be focused. That chronic always has me stuck on stupid, so I'm not going to play myself. I know that I can't smoke that shit and expect to bring back the **'MotherLoad.'** I don't know how you do it, I mean, how do you smoke that shit as much as you do and still function like a normal person?" Ed Ski asked shaking his head in wonder.

"Because it's mind over matter, I can control this shit because I'm the best that has ever done it! You got baby lungs while I got them Iron Lungs! Since you ain't smokin', hold me down while I get my lungs dirty and mind right." Henry said not wasting any time sparking the joint. "No doubt, I got you!" Ed Ski said standing post at the door just in case the CO came to the cell to call Henry for his visit. "Whoever goes down there first has to make sure that they hold the table down for the other, cause you know how crowded it's going to be.

"Anderson! An-der-son! You have a visit!" the fat, black pop-eyed female CO screamed out from downstairs because her fat ass was too lazy to come up and get Henry.

"Ah-ight! I'll be right down!" Ed Ski replied as Henry finished off the remainder of the joint. "Yo' Ed, I'll see you down there. Make sure that you keep your eyes and ears open down there. I will let you know the easiest place to swallow the *loonies*."

"Swallow the *loonies*? I never swallowed any balloons before, I just slam them." Ed Ski said as if everyone who brought Narcotics into the Penitentiary stuffed their product in their asshole.

"Well, if "slamming" floats your boat and you're more comfortable with doing it that way, I'm not mad at you playa. Just be careful, and don't start liking it!"

"Fuck you Henry!"

"No, you need to tell those balloons not to fuck you too hard! Ha, ha, ha! I'll see you down on the dance floor." Henry said laughing as he grabbed his jacket and went to find the CO so she could give him a pass to gain access to the Festival.

When Henry stepped into the yard, he saw that it was already crowded. He looked down at his watch and saw that it was 10:05 am. Henry coolly glanced around the yard trying to find his girl. He didn't want to look thirsty or lost, so he stood with a couple of guys who were also waiting for their visitors to come. They made small talk about basketball and weightlifting while they waited for their loved ones to surface. Just as Henry was starting to curse Luscious out under his breath, she came up behind him and covered his eyes.

"Guess who?"

"Uh, let me think. Alexia with that fat ass!" Henry said knowing that Luscious would get upset because he knew she envied her young and successful fine ass sister.

"Fuck you Henry!" She said smacking him in the back of his head because she knew her sister was still trying to fuck Henry behind her back.

"Damn girl!! I was just playin' with you. Come here

and give Big Poppa a hug and a big kiss!" Luscious had a frown on her face until Henry grabbed her hand and pulled her into his embrace, she couldn't help but smile.

"I missed you so much baby! You know I love you!" Henry said as he passionately kissed her. Everyone that looked at them thought they were two people deeply in love with one another, but little did they know, he had just swallowed five balloons of Purple Haze with one kiss. Instead of a half-ounce, Luscious brought two ounces with her and five twenty-dollar sacks of that Leaky-leak (*Angel Dust*) for Henry's personal stash. It took five medium sized balloons to hold a half-ounce of that fire! So that meant Luscious had 15 balloons left! Henry broke the kiss, held Luscious tightly and kissed her on her neck.

"Come on love, let's find a table, because my "Fam" should be coming down soon. They found a table off to the side with an umbrella sticking out of it. "There's a good spot right there!" Henry shouted as he rushed to claim the empty table. "Leave your jacket here while we go to get something to eat so no one else takes our table.

"Okay baby." Luscious said removing her jacket. As they waited in line to get the hot dogs and cheeseburgers, Henry saw Ed Ski come out looking lost, so he called him.

"Ayo' Ed! Ed Skiii! I'm over here!" Henry called out, waving so he could see him. As soon as he saw Henry, he started walking towards him. His girl saw him and followed him to where Henry and Luscious were standing.

"Hello" Ed Ski's woman said in the sweetest childlike voice. She was a big boned Dominican cutie that had a pretty face and the fattest ass Henry had ever seen in his entire life. She was built like a Stallion! Standing at six feet tall and weighing about 190 Ibs, she had no stomach and a tiny waist. Henry couldn't believe how well her body was sculpted. It was unreal!

"Hey Yvette, I'd like for you to meet my fiancé Luscious, Luscious, this is my homey Ed Ski and his woman Yvette. Okay, why don't ya'll take the food back to our table, and we'll get the beverages and the cards so we can play some spades." Henry said speaking to his girl.

"Okay, it sounds like a plan. Are you ready girlfriend?"

"Yes, I'm ready" Yvette responded while she helped Luscious carry the food back to the table. When Yvette's fat ass walked through the aisles, she literally stopped traffic! All the men who were there with their wives, girlfriends, etc, all stopped what they were doing to sneak a quick peek at Yvette's humongous ass. She knew they were watching, so she made her ass cheeks bounce up and down like a point guard dribbling a basketball. Once Henry saw them go back to the table and start eating, he started to build with Ed Ski.

"Yo' kid, your girl is fat to death!" He said giving his girl her props.

"Yeah she's alright." Ed Ski said trying to act nonchalant.

"Ah-ight listen, I got an ounce of that Haze for you to carry back. Once we get back, we'll split it 50-50, you think you can handle that?"

"No doubt my niggah!" Ed Ski said with certainty, even though he had never brought that much weed into the prison before.

"Okay, by the time we get back to the table, your girl will already have it. It's on you when you decide to make your move. Be careful because they watch all hand movements closely, that's another reason why I ain't into that slammin' shit. Unless you've mastered "The Hand Is Quicker Than The Eye" technique or you're a magician, it might be better to do it like me. In my opinion, the best way to get it without arousing suspicion is to get it when you kiss your broad. But you say you know what you're doing, so you gotta do what you feel is best for you, feel me?"

"Yeah, I feel you."

"If you don't think that you can't handle it, let me know and I'll bring it all back myself. Don't worry, if you can't handle it, I'll still set you out and throw a few joints your way to help get your lungs out of the street." Henry said knowing that Ed Ski wouldn't allow this opportunity to slip away, because he wanted more than a few joints to smoke, he wanted to get paid! When they made it to the table, they noticed the women chatting like they knew each other for years. They spent the next two hours playing spades, laughing and joking while Henry was taking care of business. Every so often, he would passionately kiss Luscious and feel on her soft body.

"Come on baby, you say that you got four books and a possible?"

"Well, I got five and a possible. Fuck it, give us a bubble!" Henry said excitedly giving Luscious a hi-five.

Ed Ski and Yvette both looked at their hands and threw their cards down. "Ya'll got it. We can't win." Ed Ski said giving Yvette a peck on the lips for being a good sport while they sat there and lost every single game.

"Yo' Henry, ya'll cheated! There is no way that we could lose 12 games in a row. I don't care how good ya'll play, we never got a bid over 5 books."

"Well, remember I told you about mastering the hand is quicker than the eye trick?" Henry asked with a serious look on his face.

"Yeah!" Ed Ski answered wondering what that had to do with a card game.

"Well I invented it, so now you know who the Grandmaster is!" Henry said winking at Luscious while laughing at them. "But if you would excuse us, my wife and I have babies to make!" Henry said causing both

Luscious and Yvette to blush. Luscious knew that was her cue to excuse herself and followed Henry so they could find the perfect spot to get busy!

"We'll see ya'll later." Henry said walking away with his arm around Luscious.

"No doubt, check ya'll later." Ed Ski replied, knowing that this would give him time to make his move.

"Look baby, every couple of minutes I want you to pass me the balloons one at a time, but wait until I tell you to, okay?"

"Yes honey." Yvette followed Ed Ski's instruction to a tee, and was down to the last two "*Loonies*". She passed the last two balloons to her man by kissing him. Ed Ski had initially planned to get all of the balloons from her possession before slamming them, but when he got the final two from her, he decided to try swallowing them like Henry did. He drank some juice and forced the first one down. The second one got lodged in his throat and he literally began to choke and gasp for air. Yvette tried to casually pat him on the back so she wouldn't draw attention, but when she saw the veins and his eyeballs start to bulge out, she panicked then screamed.

"Somebody please help me! My husband is choking!

The Correction Officers in the vicinity ran over to help Ed Ski. When they performed the Heimlich maneuver Ed Ski regurgitated the afternoon meal along with the two balloons on the grass. Everyone watched Ed Ski as he dived to the ground to retrieve them, but the Officers were quicker. They jumped on Ed Ski's back and wrestled him to the ground as everyone looked on in disgust. Yvette cried hysterically as they cuffed Ed Ski and dragged him into the "*Visiting Room Search Area*". One Officer gently placed his hand on Yvette's shoulder and said: "Ma'am, I'm going to have to ask you to come with me."

TWENTY ONE

Club "Speed" was definitely the place to be! Everybody and their mother were trying to get up in there. The word on the streets was that an after party was going down. Only those that had invitations were allowed inside. Limousines were pulling up front to drop off one celebrity after another, so security into the club was extra tight.

Quadel, who was in charge of Irk's security team, controlled an army of workers from inside the club by two-way radio that every one of his men had. People got their names checked off and were given a bright red band to put on their wrist. This ensured that everyone was of drinking age since alcohol was being served. Only then were they allowed to enjoy whatever the club had to offer. A pyramid was created out of champagne glasses near the bar with actual champagne flowing from top to bottom. Irk hired one of the best caterers to serve drinks and food to the club goers. He definitely made sure that everyone knew that it was Myah's night. Signs were hung throughout the club wishing her a happy birthday. Irk, Myah, Nikki, Keisha and her cousin Sherida were all seated upstairs in the V.I.P section over looking the dance floor drinking Cristal, Moet, or Dom P. They were listening to the music and watching through the picture window the different stars that came in to pay homage to the man that made it all possible.

Irk was wearing an Iceberg Bugs Bunny creme colored sweatshirt with a pair of black Iceberg jeans. On his feet was a pair of tan color Tims and hanging out of his sweatshirt was a 34" Platinum link chain with a Jesus head piece that was encrusted with yellow carnary diamonds.

As he sat next to Myah, who was getting her drink on, he looked at his watch, and saw that it was 12:17 am. He motioned for the waitress that had been serving them drinks to come to his table. The cute brown skinned chubby girl, whose legs rubbed whenever she walked, came over smiling.

"What can I get for you?" she asked in a friendly voice as she leaned over to hear him.

"Can you bring me that box in back?" Irk whispered in her ear as he caught a whiff of her cheap perfume.

"Sure can," she said as she stood up, and then turned around to retrieve the box that Irk had left there hours before. *Now is a good time to get it.* Irk thought to himself as he stood up to stretch his legs.

Myah was sipping her champagne slowly trying to figure out just what Irk was up to. He just whispered into that fat girl's ear that's been serving them drinks and flirting with him ever since they got there. "Her fat ass really thinks that she has a chance huh?" As she watched the girl turn around and walk towards the back of the room, Myah looked at Irk, who was now standing and acting as if he was really interested in that fat girl's ass, and asked, "Is something wrong?" Irk smiled and turned around to face her.

"Nah Princess, I'm just stretching that's all." If you didn't know Myah, you would have thought that Irk was her man by the way she acted when it came to him and other females. The control that she had tried to maintain was slowly deteriorating as the night continued on. The more she drank, the more she wanted him. It wasn't like he wasn't her type. In fact, Myah was feeling him more than she led on to believe. The way he carried himself, the way he treated her, and the fact that he was fine as hell was the icing on the cake. Any girl in her right mind would be crazy not to jump at the chance to be with him. Myah didn't want to be just any ol' girl. That was one of the reasons why she had to play it differently. She had to make him want her just as much as she wanted him.

Nikki didn't appreciate the way Myah was pushing up on Irk. Even though she was starting to loosen up a little from the champagne they were drinking, she still had a watchful eye on things. "I have to figure out a way to slip these "E" pills to Myah without her knowing." Nikki thought to herself as she looked around noticing that Irk was looking at her. Keisha and her cousin were swaying to the music that was thumping from speakers and mingling with some of the people that came up to greet Irk.

"Oh shit!" Keisha screamed excitedly when she saw Bleek passed by on the dance floor going towards the bar with his entourage. "There he is! There he is! I gots to meet him. Damn it! He's fine!" was all that Keisha kept saying to her cousin Sherida as she was pressed up against the glass trying to see where he was going. Irk was forced to turn around when he heard all the commotion behind him.

As he watched and listened to Keisha's hysterics, he thought to himself, *Look at this bitch, she's nothing but a damn groupie.* Then he locked eyes with Nikki and noticed that Nikki was just sitting at the table watching what Myah was doing. "And she can't enjoy herself because she's too busy trying to clock Myah's every movement. I knew there was something funny about her when she thought that I was trying to fuck Myah. Now I see what's really going on. The bitch is on pussy! I wonder if Myah knows that. She thinks I forgot about that shit she said that day. If it wasn't for the fact that she's Myah best friend, I would have flipped on the bitch a long time ago. It's only outta respect that I'm being kind to her dike-ass!"

Sherida was just happy to be around so many stars and money makers. Even though she was a little tipsy from all the drinking, she knew exactly what she was doing. As she listened to her cousin rant and rave about Bleek, she was thinking about Big Zo.

"I wonder where Zo's at. He has to break me off before I go back home."

While everyone was into their own thoughts, Quadel was outside in front of the club helping his man Russ control the traffic that continued to flow into the club.

"Man, I never had so many people try me in order to get inside this club as I have tonight." Russ said once Quadel was next to him. "Yo, what happened?" Q asked as he spotted a limo pulling up front.

"Two girls came up here looking like models. Man I mean they were bad as a muthafucka'! One was a slim redbone cutie about five-three with hazel green eyes and had an ass that looked like it should have its own area code."

"Word Son?" Quadel said trying to picture exactly what Russ was describing to him.

"That's on everything I love!" Russ replied putting two fingers to his lips, kissing them and pointing them in the air.

"What about the other one?"

"Son, this is no lie. Her friend was just as bad, but she was taller and dark chocolate, just how you like em' Her body was bangin'! She was thick in all the right places, ya heard?"

"Damn Son! Where they at?" Quadel asked wanting to see for himself just what his man was talking 'bout.

"I had to get rid of them. They offered to suck a nigga's joint if I let them inside, but rules are rules and besides, Irk would have definitely gone ballistic on a nigga if they got up in here and caused some trouble." Quadel looked disappointed, but knew that Russ was right.

"That's good looking out Son, but I know a nigga got the digits or somethin' right?"

"You know it. What's my name Son?" Russ asked as he pulled out a piece of paper and handed it to Quadel.

"Now that's my nigga!" Quadel replied as he read the names and numbers to himself. "I see ya still on top of your game nigga." Quadel was about to head back inside when someone called his name

"Yo Q! Q!" Quadel looked over his shoulder and saw Tone coming towards him with three young niggas behind him. Quadel almost forgot about Tone with all the activity going on, but then remembered what Irk told him to do when Tone came to the club.

"Yeah, Yeah, Yeah Son." Q greeted him with a pound and hug then looked over at the three young kids that were with him. They were all dressed in hoodies and jeans, but once they pulled back their hoods, Q remembered them from the concert.

"Hey Q, these are the three that I told Irk about at the Garden." Tone said in a tone of voice that let the three guys that was with him know that he meant what he said about knowing some peoples. Q looked them over and pulled out four red bands for them to put on their wrists.

"Yeah Son, ya'll in. Just put these on to let security know that ya'll good-to-go, a'ight?"

"Word, word, word, good looking out big man!"

One of the three kids said as he slipped on the band and followed Tone into the club, more hyped up now then before knowing that he was about to be around some major playas.

Meanwhile inside the club, Jay-Z's song "Hard Knock Life" was bumpin' through the speakers and everyone was on the dance floor dancing and having fun. Jay-Z and his peeps came through early to show Irk some love and was out before the crowd got out of control. Myah was just ecstatic that Irk had them come up to the V.I.P to personally wish her a happy birthday. They all toasted with champagne, but had to leave before everyone got the chance to sing "Happy Birthday."

Tone made his way through the crowded room and headed to the bar to get a drink. When he finally made it, he sat down in one of the chairs and waited for the bartender to assist him.

"I've seen you some place before," a girl that was sitting to the right of him said over the loud music.

"Probably," he replied as the bartender finally came over to him.

"What will it be?"

"I'll have a rum and coke with two ice cubes. More rum, less coke."

"Coming right up," the bartender said as he turned around to fix Tone his drink. The young lady that was sitting next to him sipped on her drink while she waited for Tone to turn back around. Her name was Tania; she was an assistant for one of the A&R's from Roc-a-Fella Records that was there because he knew Irk. She only came with him to mingle with some of the other record executives in hopes of landing another job.

Tone got his drink and turned back around to face

the dance floor and to scan the room. He wasn't in a good mood since the group he represented was pressuring him to make something happen or else they were walking. He had been managing "The PotHeadz" for over a year now and within that time he had managed to get them little gigs here and there, but nothing serious. But tonight was different. Since he knew Jay-Z's good friend Menace from around the way, he was able to convince him to let his group perform a song when the tour came to the Garden. After he listened to a demo tape, Menace told Jay about them and he agreed to give them a chance to prove themselves to a home crowd, but if they bombed, Jay said he would act as if he had no knowledge of what was going on. But they didn't bomb, and now here he was hoping to meet someone that might give them a chance and sign them to a record deal.

Tania looked at him and noticed that he wasn't even paying her any mind. She was five-seven with a caramel complexion, shoulder length black hair with highlighted tips. She was a classy full figured woman that carried her weight well. Most men were intimidated by her confidence. She normally wouldn't bother trying to talk to a guy she didn't know, but it was something about this one that made her want to get to know him.

"Excuse me!" she said loud enough for Tone to hear over the loud music.

"Yeah, what's up?"

"I don't know if you've noticed or not, but I was trying to talk to you. If I'm bothering you, just let me know, and I'll leave you alone." Tania said as she turned back around in her chair to face the bar.

"No, no, I'm sorry. I was just thinking about something. My mind was totally some place else. Hi, my name's Tone."

"Nice to meet you Tone. My name is Tania." They shook hands, picked up their drinks and turned to face each other.

"As I was saying before you ignored me, I've seen you some place before." Tania said smiling to let him know that she wasn't holding a grudge. "Are you in the music business?" Tone looked around before he answered her question trying to see if he saw his group nearby.

"Yeah, you could say that. I manage a group called 'The PotHeadz.' They're an up and coming rap group out of Brooklyn."

"Oh yeah! I was at the concert and saw them perform. They're pretty good from what I heard and from the way the crowd reacted to them. Are they signed with anyone?"

"Not as of yet, but I'm hoping that someone that was at the concert liked what they heard and give me a call." Tone replied as he finished the last of his drink. Tania's mind was in overdrive mode. She knew that this was her chance to show that she knew talent and how to find it. She definitely felt that Tone's group could be the next big thing if given the chance, so she decided to tell him who she worked for and take his number.

"Hey, you know what, since I did hear your group, I think that I could help you out."

"What do you mean?" Tone asked skeptically.

"Well, I work for Roc-a-Fella records as an assistant to an **A&R**. I could give him your number and tell him about your group."

Tone eye's lit up. He was speechless for a few seconds then said, "I would really appreciate that. Thanks!"

"Don't thank me yet. Let's see what happens first and if he does sign your group, then you can thank me by taking me out to dinner. Okay?"

"If he signs them then I'll do more than that, but

dinner would be a start. You got that." Tone said excitedly as he smiled from ear-to-ear. He couldn't believe how things were starting to look up.

Irk put the box that he just received from the chubby girl behind his back as he turned around to face the table that Myah was sitting at.

"I can't believe this nigga just took that Fat bitch's' number!" Myah said under her breathe.

"Ayo Myah, Let me holler atcha." Irk commanded forcing Nikki, Keisha and Sherida to look up to see what was going on. Myah locked eyes with him and gave him a cold stare then rolled her eyes and proceeded to get out of her seat. Her skirt hiked up a little when she slid across the chair giving Irk an eyeful of her chocolate thighs.

"Man, if she wasn't my peeps little girl I would definitely smash that ass." He thought to himself making a frustrated facial expression. Myah walked over to him and once she was standing directly in front of him, he pulled the small gift box from around his back and handed it to her.

"What's this?" she asked feeling bad for thinking that he would even consider taking that fat girl's number.

"Remember I told you that I had another surprise for ya? Well, here it is." Irk said smiling.

"Open it girl!" Keisha said excitedly from where she was standing. Everyone got up out of their seat and gathered around Myah and Irk to see what was in the box. Myah couldn't believe that he was giving her another gift. He had done so much for her already, from the concert, the birthday party and now this! Whatever it was, she knew that it had to be something big if he had waited to give it to her this late. She flipped open the top of the box and saw a thin gold chain. Attached to it was a key. Myah took the chain out of the box, held it up and looked at Irk with a puzzled look on her face. Everyone waited just like

Myah for Irk, who was the only one smiling, to explain the reason for the key.

"I know, I know. You're wondering what's the key for, right?"

Myah shook her head yes.

"Well, since you are becoming an independent young woman, I figured you might need a place to get away once in a while." Then I thought to myself, "Why shouldn't she have her own place?" So I rented you an apartment in the Bronx so that you can do just that "Get-away." But there's something else in that box Princess. Keep looking." Myah put the chain around her neck then picked up the box once again. This time, she pulls up the black velvet cloth that lined the bottom of the box and saw a thin stack of crisp brand new one hundred dollar bills. Nikki, who was standing behind Keisha, noticed now Myah was looking and knew that Irk had her mind, body and soul.

"Oh my God!" Sherida screamed excitedly once Myah took the money out of the box to count it. Myah was speechless as she turned towards Irk to hug him. "Thank you Irk! You have already done so much for me. I can't possibly accept this…" Before she could finish, Irk whispered in her ear.

"It will never be enough considering what your father did for me." He pulled her close to him and Myah cried on his chest. She was overwhelmed by all that Irk had done in order to make her 18th birthday a day she would never forget.

TWENTY TWO

When Henry and Luscious emerged from under the stage where the jailhouse band performed, they came out with gigantic smiles on their faces. As they made their way back to their table they noticed all of their contents scattered across the grass.

"What the fuck!" Henry screamed as he looked around for Ed Ski and Yvette. When he couldn't locate them he started to feel apprehensive. Out of the corner of his eye, he noticed that Luscious continued to walk towards the table. Henry felt like they were being watched, so he called her back to him until he could figure out what was going on.

"Hey Boo, come here for a minute." He said in a hurried tone, trying not to bring unwarranted heat to them. As soon as Luscious heard her mans voice she turned around slowly and walked towards him as if nothing was wrong.

"What's up baby?" She asked, noticing the solemn expression on his face. "Yo', something ain't right." Henry said as he and Luscious watched five Officers run towards the *"Inmate Search Area"*.

"Hey Henry! Where you been at dog? I've been looking for you for the last twenty minutes." The O.G. (*Original Gangster*) from New Jersey named Romerell said in a low tone of voice as he looked over his shoulder every second as if someone was after him.

"What's the deal kid? Have you seen my man Ed Ski?" Henry asked, knowing in his gut that something was terribly wrong.

"You ain't going to believe this shit, Ed Ski and his chick got knocked off a little while ago. That nigga was choking when CO Trustice ran over to perform the Heimlich maneuver on him, anyway to make a long story short, he tossed his muthafuckin' cookies all over the place! But that's not the half; the shit really hit the fan when he spit those balloons all over the grass. I've never seen a man move so fast in my entire life. He dove to the ground trying to get them "loonies", but the CO's were on him like flies on shit! He went all out, but they were too much for him to handle. They bagged his wife too. *Mike Dog* said he seen when they cuffed her and put her ass in the State Troopers car. But yo', let me get outta here, cause my wife and kids will be looking for me soon."

"No doubt, thanks for the info."

"Anytime fam, see you on the other side." O.G said giving Henry some dap as he slid off.

"Oh my GOD!!" Luscious said bursting into tears because she felt sorry for Yvette and Ed Ski. But the reality was that she was paranoid because she knew that if they ratted, the State Troopers would be coming for her and Henry as well.

"Stop all that muthafuckin' crying! Are you trying to get me busted bitch? Cause I'm the only one left with drugs on me! What the fuck is wrong with you?"

"I'm scared baby"

"Scared of what? You ain't got shit on you and I swallowed all my "*work*" (drugs) so we're ah-ight. Just act normal and we'll both make it outta here without catching a case, ya feel me?"

"Yes baby" Luscious said sniffling as she used a napkin to wipe her eyes.

About 60 seconds after Romerell left two officers approached Henry from behind.

"Anderson!"

"Yeah, what's up?" Henry asked nonchalantly. "They want to see you in the I.A. (Internal Affairs) Office, so we're going to have to terminate your visit."

The bony big head officer named Trustice said with a shitty attitude, as he waited impatiently to escort him to the Special Investigation Department.

"What the hell do they want with me? I don't know nothin' and I don't have shit to say to them!"

"I don't remember asking you if you wanted to speak to them or what you knew! I'm telling your punk ass what you're going to do. Either you say your goodbyes right now and come with us voluntarily, or you can try and buck and get your ass dragged the fuck up out of here like we did your butt buddy Ed Ski." Officer Trustice said trying to act tough and punk Henry in front of his girl.

Henry gritted his teeth because he knew that Trustice was a bitch. He smiled because he envisioned himself breaking the puny martian looking CO's neck.

Luscious was the first to notice Henry's demeanor change for the worse, so she decided to intervene before things got out of hand. "Baby, please go, I don't want you to get into any trouble. You know you didn't do anything, so don't worry about it. It's only about 45 minutes left before the visits are over anyway, plus I'll be back up here to see you on Monday. Call me tonight, okay?" Luscious said looking at Henry with pleading eyes.

"Okay love, drive safely." Henry said as he hugged Luscious tightly and gave her a passionate kiss.

"That's enough! This ain't no porno!" Trustice said like a jealous bitch, because he secretly wished that it was him that Luscious was kissing. He couldn't understand how these fine ass women wasted their lives coming to see these jailbirds year after year, when there were good single men like him out there available. As the two officers walked him towards the I.A. office, Henry took one last look at Luscious and thought to himself: "I gotta hold on to her cause she's my *Ride or die Chick.*"

"Greetings Mr. Anderson. You may be seated." I.A Officer Roscoe said in a pleasant voice.

"Nah, I'm good. I think I'll stand, cause this won't take long." Henry said looking at Trustice with revulsion. Roscoe noticed the tension between the two of them and decided that if he wanted any information from Henry, he would have to separate the two of them.

"Hey Trustice, you may leave now, I got it from here."

"Okay sir, if you need me, I'll be right outside."

"There's no need. We'll get along just fine, I'll give you a call when I'm done." Roscoe said as he opened the door to let Officer Trustice out. "Now that I got rid of that asshole we can take care of business. Now I 'm sure you know who I am, so let me tell you why you're here. First of all, your homeboy Ed Ski is in the "Hole." He is being charged with *Assault, Drug Possession, and Introduction of Narcotics* into a State Penitentiary.

The woman who was with him was also detained, but after being questioned down at the State Trooper Barracks, was released. We know she brought that shit into our prison, but we can't prove it. What I need from you is for you to sign this written statement saying that you saw her pass him those balloons. If you do this for us, I'll make it worth your while but if you fuck me over, I will make your life miserable here at Elmira State Penitentiary." Roscoe said going into a tall safe that stood in the far corner of his office. The safe held all the valuable items that were confiscated from the inmates on a daily basis such as excessive cigarettes and stamps. These things were called *"Jailhouse money"*, because it was the equivalent of having cash in the *"Free World"*. You could buy anything, from drugs to sneakers with these items. The administration knew this, so when they busted guys with more than they were suppose to have, they confiscated and stored it in a huge six foot safe so they could pay their jailhouse snitches.

Henry watched as Roscoe swung the huge iron door open, allowing him to see the contents that were inside. "Oh shit! There must be at least 2000 books of stamps and 200 cartons of cigarettes in there!" Henry said to himself in disbelief. When Roscoe saw his face light up he went in for the kill.

"Yeah, this shit ain't nothing, I got three more safes just like this one in the basement. I'm willing to give to whatever you want, just name your price."

"Well, if you don't mind, can I smoke in here?" Henry asked as he sat down in the plush office chair.

"Sure you can, as a matter of fact, here's a little something that won't cost you anything." Roscoe said tossing Henry a pack of Newports.

"Nah, I'm straight, I got my own Ports." Henry said handing them back and pulling out his own fresh pack from his pocket. He lit the cigarette and inhaled deeply to try and calm his nerves.

"Listen I am going to be totally honest with you, only because you were real with me. I am a convict and I would never tell on anyone, that's just not in my nature. As for Ed Ski, I know him, but I don't know anything about whatever went on with him. I am a simple man with a simple plan. I mind my business and I don't get involved with anyone else's business. I'm sorry I couldn't help you any further." Henry said as he finished the last of his cigarette.

"Well, I'll ask you one more time, are you sure that you don't want to be a part of my *"A-Team?"*

"I'm very sure. I'm sorry; I'm going to have to pass on that offer. I am not a Rat! So if this conversation is about me giving you information so you can bury the next man, you got me fucked up!"

"Okay, have it your way". Roscoe said calmly as he picked up the phone to let officer Trustice know that he could come and get Henry and take him back to his cell. He tried to befriend Henry with small talk while they waited, hoping that he would have a change of heart and start running his mouth like most guys did when they were backed into a corner. But Henry put the "T" in thorough and was true to the *Code of the Streets, "Never sell out!"* was the motto he lived by. He had boss game, so he recognized the bullshit psychology Roscoe was trying to administer, so he reversed it back onto him.

When Officer Trustice arrived, he had his partner stay with Henry while he went to get briefed by Roscoe.

"Look, this guy has to be the brains behind this whole operation because my *"General Informant"* told me that Ed Ski was just a mule (carrier) that was being paid to carry that shit back for Anderson. He was right about him having the narcotics, so if he says Anderson is the shot caller, I believe him. But unless he tells on himself or we get Ed Ski to turn on him, this bastard is untouchable."

"Listen Roscoe, let me and my boys lean on him a little. I guarantee you he'll start talking. He'll tell us everything we want to know." Officer Trustice said arrogantly.

"Okay, let him go back to his cellblock and monitor his every move. Spread the word to the *"Head Snitches"* in every unit and tell them whoever helps me take Anderson down will get 100 books of stamps, 10 cartons of cigarettes of their choice and free phone calls in my office for one month. I want his ass so bad I can taste it! Remember, I don't want you to give him any indication that we are investigating him, so be easy."

"Okay, I'm on it boss." Trustice said eagerly. He hoped that Henry would try to buck so he and his boys could beat him into submission. Trustice came out of the office with his bony chest poked out. "Let's go Anderson," he said in a nasty tone.

"Ah-ight, I'm ready."

"What the fuck did you say Punk?"

"I said I'm ready."

"Oh, I thought so. Don't make me fuck your ass up."

"Another place, another time" Henry said out loud to himself as he was being let back into the prison population.

"You better watch your fuckin' mouth!" Trustice said still trying to get Henry to jump out there so he would be justified in having the Goon Squad beat his ass. But Henry would not allow himself to be lured into that trap. He knew he had enough shit in his stomach to get him another 5 years easily, so he had only one mission: Get back to his cell and get that shit out of his belly!

TWENTY THREE

When Irk saw people starting to leave the club, he called Q to the V.I.P room. Together, they looked for Myah and her friends to let them know that it was time to bounce. He didn't want them getting pissy drunk if they were planning to drive back to Long Island tonight. If they all continued to drink, none of them would be in any shape to drive. So he was going to make sure that his guests would be okay.

Keisha and her cousin Sherida finished off their second bottle of champagne and ordered another one. Nikki stared straight ahead, looking like she was mad at the world. She watched Myah's every move. When she made eye contact with Irk, she rolled her eyes. Lucky for her, he was in a good mood, so he disregarded her bitchy attitude. Before he dropped them off at Myah's car, he would swing by her new apartment, so she could see her second home. He figured that once they got there, they would want to chill for the night, sleep off the alcohol in their system and drive back to Long Island in the morning.

When Q entered the room, he saw Irk standing by the bar and started to walk towards him. Before he could take three steps, Keisha jumped up from her seat and verbally attacked him.

"Damn! Where the hell have you been?" she said acting like she was his girl.

"Out front doing my job, why?" Q responded hastily. He knew Irk was waiting, so he really didn't have the time for the third degree interrogation. He believed whole heartedly in the old adage: *"Business before Pleasure."*

Before Keisha could say another word, Q held up his index finger and motioned for her to wait a minute.

"You ain't all that Nigga!" She mumbled under her breath as she watched him walk over to Irk and Myah.

"What's up?" Q asked Irk as they gave each other dap. "You know we're about to bounce, so shut down shop and make sure everything's secured, ah-ight?" Irk asked as he pulled out a roll of *Grants and Bejamins.*

"Make sure you pay our staff off after you close down."

"Ah-ight kid, I got you!" Q replied as he pocketed the stack of bills. Irk noticed Keisha sweating his man, so he told Q to make sure that he hollered at her before he bounced. "There's nothing wrong with a lil' chicken in your life sometimes!" Irk said looking in Keisha's direction with a smirk on his face. Q looked at Keisha and fought the urge to break out in a fit of laughter. Her disposition told him that she was a Diva chickenhead and he loved it! He smiled as he watched Keisha whisper in Sherida's ear while pointing in his direction. He turned to Irk and said

"Do you want me to walk you out?"

"Nah, just have *D* and *Hass* meet me downstairs in ten minutes."

"No doubt!" With that, Q gave Irk dap and a brotherly hug then proceeded to the door. Before he reached his destination he stopped by Keisha, called her over and in a low voice said, "Hey Boo, I'm sorry that I couldn't holler atcha before, but I'm here now. Here's my number, give me a call tomorrow and I promise I'll make it up to you, ah-ight?"

"I'mma hold you to that!" Keisha quickly replied licking her lips as she took his number, putting it in her bra.

When Myah saw the way that Keisha was acting, she knew that whatever Q said to her pertained to sex. She always took a lot of numbers when she met guys in the club. But whenever she put a guys number in her bra, that was her way of saying, "I'm fucking you tonight!" But nothing Keisha did surprised Myah; she knew that she was nothing but a slut anyway.

Nikki walked over to Myah, sat down next to her and asked. "Are you ready to go yet?"

"Yeah, what about you?"

"I've been ready for at least an hour. What about Irk?" Nikki asked as she looked in his direction.

"Yeah, he's going to take us by the apartment before he takes us to my car. I'm dying to see what it looks like! Can you believe it? Not only did he make sure I had the best birthday ever, he even paid for an apartment for me. Damn! My very own apartment!" Myah said excitedly as she looked around the room enjoying the party atmosphere. She continued to sip from her glass of champagne feeling like she was on top of the world.

Nikki slowly pulled a small bag out of her pocket and patiently waited for Myah to put her glass down.

"Hey girl, pour me another drink. I'll be right back, I gotta go to the ladies room." Myah said walking towards the bathroom.

"Don't worry girl, I got you!" Nikki screamed over the music. She couldn't believe how easy it was going to be! Nikki quickly dumped the powdery substance into her glass and filled it to the brim with bubbly. She watched to make sure the substance dissolved and then dropped the empty bag on the floor. She looked around to make sure that no one witnessed her devious act. She felt a little guilty slipping her best friend two crushed up "E" pills. It was too late to take back the dirty deed, it was done.

Just as she turned around, she saw Myah making her way back to the bar.

"Girl, I feel goood!" Myah said smiling as she picked up her glass to take another sip of her drink.

"Hey Myah, Irk said for you and your girls to start getting ready so ya'll can bounce." Q said, admiring Myah's beauty.

"Okay, tell him we'll meet him in the front in five minutes." She said as she finished off the rest of the champagne in her glass. "Well, I'm ready to go!" Myah said to Nikki while looking around for the other girls. Nikki knew that it would take at least 10-15 minutes before Myah would start feeling the effects of the pill. Somehow, she had to get her alone if she wanted to put her plans into action.

Tony was having a good time kicking it with Tania at the bar when he saw Irk and his entourage walking towards the exit. He wanted to thank him for giving his group the opportunity to mingle with the *'Big Willies'* of the music industry. As he was about to excuse himself, he noticed that the young lady at Irk's side kept staring at him. It made Tony a little uncomfortable, but he dismissed it and told Tania that he would be right back; he wanted to holler at Irk before he left for the night. Myah was just about to turn her head towards the door when she saw Tony walking towards her. She couldn't stop staring at him. It had been so long since she last seen him. Even with the shoulder length dreads, she still recognized his soft facial features. Myah watched him as he made his way towards them. When Tony got within few feet of them, Irk instinctively turned around.

"Irk! Hey Irk" Tony hollered when Dee and Hass both grabbed each of his arms, holding him at bay until they got the ok from their boss. Irk motioned to his boys that it was all right to let him proceed. He greeted Tony like a long lost friend, showing him nothing but love. "What's up kid? Did you and your protégés enjoy yourselves?" Irk asked as Tony gave him a hug and some dap.

"Hell yeah! I just wanted to thank you for making it happen. My group had the time of their lives."

"That's good..." As Irk was about to continue on towards the limo, he turned around to face Myah who was on his right side and introduced her to Tony. "Excuse my rudeness, Tony this is Myah, the *"Birthday girl.* Myah, this is Tony." Myah smiled then extended her hand towards him. He kissed her hand and wished her a Happy Birthday.

When Tony looked into Myah's eyes he zoned out and nostalgia consumed him. He no longer saw Myah, he saw someone that he knew it couldn't possibly be. It was like Déjà Vu. Tony looked into Myah's face, shook his head and blinked his eyes to make sure that he wasn't buggin'. "Tony, are you alright?" Myah asked when she saw the look of disbelief on his face. Her voice snapped him out of his trance.

"I'm so sorry for staring at you like that. It's just, you look like someone that I knew a long time ago."

Irk could identify with what Tony felt, he went through the same emotions when he first saw Myah. Keisha, Sherida and Nikki looked curiously at one another as they tried to put one and one together. Myah knew exactly what Tony was talking about. She had expected him to react that way.

As Tony continued to look at her in astonishment,

Myah grabbed his hand and said

"Tony, I'm Myah, Sonya's daughter." Tony's mouth quivered and his eyes began to water as the memories of Sonya flooded his mind.

"Oh my GOD!" was all he could say because he was at a lost for words. "You are your mothers twin! You are beautiful, just like your mother!"

Myah felt good as she listened to him talk about her mother. He was one of the last people to spend time with her before she died, plus her mother loved him. Everyone stepped to the side to allow them some private time.

"Where are you staying now?" Tony asked as he regained his composure. "I live on Long Island with my Aunt and Uncle. I've been there ever since that day they found my mom." Myah explained. "How have you been?" Myah asked in awe. She wanted to connect with her mother's last boyfriend.

"Well, I've just been staying busy. You know Myah; there isn't a day that goes by that I don't think about your mother. I...." before he could finish, Myah put her finger up to his lips and said, "You don't have to explain anything to me. I know that you loved my mom. Since I'm about to leave, I'm gonna give you my cell phone number. Please call me so we can talk, in depth. There are some things I need to know." Myah said as she grabbed a napkin from a nearby table to write down her number. After handing it to Tony, she then gave him a hug and a kiss on the cheek then whispered, "Call me tomorrow after 4 p.m." With that, she stepped away from him and headed out of the club with Irk.

Tony watched them leave and said to himself, "Yeah, I have a lot of questions for you too young Sonya." He put the napkin safely into the front pocket of his jacket and walked back over to Tania so they could finish their conversation.

TWENTY FOUR

Myah was completely shocked at what she was looking at. Nikki, Keisha and Sherida's hands flew straight to their mouths once Irk opened the front door to the apartment. It was absolutely beautiful. The only words that came out of Myah's mouth were, "Oh my God!"

"So I take it that it's to your satisfaction?" Irk asked playfully as he waved his hand in front of him to gesture for them to take it all in. He was definitely proud of the way the apartment turned out. Plus, he paid enough to an interior decorator to create the look that Myah would like. The look on her face was worth every penny that he paid.

"Irk, you have gone too far! This is crazy!" Myah said as she looked around at all of the furniture that was in the room.

"It'll never be too much. I'm just making up for lost time, Princess." He replied as he turned around to look at her.

"I can't... I can't take this, Irk!" Myah exclaimed while looking around the living room and noticing how expensive the furniture and entertainment center looked. *It must have cost him a nice piece of change. After all that he's done for me already, it doesn't feel right accepting this apartment,* she silently thought to herself.

Irk was definitely going out of his way to make her 18th birthday a day to remember. He walked them through each of the rooms, showing off just how much he put into the apartment. The kitchen was done in a simple white paint with the borders a roses color. The deep wood grain cabinets were shiny, and the kitchen table was big enough to fit six comfortably. The wall-to-wall carpet was plush under their feet as they walked from room to room. Irk made everyone take off their shoes before entering the apartment, and after walking around, they could see why. Every room was done in contemporary colors that made the rooms feel comfortable, even cozy.

Myah saw apartments like this on TV when watching "Lifestyles of the Rich and Famous," but this was *her* apartment, and that is what made it so special.

Each room that Keisha and Sherida went into drew ooh's and aah's. Nikki, being used to living the good life, was not impressed one bit. She knew that Irk was trying to shower Myah with gifts in order to win her love and respect, but she wasn't falling into that trap so easily.

As Myah was starting to warm to the idea that this was now her apartment, she started to feel lightheaded. Her body was starting to tingle. Somehow, her senses were heightened and her breathing was a little labored. She felt like her body was on fire and she needed something — anything — to cool off.

"Myah, you a'ight?" Keisha asked as she stood in front of the bathroom looking at Myah.

"I... I... I don't know. I think I might have drank too much of that champagne."

Nikki knew that she had better step in quickly before the E started to take its effect, but Irk beat her to it. He turned around and walked back over to Myah at the same time Nikki did. "Let me take you to the bedroom so that you can lie down," he stated as he grabbed her arm.

He took her to the master bedroom that was decorated to resemble a suite in a fancy hotel. The carpet was thick, and the bed had a canopy with sheer curtains surrounding it. It all looked like a fairytale. Irk picked her up, walked over to the bed and laid her down on top of the satin jade green comforter. There were small pillows surrounding two large ones near the headboard. He grabbed one of the large pillows and placed it under Myah's head to support her.

Myah's eyes started to glaze over as she looked into Irk's, and without warning, she grabbed him by the neck and pulled him down on top of her so that his face was inches from hers. She leaned up and kissed him on the lips, forcing him to succumb to her physical attraction.

While Nikki, Keisha and her cousin, Sherida were looking at the other two bedrooms, Irk and Myah were in the master bedroom going at it like two lovers who hadn't seen one another in years. As they kissed each other passionately, Irk started to run his hand up Myah's left thigh, inching his way towards her throbbing pussy. Myah was rubbing his chest under his sweatshirt. She moved her hand down to his jeans and caressed his raging hard-on that was trying its best to burst free.

They stopped kissing, looked into each other's eyes, afraid to say a word; afraid to do anything that would ruin the moment.

Irk hesitated first, not wanting to damage the relationship that they had, but that was already out of the window once he allowed her to kiss him. He moved his fingers up until they were touching the lacy material of her thong. He paused there for a moment, giving her time to object, to move away or to push his hand down, but she didn't, so he kept moving until his fingers were touching the outer lips of her vagina.

Myah smiled at him and licked her lips as she managed to get her hand inside of his jeans and around his dick, gently squeezing it as she moved her hand up and down its length. The touch alone made him want to explode right there and then, but he wanted to make it special for her. He never saw this coming, but now that the opportunity presented itself, he was going to take full advantage of it. He would be a damn fool not to.

While Keisha and Sherida were in one of the guest bedrooms, sleeping, Nikki was in the bathroom that separated the two guest rooms, looking in the big picture mirror, and trying to figure out how she was going to approach Myah. Nikki knew that the pill had started to kick in, but she couldn't do anything about it until Irk left the apartment. She finally convinced herself that she was just going to go into Myah's room and force Irk to leave them alone. She knew that Irk didn't particularly care for her, but the need to be with Myah was much stronger than her being afraid of how Irk would react.

As Nikki walked out of the bathroom, she leaned against the bedroom door that Sherida and Keisha were in, and listened to see if they were still up. When she didn't hear anything, she proceeded to walk toward the master bedroom.

Faint noises were coming from the other side of the door. To Nikki, they sounded like the type of sounds that one would make while having sex, but she knew that Irk and Myah weren't interested in each other in that capacity. When she got closer to the door, the sounds became grunts and moans. Nikki was now visibly shaken. Her worst fears were coming true. She grabbed the handle of the bedroom door and slowly turned it so as not to make a sound, and when the door opened just enough for her to see in, the sight of what she saw literally took her breath away. Tears welled up in her eyes, and her bottom lip started to quiver as she stood in the doorway, watching Irk, and Myah fucking. "Oh my God!" Nikki whispered to herself while she continued to witness the sex act that Myah was displaying before her very eyes.

Myah was on top of Irk, riding him cowgirl style, with her eyes closed, while Irk was thrusting himself within her as fast and as hard as he could.

"It feels like my pussy's exploding! Oh my Go-o-o-od!" was what Nikki heard Myah say as she bounced up and down on Irk, trying to match his rhythm.

Myah was cumming for the third time. It was as if she couldn't get enough. No matter what Irk did, it just wasn't helping her need to be satisfied.

Nikki closed the door slowly, trying not to be heard. She stood in the hallway trying to comprehend all that she had just witnessed. "I knew that bastard was after one thing! Fuck!" she said under her breath. She contemplated busting into the room and giving Irk a piece of her mind, but she didn't want to spoil the mood that Myah was in, especially since she was on the E pill. The only thing that she could do was wait it out until Irk left, and approach Myah then. Hopefully, the effects of the pill will still be working so that she could express her love to her as well.

Back in the room, Irk was exhausted. Myah was acting like a woman possessed. She kept trying to get him aroused even after the mind-blowing job he finished doing to her. Normally, after what he just did a girl would have been sore and begging him to stop, but not Myah. She acted like her pussy couldn't get enough.

"What's wrong, baby?" Myah asked in a seductive voice.

Irk looked at her and thought to himself, *Damn! She's fine as hell! What the fuck am I doing? This is my man's baby girl. I promised to look out for her, not fuck the shit out of her! Everything's fucked up now. Damn! I'm the type of guy that I promised to protect her from!*

Irk sat up in the bed and looked for his clothes. "Ayo, Princess, I gotta get outta here. Do you want to stay here for the night since your friends are all passed out in the guest rooms, or do you still want me to take you back to your car?"

Myah looked at him with lust in her eyes, and quietly said, "I want you to stay with me for the night. Let me show you how a woman is supposed to treat you, baby." Myah's body was throbbing. The slightest touch would set her off into horny fits. She grabbed a small pillow and placed it between her legs in order to grind her clitoris against it until she could get Irk back into bed. She didn't understand why she was feeling the way that she was. She knew that she liked Irk physically, but it was as if her body had a mind of its own. What she was doing was definitely not normal for her, but she couldn't think about that now. She had to satisfy her continuous desire to have sex.

Irk grabbed his watch from off of the nightstand and realized that he had to get going. He rolled out of bed, found his jeans that were lying next to the bed on the floor, and put them on. The whole time that he was getting dressed, Myah was grinding away against the pillow, trying to satisfy that burning itch she was experiencing.

She's a damn nympho! Irk thought to himself as he slipped on his Timberland boots. The look that she was giving him would have weakened others, but Irk knew that business came before pleasure, and he wasn't about to let a piece of ass come between his livelihood. "Princess, you're buggin'! Get some rest and I'll be by around ten to take you to your car, a'ight?"

"Why can't you stay with me-e-e-e?" Myah asked in a whining voice.

"Business, Princess. Business," he replied.

"You promise to come back?"

"You know I am. Why you trippin'?"

"'Cause I need it, baby! Let's go one more time before you leave," Myah begged him, batting her eyes as she slowly revealed her naked body to him.

"Nah, Princess. If I stay here with you, you'll have a nigga strung out like a junkie," Irk said jokingly.

"Oh, a'ight. Just come back when you finish whatever it is you have to do!" Myah fell back on the bed, giving up her efforts of trying to get him to stay.

Nikki, who was in the hallway quietly listening, heard every word, and before Irk opened to door to leave, she hid in the hallway bathroom until he left. She waited until he was out of apartment before approaching Myah's door.

TWENTY FIVE

As Tony sat in the living room of his two-bedroom apartment, he looked at the napkin that Myah had given him, and was contemplating whether or not he should call her. He wanted to find out how she's been since that awful day. He couldn't believe that she was all grown up now. *Time has definitely been good to her,* was what he thought to himself.

He grabbed the remote to his Bose stereo system and pressed the play button for the CD. His group, "The PotHeadz" were rapping their number one hit, "This is a Letter to My Man".

"…Who kept you up like a pack of No-doz?
Who had your back when you were fighting that nigga, Jo-Joe?
Who gave you all the weed when you were feeling so-so?
And even hit you off with cream when you needed dolo?
This is a letter to my man to explain it all.
I kept it real witcha nigga, when I took the fall.
I hope you're takin' care of business while you're
out there, black,

*'Cause when I get released, yeah, you know
I'm comin' for that..."*

Tony was feeling the words that Zolo was spitting as he walked towards the kitchen to get something to drink. He started to sing along as he went about pouring himself a glass of orange juice:

*"...Yeah, I received the money orders that you
sent for the phone,
But it doesn't help the time that I'm spending alone.
You be writing me lines like you're really
sayin' sump'tin',
And the money that you sent, yo, it ain't
doing nothin'..."*

Tony walked back to the couch and placed his glass on the table before he sat down:

*"...You said you're helping my kids and
taking care of my crib,
While taking wifey for yourself while
I'm doing this bid.
I'm only down a few years, now
she's started to hate,
By giving you the fuckin' puss like
it's meat on a plate..."*

He was really getting into it, especially as his favorite part was about to play:

*"...But when I hit the bricks, you know a
nigga gonna get rich,
And only think about the time that you
were stickin' my bitch.
Yo, I got a lot of time just to think of you,*

And I see peeps every day that are
dying to meet you.
So, P.S., watch your back where
you rest at kid,
'Cause they know that you're the reason
why I'm doing this bid..."

Even though Tony heard this song a thousand times, it still made him want to jump around. He believed in his group, and that was why he worked as hard as he did to help them get on. Hopefully, Tania would keep her word and talk to someone to help get them in the door.

He was to call her at six to find out the outcome of her meeting. Now, it was only ten in the morning, and he was trying to figure out if he should call Myah or not. He opted not to until he got himself together. Hopefully by then, he'll have the courage to do it, but for now, he took his drink and walked back to his bedroom to find something to wear. He was going to meet some A and R's later for lunch to discuss his group's future.

While Tony was listening to his group's CD, Nikki and Myah were sitting in Myah's bed, talking about the night's events.

"Gur-r-rl, my body feels like it's on fire! I don't know what it is, but I feel so damn horny!" Myah said as she looked up at the ceiling.

"What?" Nikki asked in a surprised tone of voice, even though she was fully aware of what had happened.

"Irk and I fucked like there was no tomorrow. We fucked, and it was the *bomb!* He ate my shit out so damn good... Oooh! I came instantly!"

Nikki looked between Myah's legs as if she could actually see just how wet she really was. Her mind was racing with thoughts of desire; thoughts of she and Myah going at it like two dikes. Just thinking about it caused Nikki to breathe a little harder as she watched Myah rubbing her pussy with her right hand.

Myah closed her eyes and leaned back as she envisioned Irk fucking her hard and deep. A finger slid right into her wet slit, causing her to gasp. After a few seconds, she realized that it wasn't Irk's dick that was penetrating her, but it was Nikki's finger that was feeling up her clit and pussy lips.

Nikki looked into Myah's eyes, and instead of backing away, she continued, getting bolder with each stroke of her finger inside of Myah's velvet pussy.

Myah closed her eyes, leaned back on the bed, and spread her thighs further apart, allowing Nikki full access to her lower region.

Nikki leaned in closer, placed her head in between Myah's thick thighs, moved a lock of blond hair from out of her face, and proceeded to lick around Myah's vagina. She placed her tongue on her clit and began sucking on it as if it were a piece of candy.

Myah's moans said it all as she grabbed Nikki's head to press her lips even further inside of her throbbing wet pussy. "Oooh! Oooh! Aaah! Yeah, right there! Right there!" Myah whispered as she moved from side to side to match the rhythm that Nikki was going.

Nikki's mouth was covered with Myah's love juices, but she never stopped. Myah's pussy smelled of musky sex, which Nikki knew was because of Irk, but the smell was even more intoxicating to Nikki, causing her to go berserk on Myah's pussy.

As soon as Nikki grabbed her legs to hold on, Myah's

orgasm was so strong that it caused her to let out a short scream. Her orgasm continued to come in multiples as she tried to stop Nikki from licking any further. Myah couldn't believe that she had allowed this to happen, but she was so horny that she probably would have let little Danny from high school fuck her at that moment if he was there.

Nikki continued to nibble on Myah's clit until she finally moved away. "What's wrong?" Nikki asked as she licked the pussy juice from the bottom of her lip.

Myah had to catch her breath before she could say anything. "What the fuck are you doing to me, girl?"

Nikki smiled and answered in her most seductive voice, "I thought I was making you feel good."

"It's not that you wasn't, it's just... you know... I don't go that way!" Myah couldn't even look Nikki in the eyes because she was too embarrassed about what had just happened. "I didn't know you were into that stuff," she stated, trying to figure it all out.

"I'm not. I'm just into you. Damn, Myah! Your body has intrigued me since junior high. I didn't have these feelings until I really started noticing the attraction I had for you."

As Nikki continued to spill her feelings to Myah, Keisha was in the guest bedroom, telling her drunk cousin, Sherida everything that she had seen just minutes before. She always knew that something was up with Myah and her rich, white trash friend, Nikki, but she never would have guessed that they were lesbians if she didn't see it for her damn self.

"Sherida! Sherida! Wake up, Sherida!"

"What? What? What, bitch!" Sherida yelled as she turned over to face her cousin who was sitting at the foot of the bed that she was in. "Damnit, bitch! You better have a good ass reason for waking my drunk ass up!"

"Gir-r-rl, you are not going to believe this!"

The excitement in Keisha's voice made Sherida give her full attention. "What is it? What is it?"

"I just saw Myah and that white bitch dyking!"

"Noooo! Girl, you're a damn lie!" Sherida replied.

"Word on everything I love, bitch!" Keisha shot back while holding up her two fingers as if swearing to it.

"I can't believe that. Nah! Hell no!" Sherida couldn't bring herself to believe such a thing. She liked Myah from the first time they met. Myah was gorgeous. Every guy that saw her wanted her. Now she's in her bedroom, dyking with her best friend Nikki! Hell no! "Girl, you had too much to drink and you know it. For you to say some dumb shit like that, you must be on some really good drugs. Take your crazy ass to sleep!" Sherida looked at her cousin and saw that she was serious. She quickly sat back up and said, "You're serious, aren't you!"

"Listen. I know what I saw, and what I saw was them two going at it like two hungry animals. The white girl was steadily licking away at Myah's pussy while she laid back and enjoyed the show. She wasn't complaining, I know that!"

"Oh shit! Damn, girl, I would never have thought! I never saw anything like that before, then again, I'm from the country where we are a little slower than you city folks. So that's how y'all get down, huh?"

"Bitch, don't even go there! You know I don't go that way."

"Obviously some of y'all do!" Sherida quickly added, jokingly. "Did they see you watching them?"

"Nah, but guess what?"

"What?" Sherida asked while she looked at her cousin, anticipating some more juicy gossip.

"When I saw them through the door, I quickly ran back here to get my camera, ran back to their room, and snapped a couple of quick shots."

"Nooo! Bitch, tell me you're lying!"

Keisha shook her head, motioning that she was not kidding.

"Watcha gonna do with them when you get them developed?"

"I got some plans. Yeah, I got some plans," Keisha replied as she thought about how she was going to blackmail Myah and Nikki with the copies she was going to make.

After satisfying their sexual desires, Myah and Nikki fell asleep. They didn't know that in the other bedroom, Keisha was putting together a plot that would ultimately cost her more than what she bargained for...

TWENTY SIX

After Irk took Myah and her friends back to her car, he met up with his lieutenants, Q and Big Zo before heading back to his crib in Soundview Projects.

"Yo, what's up?" Irk greeted his peoples as she walked up to them with his arms out to embrace them one by one.

"Just chillin', you know, trying to make this paper," Big Zo replied. "Last night was bananas, son! Those honeys you brought to the club were all that!"

"No doubt, no doubt," Irk said while pulling out a blunt to smoke with the fellas as they hung out, kicking the Willie-Bo-Bo.

"Yo, kid, your girl, Myah is fine as hell! Damn, son! You betta be tapping that ass before another nigga even thinks about it."

"Word is bond!" Q added as he took the blunt from Irk.

Irk thought about what he and Myah had done last night, and still couldn't believe that he let it go that far. What happened, happened, so there was no changing that. Their relationship took a turn in another direction. He had to reassess his motives and figure out just what and how he wanted to treat the situation. The sex was off the chain, especially since he wasn't even thinking about getting into a sexual relationship with her. Ever since he woke up, he has done nothing but think about her, which for him was unusual. It was just something about her that made him feel different. Could it be the fact that she reminded him of her mother, the one that he wanted to be with but couldn't? Or could it be the fact that she was too beautiful to just overlook? No matter what it was, he knew that his feelings for her have now gone beyond just fatherly. He was starting to fall for her hard.

"Yo, son, you a'ight?" Q asked as he and Big Zo were standing in front of him, just staring. Zo had the blunt in his right hand, trying to pass it to Irk, but he hesitated when both he and Q noticed that he was daydreaming and staring off into deep space. "Ayo, you a'ight, kid?" he asked again as Irk regained his composure.

"Yeah, yeah. I'm cool, son. I was just thinking that we should head over to Sadell's side of town to collect that money he's supposed to have for me."

"Yeah, I'm down for that. He's been late a few times, and personally, I don't like money like that, for real!" Zo said.

"I know, I know, but I need his connections over there since those niggas seem to listen to him. I really want to smash his ass. If it wasn't for the fact that the spot he's holding wasn't a money maker, he would have been gone."

"Word! Word! I hear that! Yeah, let's go around there. I have to holla at this girl that stays over there anyway," Q replied while clipping the blunt and heading for Irk's Benz.

"Oh, so I guess we're riding in my joint, huh?" Irk asked jokingly.

"You's the one that wanna go over there, right?" You drive, boss!"

"You niggas are stupid!" Big Zo said as he laughed at

the both of them.

"Come on, y'all. Let's go then."

As they all hopped into Irks' 600, with Q in the back, and headed towards Gun Hill Road to see Sadell, Myah was at her aunt and uncle's house, laying in her canopy bed, trying to figure out what made her act the way that she did at the apartment. She never acted that way whenever she drank, nor was she ever demanding about sex with anyone. For some odd reason, her mental was off last night, which caused her to investigate all that she did then.

That episode with Nikki was not right either, and she knew that she would have to straighten that situation out as soon as possible before it got out of hand. No one was going to find out about this, because it didn't happen. But Myah knew that it did, and as she thought about it, she did experience one of the best orgasms she ever had. She knew that she liked guys, but she found herself questioning her sexuality since she had these thoughts on her mind.

Her phone started ringing, which snapped her out of the reverie that she was in. She looked at her clock on her dresser and noticed that it read 3:46 p.m. She couldn't believe that she had slept that long. The phone rang about two more times before she finally answered it. "Hello!"

"Yeah, is Myah there?" a male voice asked.

"This is she. Who's this?" Myah questioned.

"This is Tony. What's up?"

Myah quickly straightened herself up in the bed, wiped the sleep out of her eyes, and cleared her throat. "Hey, Tony! I didn't think you were ever going to call."

Tony's mind was racing with thoughts of how to even respond or act on the phone, but somehow, he managed to find the right words to say. "You know I didn't forget ya!"

"So, whatcha doing today?" Myah asked as she jumped out of her bed and walked over to her vanity mirror. Her face was a mess, she thought, as she looked at herself trying to hold a conversation with someone from her past.

"Well, I have to meet with some A and R's later today to promote my group," Tony said excitedly.

Myah walked to her bathroom, and without thinking, pulled her cotton panties down, sat on the toilet and proceeded to urinate as she listed to Tony talk about his group.

"Yeah, my group should be the next big thing on the rap scene. You heard them last night, right?"

"Nah, I was just a little drunk from the glasses of champagne I was drinking. What did they sing?" she asked, trying to piss quietly so that he wouldn't hear. But for some strange reason, her steady stream of pee was louder than normal, which caused her to cover the receiver.

It didn't work, because Tony heard everything, and even made a comment about it. "You're in the bathroom, huh?"

"Oh my God! I'm sorry! I was trying to be quite about it, but I guess I fucked that up," she said, embarrassed.

"Shit! It ain't like I never heard that before. Do you, ma! I like a girl that can keep it real, and I see you are a real girl."

Myah was shocked by what she was hearing. She never imagined that she would be having a conversation like this with her mom's ex-boyfriend. "That's for sure!" she said as she finished up and washed her hands before heading back to her bedroom. She looked around in her closed for something to wear as she continued to talk to Tony.

"So, what's up? I think we need to get together and catch up on the past, don't you think?" Myah asked while pulling out a pair of jeans.

"I agree, but what's the best time for you, baby doll?"

Myah smiled at the name he called her. It was the first time she had heard that from anyone. "What did you have in mind?"

"Well, I'm free Tuesday or Thursday, or..."

Before he could finish, Myah said, "Why don't we meet up on Saturday? You name the time and place."

"If that's the case, we can meet at the Coliseum on Jamaica Avenue, at eleven o'clock. Meet me in front of the pizza shop, a'ight?"

"It's a date. Let me go so I can get my ass in the shower. I didn't realize it was so late," Myah stated as she sat on her bed to rest.

"A'ight, I'll see you Saturday."

They hung up, and both thought about the upcoming meeting on Saturday.

Nikki sat on her bed, wondering if she should call Myah and act as if nothing happened, or should she see if things between them changed. As she looked at the pictures on her dresser of her and Myah together, her feelings for Myah were far deeper than just good friends. Although Nikki never acted on her urges until yesterday, she knew that eventually they would surface to the top, and she would be forced to deal with them sooner or later.

Myah was definitely a beautiful girl, inside and out, and Nikki had known her for so long that they were more like sisters than girlfriends. Since that first day she laid eyes on her, Nikki knew that she liked her. As time went on and they became closer, she tried to curb her sexual desires of wanting to be with Myah. Every time she saw Myah with a guy, she became jealous, and instead of encouraging it, she would try her best to discourage it.

Nikki has had boyfriends before, but ever since she was about ten years old, she was more interested in the female body than the male body. Her first experience was at the age of nine with another little girl from school. It started off with touching and hugging, but it quickly led to loving caresses, and as they got older and more aware of their sexuality, it progressed into sneaking kisses whenever possible, or fondling each other's private parts to the point of orgasms. Nikki's first orgasm was with a girl, so it was hard for her not to feel more in tune with females. The boys were just cover-ups, which rarely led to anything more than first or second base.

After her first girlfriend moved away with her family, Nikki never told anyone about her sexual preference. She always had wanted Myah to know, but didn't know how she would react to it. Nikki was afraid of rejection, so she kept it to herself, and only admired Myah from afar. It was hard for her to be around Myah without feeling some sort of way, but Myah had no clue that she was the object of Nikki's affection.

Nikki had decided to take the chance that she did at the apartment only because she knew that Myah was on something.

Now, as she played with her cell phone, trying to figure out whether she should call or not, she was startled when it starting ringing, causing her to drop it on her bed. It rang two more times before she finally picked it up. Nikki flipped the phone open and read the LCD screen. It displayed Myah's number. She hesitated for a second, then pressed the "talk" button and prepared for the yelling to commence. "Hello…! She said tentatively, holding the phone away from her ear just in case.

"Hey, girl, what's up?"

Nikki, whose eyes were closed, opened them up and brought the phone closer to her ear to make sure she heard right. "Nothing much. What's up with you?"

Myah knew that Nikki was struggling with her conscience, so she decided not to bring up what happened, unless she did. Then and only then would they discuss it. As far as she was concerned, it didn't happen at all. "Yo, I'm trying to go out to the mall. You wanna ride with a baller that's balling out of control?"

Nikki laughed because she knew that Myah was only saying that, because they heard someone say that to them when they were leaving the mall last weekend. It was funny then, and it was funny now. "Gir-r-rl, you are so silly!" Yeah, I wanna roll with ya. When are you trying to leave?"

"In the next hour or so. I'll pick you up."

"Oh yeah, I forgot. You have a car now!"

They both laughed and said their good-byes.

TWENTY SEVEN

The rest of the week had come and gone. There was no more mention of what happened between Myah and Nikki.

People at school heard of the party Irk threw for Myah, and for a minute, that was all that anyone talked about; until Myah noticed a small note that was stuck to her locker after her homeroom class was over. As she looked around the crowded hallway full of students that were trying to get from one place to the next in the ten minutes that were allotted to them, she didn't see one person looking in her direction that would give her an indication of who might have placed it there. She opened it up and read what it said. At first, she thought it was just another guy trying to get at her, but as she continued to read further, her face contorted into a puzzled look. Then, in the next couple of seconds, fear crept into her eyes. Myah reread the note three times:

We need to talk. I know what you did after the party. I'll be in touch!

The note was signed: *The Lesbian Investigator.*

Myah crumbled the note in her hand, closed her locker and walked over towards the nearest trashcan. Her mind was racing with all kinds of thoughts as she threw the note into the garbage can. She looked around once more to see if there was anyone that might even remotely look suspicious, but everyone that was in the hallway paid no attention to her, so she turned around and walked off to Mrs. Desmond's class, clutching her books.

Keisha left her homeroom class and proceeded to walk towards Myah's locker. Missing her by a few seconds, she watched her walk down the hall with her books close to her chest. This gave Keisha the opportunity to check Myah's locker door for the note that she'd placed there earlier. It was gone! Keisha had hoped to be near when Myah read it in order to observe her reaction. Unfortunately, Keisha's homeroom teacher, Ms. Wilcox, picked today to talk longer than usual. Therefore, class was dismissed later than it normally would have been. She'd find out soon enough by observing Myah's actions at lunch. She could hardly wait.

"The Lesbian Investigator!" Keisha laughed loudly to herself as she headed for her next class, which she'd now be late for. Being late for class was the farthest thing from her mind. All she could think about was all that money she intended to collect and how she would spend it.

Meanwhile, Nikki was just opening her locker, when she noticed a small piece of yellow paper stuck to the corner of it. After peeling it off, she unfolded it and began reading it:

We need to talk. I know what you did after the party. I'll be in touch.
The Lesbian Investigator.

Nikki looked up to see if anyone was looking or staring suspiciously in her direction. If so, she might gather some indication of whomever it was that left the note, but to her dismay, no one paid her the least bit of attention.

She began to think about what she and Myah had done, and wondered if Myah had disclosed their private, yet secretive lesbian encounter. Knowing that she would never do such a thing, the thought vanished as quickly as it had entered Nikki's mind. She knew that Myah didn't and wouldn't want anyone to know.

Just as Myah had previously done, Nikki made her way down the hall, heading for her class, wondering just what was going on.

During lunch period, Myah met up with Nikki and the other girls that they hung out with. Making eye contact with Nikki, Myah's instincts told her that something was wrong. Hoping to get Nikki alone, her plan faltered, as Keisha, Tanya and Mimi approached the table they all shared daily.

"Hey, girlfriend! What's happening?" Tanya asked, smiling as if everything was just hunky-dory.

Myah noticed how Keisha was staring at her, as if she knew something...something that she was not willing to share with everyone else. Feigning that nothing was wrong, Myah decided to put on her best performance. "I'm maintaining. What y'all been up to? I haven't seen y'all all day," she stated, trying to act as if nothing was wrong.

Receiving that note made Nikki feel really uncomfortable, as if all eyes were on her. She got her lunch, casually strolled over to the table, and took a seat next to Myah. Maybe it was paranoia, but she had a strange feeling that everyone knew something... something that she didn't. "What's up, ladies?" she asked, trying to act cheerful.

Keisha sat quietly smirking until she made eye contact with Myah, causing the smirk to suddenly disappear.

Myah knew something was up with the little bitch, but she couldn't put her finger on it; not right now anyway.

She did make a mental note to confront Keisha later. Right now, her number one priority was to find out if Nikki knew anything about the note she'd found stuck to her locker.

Nikki was wearing a rather provocative skirt set by DKNY, a very short plaid skirt and matching spaghetti strap tank top. Her thick legs were beautifully tanned, and her feet were professionally pedicured and adorned by a pair of sexy three-inch heeled sandals.

She's definitely looking jazzy, Myah thought to herself.

Guys were constantly checking Nikki out, but she never once acknowledged any of them.

Keisha was observing how Nikki ignored the guys gawking at how she drank her juice. "Damn, gir-r-rl! That skirt short enough?" Keisha asked as she looked at Nikki's lower body.

Tanya, Mimi and Myah all looked at Nikki's skirt to see what Keisha was talking about.

Nikki was the first to say something. "Maybe for you, but for me, it's just right."

All the girls laughed, except for Keisha, who was looking around the cafeteria. Before Keisha could say anything, Myah jumped in. "What's the problem, Keisha? Why you starting some bullshit? I thought we were over that."

"Damn! I was just making a comment! Does everybody have to be on attack mode?"

"Naw. But I know how you get... *bitch!*" Myah stated much louder than she had intended.

"I'm not going to be too many more bitches, so watch your fucking mouth, Myah!"

Myah stood up before Keisha said another word. "Listen, *bitch!* I've told you before about your little ghetto remarks, and about downing my girl, Nikki. If you've got a problem with her, say it to her instead of talking around her, 'cause for real, you ain't shit!"

Now was the perfect time for Keisha to fire her pistol. "If I didn't know any better, I'd swear you two were fucking, especially the way you're standing up for her and all," she said calmly, as if she'd wanted everyone to ponder over what she'd just said.

Myah frowned furiously. Looking into her eyes, it was obvious that she was highly pissed. Tanya and Mimi were caught once again in the middle of Keisha and Myah's verbal attack on each other, which was about to become physical if someone didn't hurry up and step in.

"Okay! Okay! Keisha, let's hurry and get to class. We don't want to be late again," Tanya said, hoping to break up the tension that was starting to escalate.

Keisha smiled at Tanya and said, "Yeah, you're right. I'll leave these two *good friends* to themselves."

Myah was about to let Keisha have it, until she noticed Ms. Jones coming to their table. "This ain't over, bitch! It ain't over!" Myah warned Keisha through clench-ed teeth.

"Oh, I know. I know," Keisha responded while being led away from the cafeteria.

On the way to their lockers, Mimi made small talk with Keisha. "You know, it's obvious that you and Myah don't get along, so why pretend that y'all are friends?"

Keisha was still smiling when she looked at Mimi and responded, "Oh, you'll see a change in her attitude soon enough. Trust me! Myah and that white trash will soon be paying like they weigh!"

Tanya looked over in Keisha's direction as soon as she said this, and wondered what the hell she was talking about.

Keisha walked to her locker, opened it, and took out an envelope that contained eight pictures. As she looked at them, she smiled and thought to herself, *I have you, bitch! I have you right here, bitch! Let's see how tough you are when you see these pictures. I bet that attitude will change then, huh?*

TWENTY EIGHT

Myah walked through the front door of her aunt and uncle's house after parking her car in the driveway. As she passed the small table near the closet door, she looked through the pile of mail that was stacked on top. While flipping through it, she came across a letter that Henry had sent her. She grabbed it, placed it in the back pocket of her jeans and replaced the rest of the mail back on the table.

Myah walked up the stairs, heading towards her bedroom, threw her backpack on the floor and flopped on her bed. She was exhausted, physically and mentally.

The argument that she had with Keisha at school earlier didn't help matters any. She still had to find out who this "Lesbian Investigator" was, and why she and Nikki were being targeted. When she finally spoke with Nikki after lunch, she found out that Nikki had also received a note. They compared them and figured out that someone was either playing games, or Keisha, who had been acting strangely all of the sudden, was involved in some way or another.

Myah tried to replay last weekend's events in her head. When she and Nikki were in the room doing what they were doing, she remembered the door being closed…

or was it? The only people in the apartment besides she and Nikki were Keisha and her cousin, Sherida. They were both passed out drunk in the guest bedroom... or were they? All of these doubts played on Myah's conscience.

Just as she was trying to collect her thoughts, a knock at her door startled her. "Who is it?" she asked in a frightened voice.

"It's me!" her aunt replied.

"Oh, come in."

Mary opened the door and walked in, holding a manila envelope in her right hand. She walked over towards Myah's bed and sat on the edge next to her.

"Hey, Aunt Mary. What's up?" Myah asked in a concerned voice, since she noticed the puzzled look on her aunt's face.

"Well, this letter came in the mail today, and I wanted to ask you about it." She handed it over to Myah, who hesitated at first, but eventually took it. She read the return address, which she knew was bogus. When she opened it up, it contained two sheets of paper. One sheet read:

If you want the originals, then you are going to have to pay.
If not, then everyone will know!

The other sheet was a photocopy of she and Nikki on the bed in her apartment. As soon as she saw it, she closed it back up and looked at her aunt.

"Is there something wrong, Myah, that I should know about?"

Myah knew that her aunt didn't know exactly what was in the envelope, but she knew that something was wrong by the look on her face.

Myah was just about to say something when her aunt

said, "Is it a rejection letter from college?"

Right then and there, Myah knew she had a way out. "Oh, well, yeah. It's from a college that I just applied to just in case I didn't make it to Clarkson. But it seems that I made it there, and not in this one. Oh, well!" Myah placed the envelope on the bed beside her and stood up.

Her aunt followed her to the door, then bent down and gave her a hug and a kiss. "I'm so proud of you. I just wish your mother could see you now." Mary was about to cry, but caught herself. "Let me get out of here. Your uncle will be home soon, and I need to get dinner ready."

As she turned to go, Myah said that she'd be down in a few to help out, which her aunt knew would never happen.

Once her aunt closed the door and headed downstairs, Myah quickly got her cell phone from her bag and dialed Nikki's number. After two rings, Nikki answered in a slurred voice. "H-e-l-l-o!"

"Hey, what's up? You sound terrible! What's wrong with you?" Myah asked as she opened up the envelope and pulled out the picture of her and Nikki on the bed in a compromising position.

"I just got in. I stopped by Brenda's house, and when I got back, there was a brown envelope on my desk. I opened it up and saw two..."

Before she could finish, Myah told her exactly what was in it. "Two pieces of paper, one saying, 'Get money or they will tell everyone,' and another was a copy of a picture of us on the bed, right?"

Nikki was shocked. Tears rolled down her face and she began to shake. "What's going on, Myah?"

"You know who's doing this, don't you?" Myah asked in an angry tone of voice.

"No!" Nikki replied, sobbing into the phone.

"It's Keisha's black ass! She's the only one that was able to get a picture like this. That's why she's been acting funny."

"But why would she do this?" Nikki asked as she wiped the tears away from her face with a tissue.

"That bitch is trying to get paid, that's why! I'ma fix her ass though."

"What are you going to do, Myah?"

"I don't know just yet, but I'll figure it out. Let me go so I can help my aunt in the kitchen. Don't say anything about this to Keisha, or anyone else, okay?"

"Yeah, right!" Nikki responded angrily.

Myah hung up and went over to her window that overlooked the driveway. Her car was sparkling in the afternoon sun. She reached into her back pocket and felt the envelope that she had put there earlier. She pulled it out and opened it. Inside were three pages from Henry:

Dear Myah;

> *I hope your birthday party was something to remember. I'm sure you got everything you wanted. I just wish I was there to help you celebrate it in style. I just hope you took pictures for me.*
>
> *When are you coming up to visit? There are some things I want to talk to you about. I put your number on my list, but I can't call until next week.*
>
> *Have you been thinking about me? I know I have, especially after you sent those flicks last week. Hopefully, I'll get the chance to see you in person soon. I...*

Myah placed the letter on her bed and walked down the stairs to help her aunt. She really wasn't focused on Henry at that moment. Her mind was definitely on something else; revenge!

Irk was on the thruway heading south, coming back from New Rochelle, when his cell phone started ringing. He looked at the readout to see who it was. Once he saw that it was Myah, he pressed a button on the steering wheel that activated the Mercedes' hands-free phone system, which automatically turned down the volume of the stereo system in order for the driver to be able to hear.

"Hey, Princess, what's up?"

Myah just wanted to hear his voice since she was in a bad mood. She needed to talk to someone, so she decided to call Irk since she hadn't heard from him in two days. "Where have you been?" she asked with an attitude.

"Whoa! Whoa! Whoa, Princess! The last time I noticed, I was a grown ass man!"

Myah loved the way he talked and expressed himself. Ever since they had that romp in the bedroom, Irk was her man, and she was his main girl, or that's what she assumed. It was never officially made known, but he acted as if she was, and Myah never questioned it.

"If you must know, I'm on my way back from New Rochelle. I had to see someone. Is that okay with you, Princess?" Irk asked, laughing. His tone was of a playful nature, but he got his point across that he was not to be questioned about is business. He was just about the cross over the Tappan Zee Bridge when he noticed that Myah wasn't sounding like herself. "Princess, what's wrong?"

"Nothing! I can't call my man just to say hi?" she replied, trying to act as if everything was everything.

But Irk knew better. "Nah, I know sumptin's bothering you. I can hear it in your voice, baby girl."

"Damn! You're beginning to know me too well.

Yeah, there's something on my mind. I just got into it with Keisha, the one I took to the club with us."

Irk knew exactly who she was talking about. He didn't particularly like her. She was too much of a groupie. "Yeah, I remember her. What's her last name, and what did she do?"

"She's just a Bitch, with a capital B! I wanna beat her ass so bad, but I don't wanna fuck up in school or with my aunt. They already warned me about fighting. Her last name is 'Green'. Why?" Myah asked, not really thinking.

"Damn, Princess! You get down like that?" Irk asked, trying to get her talking.

"I can hold my own. You know where I'm from, baby! BX! I have to represent to the fullest!" Myah responded jokingly.

They both laughed, but Irk was already setting something up in his head on how to help her out. "Don't sweat the small stuff, Princess. I'ma swing through there in about an hour. Meet me at your apartment by seven, a'ight?"

"A'ight!" Myah was all smiles. She needed a good nut, especially after all that went down today.

When they hung up, she got herself ready to see her man, while Irk made a call to his little 'hood rat, Trish. "Ayo, Trish! I need for you and your crew to swing through Dix Hills tomorrow during school hours, and do what you do best; Slice-N-Dice!"

"What school, and who?" Trish asked as she finished painting her fingernail.

"Half Hollow Hills High School East. Look for a girl named Keisha Green."

"How bad?"

"Just a warning, noting too major. I mean that, Trish!" Irk got loud to get his point across.

"A'ight! A'ight! I hear you, damn! You owe me for

this one, Irk." Trish already knew how he was going to repay her. She needed that big dick of his, and this was her way of getting it. Her mom fucked it up last time when she came home early, cussing and fussing, but this time, they would go somewhere to finish the job. She loved herself some dick, especially when the person knew how to use it.

"I'll swing by your place tomorrow night in the white Denali. I'm only beeping once, then I'm out."

"What time?" Trish asked excitedly.

"At eight, sharp. If you ain't there, I'm gone!"

"Don't worry, I'll be there. I'll be there."

When they hung up, Irk knew that Trish would handle her business. He had no doubt in his mind after he witnessed some of her crew's handiwork. They were vicious with a razor. What they did to his old girl was classic. That bitch is still fucked up from it.

Irk drove on towards the Bronx with his system bumping Jay-Z's "Hard Knock Life, Vol. 1" CD:

"...It's a hard knock life, for us..."

To Be Continued...

About The Author

A.L. Strange is a graduate of Potsdam College. He has a B.A. in Political Science and an Associates in Sociology. He is from New York and is currently residing in FCI Loretto.

Strange is co-author of the book "Beyond Repair" with Frasier Boy and the author of "Beguiled" that will be out soon.

NEW VISION
PUBLICATION

P.O. Box 2815
Stockbridge, GA 30281

Or

P.O. Box 310367
Jamaica, NY 11431

Order Form

Name: _____

Address: _____

City: _____ **State:** _____ **Zip:** _____

Qty	Title	Price	Total
	Tit 4 Tat	$15.00	
	-Coming Soon-		
	A Blind Shot	$15.00	
	Shank	$15.00	
	Tit 4 Tat 2	$15.00	
		Subtotal	
	...Shipping Charges...	**Shipping**	_____
	Media Mail First Book ….….... $3.85 Each additional book….…..….$1.50	**Total**	$_____

(No Personal Checks Accepted)
Make Institutional Checks or Money Orders payable to:
New Vision Publication

NEW VISION
PUBLICATION

P.O. Box 2815
Stockbridge, GA 30281

Or

P.O. Box 310367
Jamaica, NY 11431

Order Form

Name: _____

Address: _____

City: _____ **State:** _____ **Zip:** _____

Qty	Title	Price	Total
	Tit 4 Tat	$15.00	
	-Coming Soon-		
	A Blind Shot	$15.00	
	Shank	$15.00	
	Tit 4 Tat 2	$15.00	
		Subtotal	
	...Shipping Charges...	**Shipping**	_____
	Media Mail First Book .... $3.85 Each additional book..............$1.50	**Total**	$_____

(No Personal Checks Accepted)
Make Institutional Checks or Money Orders payable to:
New Vision Publication